Son of Justice

Steven L. Hawk

Son of Justice

First Paperback Edition – March 2016

ISBN-13: 978-1519616357
ISBN-10: 151961635X

Cover art: Yoly Cortez
Editors: Laura Kingsley & Ty Johnson

www.SteveHawk.com

This book is dedicated to Aaron, Taylor and Steven. The best sons a father could wish for…mostly.

Also by Steven L. Hawk:

Peace Warrior

Peace Army

Peace World

Creeper Town

Son of Justice

PROLOGUE

Left . . .

Left . . .

Left, right, left.

Inexorably onward he marched.

With each tired step, vicious bolts of agony shot upward. They began at the soles of his feet and sliced through the blisters that had formed on the back of each heel. Continuing upward, the tendrils of pain cut a scorching path through aching calves and knees before settling firmly in his thighs and lower back. Having reached their final destination, the bolts turned into hot knives of torture that twisted and scraped.

Eli looked left and right at the barren, sandy Telgoran landscape and trudged forward. Occasionally, he veered to the right or left to skirt a boulder or to circumvent yet another constellation of scattered, head-size rocks—what he now thought of as "Telgoran rock gardens." At other times, he found himself staring into the distance, at one of the mysterious, dark, cave-like entrances that led to the Telgoran underground. They seemed to be everywhere, and he wondered, as he always did, if any of the planet's original inhabitants were standing in the darkness, hidden from view, watching as the exhausted humans trudged slowly past. He never saw one, but he used the thought of being observed as additional motivation to keep his feet moving. Mostly, he just fixed his eyes on a spot ten meters ahead and kept walking. Forward was the goal, and forward was the direction he always came back to.

The pack on his back—nearly half his own body weight—was burden enough to cause many of his peers to drop out. But the pack was the least of his worries. He was used to *that* kind of pain—the kind that comes from hard work, the kind that can be conquered with a strong body and a bitter refusal to say, "Flock it. I quit." By itself, that pain would be relatively easy. But when combined with all the other dynamics in play, the current trek seemed never-ending. The heavy pack, his Ginny shotgun, the loneliness of the hike, and the blistering desert they traversed all weighed heavily on the body and the mind.

And the boots! The worst pain of all was caused by the boots.

The standard-issue boots the sergeants had given them were beautiful. Made from the orange leather of the *ninal*, a Telgoran deerlike species. They were unlike anything he had ever seen. But they were worse than uncomfortable. Stiff and unforgiving, the leather didn't mold to the foot the way a boot should. While others had marveled over the receipt of such an important part of their gear, he had held them in his hands, and after a quick, five-second inspection, recognized them as a problem. Armies lived and died by their feet. While others took care not to scratch their boots, he took every opportunity to abuse them and work them into shape.

Despite the tired aching of his feet, a quick look over his shoulder at the forms struggling along behind him proved that his efforts to break in his footgear hadn't been completely in vain. Although he struggled, the rest of the training unit stretched out for more than a kilometer across the sandy terrain behind him—the closest, no less than a hundred meters away. Most of them were hobbling or limping.

At a few centimeters under two meters, he was shorter than many of the other recruits. Most would describe him as wiry and lean. Few, if any, random onlookers would have placed their bets on him to be leading the pack in such a grueling, lengthy forced march. Yet here he was. His body, well toned from a lifetime of physical training, was not as bulky as a majority of his male counterparts, who, without exception, had been raised on Earth. Unlike his peers, Eli hadn't called the planet where he was born "home" for nearly a dozen years. Fully two-thirds of his life had been spent on Waa, the planet where the Shiale Alliance was headquartered. He kept that fact to himself, though. He had no desire to open himself up for the inevitable litany of questions and probing the knowledge would provoke.

Although he doubted they would need to be told after this fiasco, Eli made a mental note to ensure every other recruit worked on breaking in their boots before the next march. The need for him to pass along such obviously important information made him shake his head. Their Minith sergeants had to know about the problem and should have warned their charges before throwing them into the first forced march of their training. He wondered if withholding the information was an oversight, or if it was done with some purpose in mind. He couldn't fathom any rational reason, but it was possible the boots were some form of cruel test.

One thing was certain, though. Their footgear was an excellent example of form over function, and form failed miserably. If he had his own well-worn boots on his feet, he'd be kilometers ahead. His feet would be tired, but not blistered. Every step wouldn't be a rage against the torture that threatened him.

Left . . .

Left . . .

Left, right, left.

When his body demanded that he stop moving—cried out that he couldn't take another step—the litany moved him forward. The unspoken words beat out a worn rhythm he had come to rely upon. As long as the words continued to generate forward movement, he would place his faith in them. He had no idea what he would do if they ever failed him. He refused to consider that possibility.

Left . . .

Left . . .

Left, right, left.

The heat of the Telgoran sun beat down on his shoulders, creating bothersome rivulets that began beneath his helmet and flowed downward. His uniform was soaked with the salted clamminess of his body's sweat, and he paused his silent chant long enough to turn his head and suck down a quick gulp of water. The plastic spout that trailed over his shoulder and into the water pouch stored in his pack was hot, as was the mouthful of life-sustaining liquid it dispensed. He wanted a second gulp. Hell, he wanted to drain the reservoir dry, but he kept his desire in check. He didn't know how much farther they had to go, and the last thing he wanted was to drop out because he couldn't ration his water allowance properly.

Discipline. They're teaching you discipline. Ah! It's another test.

Despite his intense discomfort, the sudden flash of understanding caused him to smile. There was a reason behind the madness. Somehow, that made the harsh reality of his situation bearable. He silently scolded himself for wallowing in the pain of his present circumstance and made a personal commitment to expand his view of the nonstop training and torture—to look for explanations and reasons, to view the cruelties of the *right now* through a broader lens. With a nod to himself, his mind turned to the long-term. *This hell can't last forever,* he told himself for the hundredth time. For the ten-thousandth time, he repeated the mantra.

Left . . .

Left . . .

Left, right, left.

A sense of renewed purpose and strength flowed through Eli's body. He lengthened his step, increased his pace, and pushed on through the pain.

CHAPTER 1

General Grant Justice, Supreme Commander of the Alliance Defense Force, scanned the holo-page that floated above the shiny agsel surface of his desk. The memo took less than five seconds to digest. With a curt wave of his hand, he deleted the irritating message and swallowed the curse that was trying to force its way past his lips.

The Minith general in charge of the forces on Telgora was complaining again. Apparently, the posting didn't meet the standards "appropriate to one of his social position," and he needed more authority and resources. As if two hundred thousand soldiers—nearly half of their entire contingent of ground troops—weren't already posted there under his direct control. It was typical Minith posturing, meant to position the general for the next plum assignment. For Grant, it was just one more thing that demanded his attention. His demeanor and skills weren't suited for administration. Unfortunately, administrative tasks represented the majority of his job.

Grant was a soldier, trained to fight and lead men in battle. Despite turning fifty on his last birthday, he still preferred working with fellow soldiers in the field to manning a desk—even when that desk was the senior military desk in the Alliance.

The old soldier stood up and walked to the large window that looked out over a northern view of the Waa capital. It wasn't Earth, but from forty stories up, it was still quite a sight. Over the tops of the shiny metal and glass buildings that made up the skyline, he spied the launch area for the alliance mother ships in the distance. He wondered briefly if any of the departing ships were bound for Earth. He felt a sudden pang of longing that quickly dissipated. Earth wasn't his home now. It hadn't been his home for a long, long time.

The general stared out at the planet that was now his home and considered how unlikely it was for him to be standing where he now stood. *What were the odds*, he wondered? Man wasn't the strongest species in the universe. The Minith, with their large, apelike bodies could easily beat most humans into submission when they met hand-to-hand on a battlefield. No contest. Even the Telgorans—those thin, seven-foot-tall warriors with muscles like corded steel—could defeat the strongest human in a contest of pure strength. And their quickness, oh, the Telgoran quickness. Again, no contest.

At best, man came in a distant third—and that was only when comparing the species with which they were intimately familiar. No doubt, there were even stronger species as you left the tiny corner of the universe where humans existed and delved deeper into the stars.

Nor was man the smartest species. The Waa, those little green aliens, with the large, dark, almond-shaped eyes, claimed that trait. Their unparalleled ability to design and build remarkable spaceships and other technological wonders gave credence to the claim. Though they held a secret most non-Waa would never know—the ability to read minds. They could learn a task or a process simply by observing your thoughts as you performed the work or thought through a problem. It was, without a doubt, the most efficient self-learning method possible. Yes, it was hard to argue with their claim of being a “nine” on the intelligence scale. Humans and Minith, in comparison, were a “six” and a “four,” respectively.

Yet, despite not being the strongest, nor the fastest, nor the most intelligent species, of the four sentient species that were involved in the Peace Wars, man had come out on top. Aided by the tall, reed-thin Telgorans and the diminutive, green Waa, the humans of Earth defeated the aggressive, planet-robbing Minith on the three primary planets where the four races now lived: Earth, Waa and Telgora. The Minith home planet was destroyed during the war, along with most of their people.

Grant understood his place in the scheme of things. He had played a significant role—perhaps the most significant, he conceded with a sigh—in humanity’s eventual victory over the Minith. But it wasn’t because he was the strongest, fastest or smartest person on Earth. He was merely a solitary warrior who possessed a rare set of skills and a unique view.

While most on Earth believed that peace and conformity were ideals humanity should endeavor to achieve, Grant’s personal philosophy was somewhat more antiquated. While he believed in the concept of peace (not the capitalized “Peace” that most humans worshiped), he understood that true peace requires the ability and willingness to protect yourself from those who would take advantage. Like the Minith, who had used the humans’ unwavering obedience to peace to enslave Earth and steal its resources.

Grant was the catalyst that saw mankind build its first army in more than four hundred years. It was an army that defeated the Minith invaders on Earth and then took the battle to the planets of Telgora and Waa, where the aliens also held power. Eventually, the Minith were soundly beaten, and their home world was destroyed.

With the Minith defeated, the citizens of Earth wanted nothing more than to retract back to their lonely, overcrowded planet, bury their collective heads, and forget about life beyond their tiny solar system. But Grant refused to let that happen. Nature abhors a vacuum, and leaving Waa and Telgora to their own fates would have created an atmosphere for the Minith to reclaim what they had lost—or worse. Grant recognized the threat and quickly started the process of forming an alliance between the four races.

Bringing the Waa and the Telgorans into the alliance had proved easier than getting his own race engaged. Despite their victory over the Minith, most humans still despised and feared their former enemy. It took months of intense deliberation and debate within Earth's Leadership Council, before the surviving Minith were grudgingly recognized as war refugees. It took even more time for humanity to finally accept them as an equal member of an alliance.

Grant argued tirelessly on behalf of his previous foe, and for very good reasons. The Minith were already residing on Telgora and Waa. With their home planet destroyed, it was obvious they weren't going anywhere. Add to that the Minith culture norm that required subservience when defeated in battle, and the decision was a no-brainer. Perhaps most importantly, threats far greater than the Minith existed outside of their backwater corner of the universe, and Grant needed experienced fighters. Although their political influence was minor, they filled the need for soldiers, and were now a major component of the alliance military. Their willingness and ability to fight readily offset the distaste that most humans had for war.

Now, a dozen years after the end of the Peace Wars, the Shiale Alliance was still in its infancy. In some ways, it was doing well. Prosperity seemed within reach. The mining and sale of agsel ore to the planets and races that existed outside the Alliance provided resources and wealth. This wealth supported all partner-members and fostered growth on the two dozen planets that made up their tiny corner of the galaxy.

In other ways, survival was an ongoing struggle. Cracks were appearing—caused by both internal and external forces—that threatened the alliance. Those cracks now kept Grant awake at night.

He rubbed his eyes and shook his head at how he had come to be here in this place, at this time. He hadn't asked for this, had never wanted the mantle that had been forced upon his shoulders. On the other hand, he knew it hadn't been possible to refuse the demands of three disparate races. The Waa hadn't cared, but the leaders of Earth, the Minith, and the Telgorans had all made his oversight of their combined fighting forces a requirement of their signing onto the Shiale Alliance. It had been twelve years and he wondered if they would ever allow him to retire the post—or if he'd be locked into the position until he croaked. Hell, the thought made him want to jump on the next ship bound for the outer ring and lock horns with the next Zrthn battle carrier ship that crossed the demarcation line that delineated Alliance territory.

Now there was a real problem. The Zrthn threat, always a looming presence, had grown more worrisome over the past six months. Instead of an occasional foray up to the demarcation line, followed by an immediate retreat, they had begun crossing deep inside Alliance space. Grant knew they were probing for weakness, testing the Alliance response to the incursions. So far, neither side had done anything more than posture, which was good. The last thing Grant or the Alliance wanted was another war, especially with an enemy that he knew so little about.

Grant's musing about the Zrthns was cut short by a knock on the door.

C'mon in, Sha'n, he thought.

His office door opened at the unspoken permission and Sha'n entered. Although her official title was Assistant to the Commander, the Waa female was more of a trusted adviser than anything else. Standing an inch above four feet tall, the diminutive aide had the same green skin and large black eyes that were common to all Waa. Not for the first time, Grant smiled at the thought that the Waa were the little green men that were rumored to have made numerous visits to Earth in the mid- to late-1900s. Only they weren't rumors, he knew. The Waa visited Earth regularly in the latter half of the twentieth century. What was really funny was that they looked remarkably like the cartoon- and movie-based characters that had become so popular after those visits began. Green skin. Large, bald heads. Enormous, almond-shaped black eyes. Even the flowing, light-colored robes they wore fit the ancient-human stereotype.

It had taken Grant nearly a year before he could identify Sha'n as an individual, distinct from the thousands of other Waa who resided in and beneath the city. Eventually, he came to recognize her from the tiny wrinkles covering her skin, the distinctive angle of her eyes, and the way she walked. Grant had once tried to describe his efforts at distinguishing a single Waa to an acquaintance on Earth. The best example he could come up with was to ask his friend to imagine a thousand oranges. At first, they all looked the same, but if you removed a single orange and examined it every day for a year, you might eventually be able to pick it out of a pile of oranges with some effort. You just had to make sure it was a small pile.

After more than ten years by his side, Sha'n had become one of the most important and trusted individuals in Grant's life. She wasn't just an aide or an advisor; she was one of a small handful of his true friends.

Good morning, Sha'n, he greeted his aide.

Good morning, Commander Justice.

While the Waa could speak normally, mind-speak was infinitely easier, and the advantages over verbal communication were significant. Mind-speak was like communicating in 3-D. It permitted the full use all of one's senses. Complete thoughts, feelings, smells, and sights—among other things—could all be relayed during a conversation. For example, Grant's simple greeting to Sha'n had informed her of his mood and relayed his pleasure at seeing her enter his office. It was a far superior method of communication to simple verbal-speak, which was limited by each individual's vocabulary and ability to express themselves through words and body language. Grant often wished he could use mind-speak with other humans. It would make things so much easier. But humans, while capable of interacting with the Waa on a mental plane, weren't built for communicating with one another on that basis.

Of course, it was possible for the Waa to act as

"mental interpreters" between humans, which could enormously improve human interactions, but there were two problems with that scenario. The first was simple logistics and availability. The Waa were the premier builders and thinkers of the Alliance. Their skills would be poorly spent acting as simple interpreters between humans.

The second problem was the more important, however. Their ability was one of the most closely held secrets of the Shiale Alliance. Other than Grant, only two other humans and the Telgorans knew what the "little green men" could do. The Telgorans kept to themselves, they detested the Minith and rarely interacted with humans. Even if Grant hadn't received their agreement to keep the information secret, he had little fear they would ever disclose it. It didn't serve the Alliance for the knowledge to become more wide-spread. The Waa were incapable of reading the minds of the Minith, the most aggressive, warlike contingent of the alliance. Grant trusted his large, green allies—somewhat—but he didn't feel a responsibility to disclose information the Minith could potentially use against them. Also, and more importantly, if the Zrthns learned of the Waa's ability, the not-so-small advantage the Alliance held in their fight to keep the foreigners at bay might disappear.

You are concerned about the upcoming negotiations. And about things on Telgora.

Grant mentally kicked himself. He hadn't meant for either piece of information to slip out. Sha'n had been working with him on methods for preventing the Waa to peek into his mind. He was getting very adept at cloaking his inner thoughts, but he had to concentrate in order for it to be effective. He had nothing to hide from Sha'n, but immediately began the cloaking techniques she had taught him. He felt confident that with more practice he could train himself to shield all of his waking thoughts without significant effort.

He pushed the Zrthn threat to the back of his mind and focused on the situation on Telgora.

Yes. Any word from our sources there? Grant asked.

We received the weekly update. Eli is doing well in his training.

Excellent. His identity?

Still hidden from all parties. No one knows he's your son.

Grant nodded and turned back to the window. He heard the door close behind him, signaling Sha'n's departure. She came and went as the need, or his mood, dictated.

Despite the attempt to hide his feelings, he knew she had picked up on his worry. It hadn't been his choice to send his only son into the hell of Telgora. It certainly hadn't been his idea to send the boy—even as an eighteen year old, Grant still considered him his boy—into military training as an ordinary foot soldier. Eli had grown up in an environment that groomed him to be a soldier. He could have easily qualified as an officer based on the standard qualification tests had he wanted. He was proficient in virtually every aspect of military life, Grant had personally overseen his training since he was seven. But Eli was his own man, and had refused what he considered "the easy way." He wanted to enter the military the way a common soldier did.

Despite his worry as a father, he was proud of his son for his choices. Few of the most important things in life were ever gained by taking the easy path. Hard work, commitment, and sacrifice led to success.

Yes, Grant was very proud indeed, and how could he not be? After all, it's what he would have done.

CHAPTER 2

With a groan of effort, Eli slipped the overstuffed pack from his shoulders and dropped it to the barracks floor. The nondescript, cement block building where they were housed wasn't home, but it was the only place where he and his fellow recruits could unwind out of sight and mind of their Minith task masters. As such, it was a welcome sight whenever they came in from a long day of training. The room where he bunked was painted a light green and housed twenty soldiers—men and women mixed. Each trooper was assigned a standard bunk and a storage closet for their equipment. A large, communal latrine was just down the hall, and served five of these twenty-person rooms.

He stared at the name "Jayson" stenciled on the top of the pack for just a moment. It felt strange to use a last name that wasn't his own . . . but also good in a way. All of his life, he'd been known and treated as the son of the most important—and most famous—human in the entire Shiale Alliance. Here, he was his own person, and the anonymity the alias provided was as frightening as it was liberating. He was intensely proud of his father and of the family name, but for the first time in his eighteen years, he would succeed or fail on his own merit, without the influence, prejudice, or stigma that came with the name "Justice."

He carefully leaned his weapon against the pack, then executed a flawless, rolling flop onto his bunk. The relief of being off his feet for the first time in over twenty-four hours swallowed him whole.

Around him, the sounds of platoon-mates collapsing into their own bunks filtered through his fatigue. The wrinkles and lumps caused by his flop would need straightening soon—everyone's bunk would need to be perfect for evening inspection—but for now, he soaked in the pleasure of the not-so-soft mattress. Although there were only humans assigned to his training unit, the bunk was oversized, built to accommodate any recruit—human, Minith, or Telgoran. Eli's slender frame fit easily into the bed, with plenty of room to spare.

"Ah, crud," he heard Private Gale Benson mutter as he approached. His feet scuffed across the floor in that exhausted, shuffle-walk manner that had become so familiar. It also meant they would need to buff out the minute scratches that Benson was leaving in his wake. Another wonderful chore. "How the flock am I gonna make it up there?"

Eli buried his smile in his pillow and grunted a noncommittal response. On the first day of training, Benson had demanded that they switch bunks. Ignoring the hint of violence that had accompanied the demand, Eli had agreed at once. Giving up the top bunk he had been assigned for the bottom bunk Benson had been issued was a no-brainer. Not only were the bunks larger in order to accommodate the size of the average Minith soldier, the top bunk was also considerably higher than a standard human bunk for the same reason. Unfortunately for Benson, he hadn't had the foresight to consider the energy needed to climb to the top every night.

Exhaustion threatened to drag Eli into sleep, but he fought the temptation. He waited until Benson finally reached the summit, then turned over and stared at the bottom of the other man's bed. He went through a five-minute routine of horizontal stretching exercises, then slowly coaxed his aching body into a seated position and lowered his still-booted feet to the floor.

"What're you doing?" The question drifted down from the top bunk. Benson sounded completely spent from the recent march.

"Gotta get these boots off, man," Eli replied.

"Ah, hell. Should I even ask why? We gotta be outside again in an hour anyway."

"That's the reason. Do you want to head out on another march without taking care of your feet?"

"Crud, EJ! You waited until I got up here to tell me that, didn't you?"

Eli grinned and began unlacing the orange-tinted boots. Benson had taken to calling him by his initials weeks ago, and to Eli's surprise, he kind of enjoyed it. He had never had a nickname, and EJ was as good as any. He sighed when he kicked off his first boot, groaned in pleasure when the second one came off. The relief was immediate, but temporary. Both boots would be put back on shortly.

"Nah. Too tired to think of it before now. That's all."

"Yeah, yeah. Save it for the Minith. You just like to see me suffer, admit it."

"S'what you get for talking me out of the top bunk on day one," Eli chided.

"Yeah, and you refused to trade back on day two. But the offer still stands."

"I'm good, but thanks. Still . . . you need to wash your feet and put on fresh socks before evening formation."

"Crud."

Despite their early, rocky start, the two men had come to like each other. Eli enjoyed the other man's humor and his ability to do whatever was needed to survive the torture their Minith trainers put them through. He also knew the other man had come to rely on his experience and guidance. As their training progressed, more and more of the individuals in their unit dropped out, casualties of the stress and conditions to which they were subjected. Interestingly, whatever they were required to do, Eli always seemed to come out near the front of the pack. He wasn't always the best, but he was never far behind the leader. Benson had quickly taken note.

Others had taken note as well.

As Eli limped across the barracks floor to the latrine, he saw several heads turn in his direction and take note of his actions. As he was leaving the washroom, his feet now clean, most of his unit—Benson included—passed him going in the opposite direction.

* * *

An hour later, the fifty-four men and women that remained in their training platoon stood silently in rank and file. The hot, Telgoran wind whipped viciously through their battered ranks, causing several of the soldiers to sway or stagger against the invisible assault. The hard-packed ground they occupied was kept clean by the wind, but rogue grains of sand and grit were regularly found by the invisible cyclone and cast angrily against an unprotected hand or face. Random yelps or flinches from his peers punctuated each occurrence, and gave notice that it was just a matter of time before another of the tiny missiles found a target. The anxious wait for the next surprising sting was worse than the sting itself, Eli thought, and he took a deep breath of hot air and forced his tense muscles to relax as best they could. This experience was temporary and wouldn't last forever, he reminded himself. A sudden bite of pain to his left cheek reminded him that the experience, though temporary, had to be endured just the same.

The two sister platoons in their training company stood to the left and right of Eli's platoon. Neither of the other platoons held more than fifty recruits each, Eli noticed. The forced march that weeded out five of his platoon-mates had taken a much heavier toll on the other two units. A quick peek showed the boots of all but a few in the other platoons were still covered in dust and sand. Few of them had bothered to treat their feet during their short break. A whisper of concern tickled the back of Eli's neck at the oversight. It also resurrected the still-lingering question of why the Minith sergeants didn't look out for them? Weren't they invested in the health and well-being of their charges? Along those same lines, he wondered what had kept him from looking after his peers. It wasn't his job to look after everyone, but if he could help, why not? He had been training to be a soldier for years, he knew things that those around him obviously didn't. It made no sense to keep that knowledge to himself. With an internal nod, he made a decision to step up and fill in the gaps where he could. Maybe their instructors couldn't be bothered, but he had no such qualms.

The assembled humans immediately snapped to attention as three Minith instructors exited the building to their front. The aliens were outfitted in the same dirty-copper colored uniform as Eli and his peers, but that's where the resemblance ended. The giant warriors had greenish skin, stood in excess of eight feet, and weighed more than three hundred pounds. Their simian appearance was offset by large, batlike ears. Those ears were the reason they didn't wear the black beret that the humans sported. It was safe to say, the Minith were intimidating and Eli had noted early on that the instructors leveraged their physical appearance to push, taunt, and torture their human charges.

Each was a sergeant in the Alliance Defense Force and all had several years of military experience. At least one of them had seen battle against humans on Earth, Eli had learned a week earlier. His instructor, Sergeant Twigg, had dropped that nugget of information during a class on hand-to-hand combat. The way his eyes had searched the recruits surrounding him seemed full of menace, as if he was daring one of his human charges to make a comment or offer an affront to his honor. No one had accepted the unspoken challenge. It was likely the other two sergeants had similar battle experience.

The three huddled in front of the assembled platoons and openly ignored the humans. Although Defense Force regulations required that all military personnel speak Earth Standard language whenever a second race was present, the three Minith sergeants set that rule aside in favor of their native tongue. It was apparent the Minith did not anticipate any of the humans could speak their language.

Interesting, Eli thought as he strained to hear what they were saying.

"Stupid monkeys," the soldier next to him

muttered. A quick glance showed the soldier to be Private Jerrone, an orphan from Earth. "They're supposed to speak Standard."

"Shhhh," Eli whispered. "I'm trying to hear." The comment prompted a gasp and a sideways look from the other recruit. Apparently, he hadn't expected any of his peers to speak Minith, either.

". . . only five were lost?" Eli heard the Minith sergeant for First Platoon, Sergeant Brek, ask.

"That's unacceptable," Sergeant Krrp, the sergeant for Third Platoon replied. "We can't let that many of these sheep pass."

Sergeant Twigg's ears twitched, and the look that crossed his face showed that he agreed with his fellow instructors. "What do you propose?"

"Another march?"

"Humpf! I'd agree, but what if the humans sitting in power hear of it? It could undo years of work," Brek offered. "So what if we put an additional twenty humans in the ranks? It's not as if they could harm us or change our plans."

The three looked over the assembled humans once again. Eli, who had spent most of his childhood with Minith friends, and being tutored by Minith warriors, recognized the look of contempt on the faces of the three trainers. By nature, Minith were contemptuous creatures, so seeing the expression was no surprise. However, observing a Minith openly express contempt toward a human was a new experience for Eli. He wondered what it meant.

"Let's put them through another ten kilometers," Sergeant Twigg announced. He waved a large, greenish hand at the humans assembled behind him. "They look ready to drop, and that should be enough to weed most of them out."

"And if we get questioned by the masters?"

"We'll explain it away, of course. Just a standard training exercise." It was apparent that Twigg was senior, and the other two nodded at the decision. "And stop calling them 'masters.' They're sheep, just like the pitiful creatures behind us."

"Very well. Shall we feed them first?"

"Yes," Twigg replied. "They'll be emptying their stomachs on the side of the road within the first kilometer."

A cloud of anger passed through Eli's being. He didn't know what their motivations were, but it was apparent they were no longer bound by the Minith culture principle that dictated their subservience to the humans who had defeated them. Eli wondered if all Minith felt the same or if this new behavior was limited to a small group. Regardless, it was suddenly apparent why these three were blatantly ignoring their responsibilities as training sergeants. They wanted the humans who had been placed under their tutelage to fail.

CHAPTER 3

They were released with instructions to eat quickly and be back in formation in thirty minutes.

"You've all put in a good day of work," Sergeant Twigg announced before releasing Second Platoon for the evening meal. Typically, a comment of that nature could be accurately interpreted as confirmation the worn-out recruits would soon be done for the day. In this instance, though, Eli knew that wasn't the case. The Minith sergeants were setting them up for failure.

As the recruits fell out of formation and began moving toward the mess hall, Eli debated quickly on what action he should take. Until now, he had managed to stay under the radar of the instructors. And while his platoon-mates may have recognized some of his actions as potentially noteworthy, he had resisted taking steps that would designate him as a leader to the training cadre or the other platoons. Basically, he'd kept his head down, his mouth shut, and done his own thing.

But now . . . now, he felt he had to take some sort of action—warn his platoon and the others of what was coming. Having made up his mind, he scanned the crowd and found the person he wanted.

"Yo, Benson," he called. "Hold up!"

Benson looked back, saw who had called out to him, and waited for Eli to catch up.

"What's up, EJ? I'm starving, and we've only got thirty."

"Yeah, but we've got bigger problems right now."

Benson raised an eyebrow and waited for Eli to continue. "We're going to have to march again after chow."

"What! No way, man," the other private argued. "You heard Twiggy. We're done after chow."

"He never said that. And you better not let him hear you call him 'Twiggy'."

"Yeah, yeah," Benson countered, trying to sound tough, but not quite pulling it off. His quick scan of the immediate vicinity to make sure the big-eared sergeant wasn't around gave him away. He was about to say something else when Eli felt a tug on his sleeve and turned to find Jerrone at his side.

"So, you speak the green monkey's language, Jayson?" Eli bit down on his irritation at the question. He had a lot of respect for the Minith. Hell, his best friend, Arok, was Minith. As a result, he had come to despise the derogatory names many of his fellow humans used when referring to the other race. For the thousandth time, he reminded himself that few humans knew anything about the alien race that once enslaved Earth. And what they did know, wasn't very positive.

"Well?" Jerrone persisted. "What were they saying?"

Benson took a step backward and looked at Eli anew.

"You speak Minith?"

"Shhhh, both of you," Eli whispered and motioned for the two to keep it down. "Yeah, I understand a bit of Minith."

Benson whistled and shook his head. Jerrone studied Eli's face, apparently unsure if he could believe what Eli was telling them. As far as most Earth-born humans knew, the number of people that could speak an alien language could be counted on the combined fingers and toes of the three recruits standing in their small circle. It's why Earth Standard was the official language of the Shiale Alliance—well, that and the fact that Earth had defeated the Minith in the Peace Wars a dozen years earlier. Victory carries its perks. Being able to designate an official language was one of those perks.

"How do you—"

"That's not important," Eli waved away Benson's question before he could finish it. "What *is* important is that we let everyone know what's going on. Our beloved sergeants are going to be putting us back on the road for another ten-kilometer march as soon as chow is over."

"Is that what they were gabbing about?"

"Yeah. Apparently, we didn't lose as many people as they'd hoped for on the last one."

"What, do they have a quota to meet or something?" Benson asked. It was in interesting question and one that Eli wanted to pursue. But not now, there wasn't time.

"Not sure." It was all Eli could offer. "But we need to spread the word. Can you guys let the folks in our platoon know?"

"I guess." Benson agreed. "What do I tell them exactly?"

"Tell them we've got another march right after chow. Don't overeat. Take in lots of fluids. And stay away from the *chakka*."

"They won't like that. That stuff is pretty tasty."

"Yeah, but it makes you sleepy, sits like a stone in your gut, and doesn't provide enough calories. If they eat it right before we hit the sand again, they won't make it to the halfway point."

Chakka was one of the few Minith foods that humans would touch, but those who tried it often overdid it. It tasted wonderful—offering a nuanced blend of alternating flavors that seemed to change with the eater's particular palate. The first time Eli tried *chakka*, it tasted like a blend of dark chocolate and salted nuts. The second time, he could have sworn he was eating some delicious form of beef that had been perfectly seasoned. It had also provided him with a sense of mild euphoria, quickly followed an hour later by a two-hour nap on each occasion. He had sworn never to eat it again after that. Despite his personal abstinence, it was a popular evening meal for the trainees in their unit when they knew they were going to be done for the day. It definitely beat the pastelike foodstuffs that were the standard human fare.

"Fine," Benson agreed. "What about the other two platoons?"

"Let 'em hang, I say," Jerrone offered. "Second Platoon is our home."

Eli considered agreeing—there was serious competition between the three platoons. Each consistently tried to outperform the others, and bragging rights had become an important aspect of their training. But the recent revelation that the Minith sergeants wanted them to fail changed things. The sergeants had turned this into an "us versus them" scenario that removed any doubt over what needed to be done. He had an obligation to let the other two platoons know what was up.

"No, we need to tell them," he decided. "They can choose to ignore the warning if they want, but we have to let them know. It's only fair."

"Hey, whatever," Jerrone shrugged and turned to head inside. "Do what you need to. I'm off to spread the word to our folks."

"I can tell that Johnson guy," Benson offered. "He seems to run things over in First Platoon. Not sure who's in charge over in third."

Eli swallowed, suddenly nervous. He knew who the unofficial leader was in the Third Platoon. He'd been keeping tabs on both of their sister units since day one.

"I know who to speak with," he replied. It was all he could manage, and he suddenly didn't feel well. For Eli, the sudden absence of self-confidence was an unusual state of being, and he shook off the unwelcome feeling like a coat of dust. "Tell Johnson his folks need to change their socks too. They'll need those just as much as they need chow."

* * *

"Private Tenney, can I speak with you for a moment?"

The recruit from Third Platoon looked briefly at Eli, then turned her attention back to the chow line ahead of her. At least twenty other soldiers stood between her and the serving line where their daily meals were slopped out. At least half of the company had already gotten their chow and were seated at the tables scattered throughout the large room.

"Shove off, pal," the dark-haired private replied with a dismissive tone that easily cut through the growing din of the chow hall. "You're cute, but I'm not interested."

It took a moment for Eli to understand what she meant. When the words sunk in, he felt the blood rush to his face. *What the—?* He gritted his teeth and tried again.

"You lead things in Three, right?"

The unexpected question got her attention. She turned her green eyes on him and searched his face. He felt his guts tighten and waited for recognition.

"You know we don't have leaders . . ." Her eyes dipped to read the name inked on his left sleeve. "Private Jayson."

"I know we don't have *official* leaders, Tenney. But I've seen how you take charge of the rabble in Three." The comment caused her eyes to harden for just a moment before realizing he was taunting her. "They look to you for just about everything."

"I don't know what you mean," she answered, once again offering him the dismissive tone. For good measure, she added a snide curl of her lip and a casual wave that meant nothing short of "get lost."

"Yes you do," Eli snapped, angry at her obstinance. He was running out of time. The first two members of Third Platoon were already getting food plopped on their plates up ahead. "No time to explain how I know this, but we're getting tossed back into the sand right after chow. You need to get your folks fed and their feet taken care of before we land back in formation in"—Eli checked the time—"twenty-five minutes. And I'd recommend laying off the *chakka*, if you know what I mean."

Her eyes bore into his—searched for signs of deceit, truth, or something else. He couldn't tell for sure, but apparently she found what she needed.

"You had better not be mucking with my platoon on this, Jayson."

"I enjoy friendly competition as much as you do," he answered. "But mucking with another platoon for no good reason just isn't my style. We're spreading the word to our own platoon, as well as to first. Even if they don't put us back on the hump, what's the harm in being prepared?"

"Fine," she said, roughly poking a finger into the middle of his chest. The action nearly caused him to retreat a step, but he just managed to hold his ground against the offending digit. "But you'll answer to me if we're not back in the sand before lights out."

Eli did his best to ignore the finger drilling into his chest. He sorely wanted to produce a witty, but sarcastic response to her threat, but all he could think of was "Oh no. I'm so scared." That didn't seem like a response any self-respecting adult would give, so he bit his tongue, offered her a weak, closed-mouth smile and nodded. The finger pushed angrily into his chest for another second, then was gone. Without another glance in his direction, she was off to the front of the chow line. He watched as she intercepted the first few members of her platoon and issued quiet instructions, then began working her way backward. Eli released the breath he hadn't realized he'd been holding, then turned to return to his own platoon, lined up at the rear.

All in all, it had gone much better than he had expected. Private Adrienne Tenney was passing the word to her team.

Best of all, she hadn't recognized him.

Then again, twelve years was a long time, and he wasn't six years old anymore.

CHAPTER 4

A forced march is a grueling test of mind over matter. There are two simple rules: keep moving until you reach the end, and reach the end within the time allotted. That's it. Armies have been doing it for thousands of years.

For the most part, the Alliance Defense Force version of the forced march was little different from previous versions. Everyone carried the same amount of weight, everyone traveled the same distance, and had the same amount of time to finish. The experience was as much a mental test as one of strength and endurance. The keys to success were as simple as the rules: Don't give up. Push through the pain. Beat the pacer.

The pacer was a new twist. Earlier armies used timed finishes, or had sergeants bringing up the rear, to determine who made the cut and who didn't. Eli and his peers had the pacer—a mechanized device that hovered at the rear and move at a steady, controlled pace. The shiny metallic orb floated a meter off the ground and identified the wash-out line for the marchers. Every five seconds, it issued an ominous, tinny *beep* to alert those it was nearby. Anyone who failed to cross the finish line before the pacer, or who fell behind the orb for longer than ten seconds, was deemed unfit for service and sent home. For those currently present, home was Earth. Overcrowded, peaceful, boring old Earth. The same planet that millions of men and women—mostly young adults—were trying to leave.

Eli found it strange that humanity had never really tried to leave their planet through their own will and engineering. They were content to grow and expand across the face of the planet, using up the resources as if they were limitless. Until they realized there was something else out there—something more. Military service was the primary method of escaping the socially compliant existence that had become the norm for a life on Earth, and training spots were as coveted as they were few. The need for soldiers was greater than ever, but skilled fighters who could train recruits were scarce. As a result, washing out of training meant spending the remainder of your life performing rote, undesirable tasks that no one else wanted. Washouts weren't selected for engineering, admin or leadership positions. The feeling on Earth was you had your chance, and through your own fault, wasted it. With sixty billion people to care for, second chances at a plum assignment were as common as blue unicorns.

Left . . .

Left . . .

Left, right, left.

A kilometer into the second forced march of the day and Eli—though tired and sore—felt strong. He had something to prove, not only to himself, but to the three Minith who wanted to see him and his kind fail. For him, proving he could take whatever they threw at him was all the motivation he needed. He put his head down and trudged against the hot, swirling wind that battered relentlessly against his body. It was an invisible force that did its best to hold him back and keep him from his goal. Lowering his head made it harder to breathe the overheated air, but it helped protect his face from the ever-present sand bites. It was a trade-off that he gladly made.

The three platoons had started the march in loose formation, but that quickly fell apart once the march began. As usual, the trek became an individual event—every person for themselves. The fast moved to the front. The slow dropped to the rear. Those who moved too slowly would eventually drop behind the pacer. If they fell behind for more than ten seconds, they washed out.

Left . . .

Left . . .

Left, right, left.

Eli was in the zone. His head was down against the wind, and he was pushing relentlessly forward.

And then he wasn't. His momentum slowed as he fully considered his position and the position of those behind him. As he thought about the alien sergeants, and their desire for human failure, his temples began to throb and his heartbeat—already elevated—increased. Anger. Resentment. Disgust. All of those emotions and more began working their way through his being as he thought about his fellow recruits. They deserved a chance to break out from the overpopulated world they had so recently left behind. They didn't deserve to be treated like cattle or sheep by a cadre of alien underlings who had already been defeated by humanity. By Eli's very own father, no less.

Instead of pushing forward toward the finish line, he slowed, turned around, and began a slow backward walk. He stared back along the path he had already crossed, his eyes searching for and taking in the sight of his fellow recruits. Fellow humans.

He had been moving well, staying strong, well

ahead of the pacer. Unfortunately, there were plenty of others—from all three platoons—who weren't doing as well. No one had fallen behind the pacer yet, but several were beginning to lag. If they didn't pick up their pace, it was just a matter of time. Scenarios ran through his mind and his feet stopped moving altogether.

He suddenly understood that this march wasn't just about *his* success. It was about the success of his race. It was about meeting the cruelty of their Minith trainers head on, and showing them the true nature of mankind. *They lost the Peace War*, he raged. *We didn't.* Eli decided it time to remind them that they had been beaten a dozen years earlier, and would be beaten again in another dozen years, if necessary.

Before he could change his mind, his feet were moving again. Only this time, they—and an anger that seemed to grow hotter with each step—carried him *away* from the finish line. This time, they carried him toward the pacer. The wind—now at his back—was a welcome nudge aiding his movements.

"What the crud are you doing, EJ?" Benson passed Eli going the other way. Eli didn't answer; he just kept moving toward the back of the pack.

He passed several more recruits and all of them looked at him as if he'd lost his senses. For all Eli knew, he had.

Flock the pacer and flock the Minith!

First, second, or third platoon—it didn't matter. These were his people. It might be crazy, and he didn't know how, but he was going to do whatever he could to help those at the rear of the pack.

He passed Private Tenney at the midway point and she stared at him as he got close. Eli stared back, suddenly not caring if she recognized him. He was who he was and wouldn't deny it if challenged. His father had beaten the Minith in war. All he had to do was beat them on a forced march. And to beat them, he had to save every human he could from washing out.

It took only a few minutes to reach the back of the pack where he noticed four recruits, two women and two men, struggling. The pacer was less than a quarter of a kilometer behind them—close, but still too far away to hear the dreaded warning tone. That was good, but one look at the group told the story. With nine kilometers left to go, there was no way this group would make it unless they moved faster.

He slowed and waited for them to reach his position. Each looked up at him as they neared. Fear, pain, and desperation were written clearly across their faces. Surprise and curiosity at his approach quickly followed. He offered a single nod to the group as they reached him, then turned around and settled into the wind beside them. His legs and feet told him what his mind already knew. Their pace was too slow. They had to pick it up.

"What . . . are you . . . doing?" one of male recruits asked.

"Did any of you eat the *chakka* at dinner?" A chorus of "yeses" confirmed his suspicions. They either hadn't gotten the word or had disregarded it. "Well, do you regret it now?"

"Yeah," was followed by two "uh huh's," which was followed by, "never eating . . . that stuff again."

"Glad to hear it," he replied. He wanted to chastise them for putting themselves—and now him—in this position, but wasn't certain if now was the time. Instead, he lowered his head and picked up the pace just a bit to see if the group matched his step—was pleased when they fell into the new, but still-too-slow rhythm. He couldn't resist a slight, teasing rebuke. "I'd hate to think I came back here to help your sorry asses unless you learned your lesson."

"Not sure how much . . . help you can give," the female recruit next to him said. "Just a . . . matter of . . . time."

"True . . . we're pacer bait now," one of the men added.

"Is that what you all have been discussing back here? How hopeless things are?" None of the four responded, but he could tell that they'd been thinking it, if not actually saying it out loud. He tried walking a bit quicker but only two of the four kept up with the faster pace. The other two dropped back and didn't try to close the widening gap, so he slowed back down to match their pace. Eli took a deep breath to release some of the anger that had delivered him to this point, and thought about what he could do to get them to move quicker.

"I'm usually at the front of the pack," he tossed out to the four. "Would you like to hear how I do that?"

"All ears . . . buddy," one of the men answered.

"First, I tell myself that this walk, this pain, this phase of training . . . Well, I tell myself that it can't last forever. At some point, it's going to end. Then I remind myself it will either end with me behind the pacer, bound for a trip back to Earth, or it will end with me in front of the pacer, ready for the next challenge."

"You're a . . . genius," the man gasped. The sarcasm was evident despite his lack of breath. "How come I . . . never thought of that?"

"But that's just the start," Eli continued. He flinched as a grain slapped him in the chin. He wiped the back of his hand over the sand-bite, noted the tiny streak of red it came away with, and erased the tiny stain against his pants. "After I remind myself of that, I put everything out of my mind except for one thing."

Several moments passed, but he refused to speak until someone asked the obvious question. Finally, the second man spoke up.

"And what's that?"

"Left . . . left . . . left, right, left," Eli answered. He stepped onto his left foot and began. "I just keep repeating it over and over and over, like a mantra."

He kept on repeating the litany, matching the words with the footfalls hitting the ground. After a minute, he felt more than saw the four walking beside him, each now in step with his cadence. He repeated it over and over and over.

"Left . . . left . . . left, right, left." They didn't say a word, but fell into his rhythm, matched him pace for pace as they covered the ground. He increased the pace by slow degrees until—finally—they were moving faster than the pacer following silently but steadily behind them.

Ten minutes after starting, the small group caught up with two more stragglers. Eli didn't stop calling out the pattern. He just jerked a thumb at the two, indicating they should fall into line behind them. The two fell silently into place and kept up. The group soon fell into a rough semblance of a formation, with two troops in front, two in the middle, and two in back. Eli marched to the left of the small formation and called out the pace.

By the five-kilometer point, the group had grown

to fourteen. Eli continued calling out the steps, but the group could move only as fast as the slowest person. And some were faltering. Despite his best efforts, they began to lose ground to the pacer. A quick glance behind showed the hovering orb had regained its former position a quarter of a kilometer back. He was beginning to doubt if they could all make it, but refused to concede a single person to the Minith unless there was no other choice.

"Left . . . left . . . left, right, left."

At seven kilometers, the group had grown to twenty. They were aligned four wide, with five rows total. After some consideration, Eli instructed the four in front of the formation to fall to the rear. Those in the rear had some protection against the heated wind blowing in their faces, and trading off the forward positions made sense. They kept it up on a rotating basis, with the front row dropping to the rear every five minutes or so, and the action seemed to help. The group picked up the pace. Hopefully, it would be enough.

At the eight-kilometer mark, with only two kilometers left, the first person dropped out of formation and stopped. Eli kept calling out the pace, but immediately pulled one of the stronger recruits from the formation. He pointed at her—she was one of the original four, he noticed—and then pointed at his spot next to the formation.

"Left . . . left . . . left, right, left."

With hand motions, he let her know that he wanted her to begin calling the cadence. She started tentatively, but he called out the steps with her. Together, they counted. When he felt she had it, he turned back toward the recruit that had fallen behind.

He retraced the twenty meters to the young

private, who was now bent over, throwing up. The private still had his pack on his back, but his plasma rifle was on the ground, and his hands were planted firmly on his knees. He didn't appear to have any inclination of continuing. Eli read the name on his sleeve.

"Simms, that pacer isn't going to wait for you. You gotta get moving." Simms just waved a hand dismissively and dry heaved. Eli looked behind the man and saw the metal orb approaching. He knew it wasn't coming at them any faster, but it sure seemed to be eating up the distance now that they weren't moving.

"Can't . . ."

"You want to wash out? Get sent back home?" It was a question that they both knew the answer to, but Simms didn't seem capable of moving another step. Eli scrambled for a solution, any solution. Only one possible answer came back. He didn't stop to second guess. "Drop your pack. Now!"

"Huh?" Simms looked up from his feet for the first time, unsure of what he was being told.

"Drop your pack," Eli repeated. "Can you move on if you don't carry the pack?"

"I can't just . . . leave it here and move on. What good is . . . that?"

"We're not leaving it behind, Simms." Eli didn't wait for the other man to reply or understand. Instead, he handed his shotgun to Simms, then reached out and pulled the pack from the exhausted man. He met no resistance, and let the pack drop to the sand. Simms straightened, noticeably relieved to have the weight lifted from his shoulders. Eli readjusted the load on his own back, then reached down for Simms's pack. "Hand it up to me."

Simms stared at Eli, his mouth open in shock.

Beep.

"Now, Simms! No time to waste," Eli shouted while pointing at the discarded pack.

As if in a daze, Simms slung Eli's shotgun over his shoulder, reached down, gripped the shoulder straps and hoisted the weight up. "Turn it around so the straps face me."

Beep.

Simms turned the pack around and watched as Eli reached his hands through the straps and hugged the bulk to his chest. He used his right thigh to help hold the pack in position.

"Now loop the straps over my shoulders," Eli grunted. He couldn't believe what he was attempting to do, but it was the only thing he could think of. Without a word, Simms pulled the straps over the back of Eli's shoulders and stepped back. Eli bent his knees, tested the security of the load, and began a slow, but steady walk in the direction of the finish line.

Beep. The short hairs on the back of Eli's neck itched in response to the warning sound. He refused to turn around, but it seemed as though the pacer couldn't get much closer without passing them.

"Let's go, Simms. *Now*!"

Without thinking, Eli quickly fell into step with the female recruit's cadence. She and the formation were sixty meters ahead, but the wind blew her words back toward the duo. Ignoring the hot stabs of agony that tortured his being and struggling against the weight of two packs, Eli extended his step, anxious to leave the pacer, and its obnoxious "beep" behind. Simms now carried both their weapons and managed to keep up.

"Left . . . left . . . left, right, left."

He pushed everything from his mind, including the newly discovered inability to draw enough oxygen into his lungs, and concentrated on her voice. He suddenly regretted not getting her name.

At kilometer nine, Eli saw another person fall out of the formation ahead. He groaned, his body running on fumes. He knew he was too spent to help.

"Don't worry, Jayson," Simms said from his side, before stumbling ahead. He appeared tired, but could obviously move quicker now that he wasn't carrying the additional weight. "I've got this one."

Eli managed to lift his head from and watch as Simms reached the female recruit and spoke a few words. By the time he reached their position, each had a strap in one hand, and with the load hanging between them, they struggled toward the finish line. For someone who had been ready to quit just minutes before, Simms seemed determined now. Eli wanted to pat him on the back, tell the pair "Way to go" or something, but he couldn't. His hands were full, and he no longer had enough strength to do more than take the next step and gasp hungrily for his next ragged breath. The anger that had set him on this path had passed. He imagined the pacer breathing down his neck and wondered if he'd be the one to wash out. For a moment, he wondered whether he should have ever turned around, but it was a fleeting thought. No, he'd do it all over again, if it meant saving just one of his fellow humans.

Onward he pushed, refusing to give in to the pacer on his tail, the Minith who controlled it, or the pain that racked his body and threatened to keep him from his goal.

Step after step. Ragged breath upon ragged breath. Pain on top of pain.

With less than half a kilometer to go, Eli stumbled over a rock and his right knee buckled. He managed to utter a slight curse before his body—and the weight of the two packs he carried—smacked the ground in a tumbled mess of clatter and exhaustion.

His mind screamed "Get up!" but his body refused to listen. The arms that held the pack to his chest were quivering bowls of jelly. The legs that had carried him so far, nothing more than useless slabs of dead, tired meat. He rocked side-to-side in frustrated anger but couldn't even push himself to his knees, much less regain his feet.

Beep.

The worst agony—that of defeat—crashed down upon him, and he cried out in rage. The weight of his failure felt like all the dirt in the world being shoveled onto the lid of his casket.

Beep.

Unable to move, his chin sank into the sand-covered soil of Telgora, and he raged silently against the inevitable. His eyes closed against the tears that threatened and spent his final speck of energy to curse the Minith sergeants.

Beep.

He was done.

* * *

Dark. Heavy breathing all around. Snoring?

If he hadn't known better, Eli would have thought he was back in the barracks with the outer shutters closed against the perpetual Telgoran sun. The sounds he had come to know over the past few weeks surrounded him. The feel of the mattress beneath him was familiar. Even the unique smell of the place—a worn combination of body sweat, oil, and stale farts—was spot on. But that couldn't be. He was a washout.

Wasn't he?

He tried to sit up, but a hot blast of pain knocked him flat on his back again.

"Uhhh," he groaned and agreed with his body that lying down was preferable to sitting. He heard a rustling from above and saw a shadow appear over his head.

"EJ, you okay, man?" The shadow was Benson's noggin looking down at him from the top bunk. He *was* back in the barracks.

"What . . . what happened? Why am I here?"

"Private Jayson, you pulled a real-life Justice on that march," the shadow-head offered. "Who knew you had it in you?"

"I pulled a . . . a what?"

"A *Justice*, EJ," Benson said as if talking to a five-year old. "You know . . . something a hero would do. Where the crud are you from, anyway?"

Eli had no intention of answering *that* question. At least not completely. He had been born on Earth, but had spent the last twelve years of his life on Waa. He wasn't up to date on Earth-side slang, but he had a good idea of what "pulling a Justice" meant.

"What am I doing here?" he asked, still confused. "I washed out."

"Um. No," the other man stated. "You didn't."

"I didn't finish."

"Well, that's not exactly true. You didn't finish on your own, but you finished."

"What?" Despite the pain, he turned to the side and pushed up to prop himself on his right elbow.

Nothing was making sense. He remembered hitting the ground, trying—and failing—to get up, the pacer's beeping, then . . . nothing.

"That female from Third. Tenney. She crossed the line about two minutes after I did. She pointed at me and asked if I was Second Platoon," Benson explained. "She didn't even wait for an answer, just yanked my arm and said 'Let's go.' I'm not sure how she knew you were in trouble, but the next thing I know, we're headed back out. Only this time, we're heading *for* the pacer, not away from it.

"Johnson from First and a couple of others saw us heading back out and they followed. Five minutes later, we come up on you lying face down in the sand. I'm not sure how she knew you were in trouble, but the pacer couldn't have been more than twenty meters away when she tossed one pack at me and another one at Johnson. How the crud did you end up with two, anyway?"

"Long story," Eli replied. "So, what happened then?"

"Well, then Tenney pulled her own Justice." Benson sounded both awed and amazed at what he was relaying. Eli couldn't help but feel some of that as well. "That lady picked you up, tossed you over her shoulder and started humping your body back toward the finish line. She had to hand you off to me before we got all the way back—you're not all that light, it turns out—but just seeing her lift you out of the sand was a sight I'll never forget. When she did it, Johnson and I just stared at each other and trudged along behind."

"Wow," Eli mumbled, not knowing what to say. Adrienne had saved him from washing out. "Why would she do that?"

"Same reason you went to the back to help the laggards, I guess. It was the right thing to do."

Eli thought about Simms and the other recruits he had helped keep ahead of the pacer. He was afraid to ask how many of their fellow humans had washed out, but did anyway.

"Not a single one," Benson replied. "That was your doing, EJ. That was *your* Justice."

Eli plopped back down on the mattress. The previous agonies of aching muscles and shredded feet were nearly forgotten, little more than echoes. Amazement, and a sense of wonder at what the three platoons had done, washed over him. He remembered something that his dad had once told him. He now knew it was true. A single unit working together can do what an unlimited number of individuals could never hope to accomplish.

"Wow," he repeated. Further words escaped him.

"There's only one problem," Benson mumbled just before the shadow that defined his head disappeared. The slight tremble of the bed indicated that he had flopped heavily onto his back. "Twiggy wasn't very happy. Neither were the other two sergeants."

Eli smiled, pleased to know that their effort at winnowing out more humans hadn't succeeded.

"He wants to see you first thing in the morning."

Eli's smile disappeared. His ability to keep a low profile had apparently ended. He considered how the sergeant might react to his actions and wondered what kind of trouble those actions had called down on his head. It was a brief thought, though. With a realization that was as sudden as it was unexpected, Eli found he didn't really care what the alien thought, or how he might react.

"Hey guys," a female voice interrupted. He lifted his head and saw Adrienne Tenney approaching the bunk. The unofficial leader of third platoon nodded to Benson, then ducked under the top bunk and sat down on the edge of Eli's bed. "How's the patient?"

"The patient's fine," Benson replied, still looking down from his perch. "For now, anyway. He's got a date with Twiggy in the morning, though. You might want to check back then."

"I'm not worried," Eli offered, but the titled head and blank stare he received from Benson informed that maybe he should be. "Okay, maybe I'm worried a little bit. Not much I can do about it now, though. What's done is done.

"I understand I owe you a 'thank you," he said to Tenney as he pushed his tired body into a seated position. Somehow, it didn't feel right to be lying down with her sitting less than a foot away.

She waved a casual hand at the suggestion. "Don't mention it, Jayson. You saved a bunch of my guys with the advance warning. And those theatrics at the end of the march. What made you turn back and help the stragglers?"

Eli pondered the question. He knew what made him do it—his loathing for the Minith sergeants, and the overwhelming need he'd felt for his kind to succeed—but he didn't think he could adequately verbalize any of that, so offered up a simplified version. "I didn't want to lose another person. That's my new motto: 'No more washouts.' From here on out, I'm going to help anyone who needs it."

"Very nice," Tenney nodded, then cocked her head and squinted, as if studying him. "I like that." She then reached out her right hand and gently squeezed his knee. Eli swallowed the knot in his throat and tried not to shy away from the unexpected attention.

"Well…feel free to use it," he said. His tongue seemed thick in his mouth and he felt a flush of heat cross his face. He wondered if she'd notice. He didn't know why she made him feel so self-conscious, but it had nothing to with her recognizing him. No, it wasn't that. This felt… different. He'd never had much opportunity to speak with girls; there weren't many on Waa. "And really. Thank you for saving my skin. You're the only reason I'm not a washout."

Tenney nodded and stood up. The height of Benson's bunk meant she didn't have to duck to be seen.

"Well, this guy here helped," she said, pointing her chin up at Eli's bunkmate. Benson had grown quiet over the past two minutes, which was completely out of character. "I'm going to head back to my platoon now. Good luck with your sergeant tomorrow. I'll check back to see how it went."

"Great," Eli replied, his voice cracking with the single word. He cleared his throat. "I'm sure it will be fine. As far as I know, I didn't break any rules."

She offered Eli a small wave, nodded a goodbye to Benson, and turned. Eli couldn't help but watch as she walked down the aisle and out the door. When she was out of view, he turned to find Benson staring at him, a wide grin plastered to his face.

"What?" he asked the upside-down face that peered back at him.

"I think she likes you, EJ," Benson said, retracting his head. The bed shook slightly as he flopped heavily onto the mattress of the top bunk. "And I *know* you like her."

Eli found his mouth moving to contest his friend's assertions, but he suddenly—surprisingly—found himself incapable of forming a single word.

* * *

"Two years," Grant sighed and absorbed the information. Two more years until the ship is completed. There was nothing to be done to expedite the timeline, so he merely nodded and kept walking. He automatically shortened his pace to accommodate the shorter legs of the three Waa conducting the tour. They were in one of the large, underground facilities where the Waa engineers constructed all alliance ships. This particular facility was larger than most, having been built specifically for this new breed of vessel. Due to the secrecy around its construction, Grant was the only non-Waa to have access to the area and he stared up at the behemoth that had been his brainchild.

The outer hull and all of the interior walls, walkways, and crew compartments were completed, which gave the initial impression the ship was further along in production. But he knew the delay was always the command and control systems—the components of the mother ship that governed the electrical, fusion, and drive systems. And—in this ship anyway—the weapons systems.

"How are tests of the ship-born cannons coming along?"

They have all been successful. The Waa's "words" were accompanied by a sense of proud accomplishment and visions of the large cannons being fired, both in underground testing facilities and in the orbiting firing range that had been built specifically for the purpose of conducting the test. It was important to test the device using the real-world conditions that came along with space-based use.

"Very good, Yuh. You and your workers have done an admirable job." Grant stopped hiding his thoughts just long enough to communicate his feelings of pleasure, pride, and appreciation for what the Waa had accomplished. He was getting better at keeping his thoughts masked and, at Sha'n's suggestion, was using this tour as a test of his abilities. She was trailing the group at a short distance, with the sole purpose of "listening in" on his thoughts.

Ten minutes later, the tour concluded, and the general and his advisor were promptly escorted to a carrier vehicle. At a nod from Grant, the pilot lifted off and began the short, thirty-minute trip back to the Shiale Alliance Defense Headquarters compound.

How did it go? he asked Sha'n.

It went well. I could not detect your thoughts, nor could the others. She transferred a feeling of consternation and confusion that conveyed how the other Waa had felt at the unexpected situation. Grant chuckled. He didn't have to imagine the surprise the unsuspecting Waa had felt at finding a human whose thoughts couldn't be read. Sha'n communicated it perfectly.

"It only works when I verbalize," Grant relayed. "I couldn't mask anything using mind-speak."

Agreed.

"What is it, Sha'n?" He had detected a note of concern in her "voice."

I could not see your thoughts on the ship, but I did capture a hint of unease in your being. So did the others. They suspect it had to do with the timeline. But I know it has to do with the ship and the weapons it is designed to carry. Why does this worry you?

I don't know, he admitted. *It shouldn't.*

He let his thoughts wander, knowing she'd pick up on whatever crossed his mind. Sometimes it was best to just think and let her observe. It was the nonverbal version of talking out loud.

This new mothership we're building. It will be the first of its kind. There's never been a ship that's carried its own arsenal of weapons, which means we're looking at a paradigm shift—a new way of fighting our enemies. On the surface, that seems good, because it could shift the balance of power firmly in our direction. Until now, these ships have been limited to carrying planet-bound armies and fighters. That means battles have been fought on the ground, soldier against soldier, army against army. But now we're introducing a weapons-bearing mothership that has the ability to destroy other ships in space, before they ever reach a planet's surface-based defenses. In other words, we win the battle before it starts. Honestly, I don't know why this has never been considered before. I mean, I know why the Minith didn't think of it—they're all about the ground and pound. But why haven't the Zrthn or some other race out there somewhere thought about this capability? It boggles the mind. Six hundred years ago, humans had funny little devices called televisions, where fictional stories told about space-going battleships. Even then, long before humans ever reached the stars, our minds considered the creation and plausibility of starship-born weapons. We gave them interesting names like photon torpedoes, plasma cannons, and neutron mines.

Grant released a long sigh.

Then again, maybe we're just built that way—to keep progressing, to find the next big thing, even if the next big thing is something designed to kill.

Grant struggled with how to express his thoughts in a way that delivered his concern to Sha'n without the overwhelming burden of the emotions he was feeling.

But the problem with introducing a new weapon is the same problem that mankind has been dealing with since we first picked up a stick to club our enemies in the next village. Once the genie is out of the bottle—once we pick up that stick—there's nothing to keep our enemies from reaching for their own stick. Any advantage we gain from putting a new type of mothership into service is only momentary. Once we cross that threshold, others will soon follow. Then we have a race to see who can build the most ships or the biggest ships. It opens up a can of worms that might eventually destroy the Alliance.

I see, and I understand. Should we cease production?

"No, Sha'n," Grant replied and tried to rub the ache of fatigue from his eyes. "It's too late to put the genie back in the bottle. And we might need her to survive what's ahead. We just won't use her unless there's no other option."

CHAPTER 5

Eli exited his barracks building and turned left toward the building where Twigg and the other sergeants resided. The training complex was made up of four similar cement block buildings, set in a box pattern. A large, open space, known as the quad, resided in the middle of the building group and was where their daily formations were held and much of their training took place. He bowed his head against the ever-present wind, and hurried his steps. The gusts were always worse in what they called "morning." Morning was such a discretionary concept when the sun never left the sky. For their unit, morning was merely the time of the day when the sleep cycle ended and the next training day began. It took some getting used to for everyone, but most were now in tune with the new normal.

Not for the first time, he looked around at the world around him and marveled that he was on another planet. Most humans never left Earth. He had been born there, but had been relocated to Waa as a child. Now he was on his third planet, and he marveled at how different it was from the other two.

Almost all of the differences were caused by Telgora's rotational axis, he knew. The planet spins on a near-perfect ninety-degree axis, which means it rolls around its sun like a giant marble. The southern hemisphere resides in perpetual daylight—the north, in perpetual dark. At the sun-facing south pole, temperatures remain a constant four hundred degrees Fahrenheit, two hundred degrees Celsius. Temperatures at the bitterly frozen darkness of the northern pole are just the opposite.

As a result of the world being tipped on its side, only the thin band of planet that exists between the two extremes is habitable. That's where he and all the other living creatures on the planet were currently located—within a roughly ten kilometer-wide ring that circled the entire planet. Here, Telgora is a blend of green, flowing meadow mixed with wide stretches of barren dirt and rock. Orange, deerlike creatures, called *ninal*, roam freely between the meadows and the barren areas and represent the primary source of food and leather for their underground-dwelling cohabitants. Outside of the band, very little survives above ground for long. Native Telgorans—reed-thin, seven-foot tall warriors, with muscles like steel—live most of their lives underground, protected from the often-bitter winds and extreme temperatures that assault most of the planet's surface.

Eli could quote these and other facts about the planet from memory. He hadn't spent all of his youth studying only fighting and ancient battles. He had given time to other topics as well, and knowing about the planet where he knew he'd eventually end up only made sense.

Although he considered the rotational axis, and the resulting weather patterns, the most interesting aspects about the planet, he understood—as did everyone in the Shiale Alliance—that the agsel beneath the planet's surface is what most thought about. Telgora is a remote planet, residing on the edge of the Milky Way galaxy. To the casual observer or passerby, it would be deemed unworthy of investigation or consideration, and dismissed as another worthless backwater planet. But the casual passerby might not know that far below the catacombs where the native Telgorans make their homes, expansive deposits of precious agsel ore reside, waiting to be extracted, processed, and shipped off-world. For the majority of the scatted species and races in the universe, the possession of agsel, and the ability to incorporate it into space-worthy craft, represents the difference between being planet-locked or space-able.

Only with the ore is faster-than-light travel possible. This made Telgora anything but worthless.

The human and Minith workers that mine the planet's ore keep themselves holed up in a series of giant bunkers scattered across the thin, habitable band. Totaling nearly thirty in all, each bunker is a veritable city that provides for the needs of the miners living inside. Hospitals, restaurants, bars, housing, and other necessities—legal or illegal, moral or not—are provided for the inhabitants. Life on the mining planet is tough, and the Leadership Council that has been established to govern Telgora learned early on that concessions were needed to keep workers happy and maintain production. One such concession was segregation. Only the underground communities that held the Leadership Council were fully integrated—home to both Minith and humans alike. All others were not, only housing a single species. Humans and Minith had come to an understanding in the dozen years since the end of the wars, but that understanding didn't always lead to acceptance or tolerance. Distrust was commonplace among the races. Violence—once a criminal offense for the humans—was becoming more acceptable within the rugged communities so far from Earth.

Except for the massive herds of the orange-colored *ninal* beasts, the bleak, uninteresting landscape keeps most of Telogra's inhabitants firmly entrenched inside their living and work spaces. Few care to venture outside, and those that do, usually cut their visits short.

The exception, obviously, are the soldiers of the Shiale Alliance defense forces. They traverse the Telgoran surface voluntarily, and they do so regularly. Housed in thousands of large, concrete buildings placed strategically near the mining bunkers, the soldiers—human and Minith—adapt to the conditions as best they can.

Eli was thinking about his need to adapt to the windy, sand-blown planet as he followed the stone path that separated his barracks from the dozens of others that had been erected a kilometer east of Mining Bunker Thirteen. Bunker Thirteen was the official name, of course. The inhabitants not-so-lovingly referred to their Telgoran home as "Titan City" in deference to one of the main heroes of the Minith Wars. Titan was now Earth's Emissary to the Telgorans, and lived with the natives in their underground system of caves. The bunker was one of the original five mining sites on Telgora, and it was rumored that Titan had fought there.

Eli smiled at the thought. He was one of the few on the planet that knew the "rumor" was true. When Eli was ten, "Uncle" Titan himself had described in exquisite detail the battle plan that the youngster's dad had drawn up to defeat the Minith on this planet. That battle had taken place just before Grant Justice and his army had taken the fight on to Waa. The need to protect his identity from those around him—human and not—settled onto his shoulders even more firmly with the memory. Now that he had begun the process of being just another name on the training list, it was doubtful those around him would understand if the truth came out. He wanted—no, he needed—to see this through on his own, without his father's influence hanging over his every move. He hadn't realized until just recently, that not being tied to his father's legacy was . . . liberating. For the first time in his life, he was free from the heightened expectations and constant scrutiny that came with having the name Justice.

He halted outside the door and took a deep breath before lightly tapping. He heard a muted voice call out "Enter" in Minith. Eli ignored the alien invitation and tapped again. His second effort was rewarded with the appropriate English Standard, and he pushed his way inside the tall, wide door that identified the office as belonging to a Minith.

Inside, he found Sergeants Twigg and Brek standing behind a large, plain desk. The room was painted purple—the aliens' preferred color—but was otherwise barren except for the desk, a large (again, purple) chair, and a map of Telgora on the far wall. Eli noted the highly scuffed path that circled the entire room. It was no doubt a result of the Minith's characteristic need to pace. Every Minith office he had ever been in—and he had visited quite a few—seemed to have a similar path. The two sergeants appeared to have been studying the map, but both turned as he entered the room.

Eli approached the desk, whipped his body smartly into the human version of attention, and announced, "Private Jayson, reporting as ordered."

Sergeant Twigg released a noise that might have been confused with a kitten's purr by most humans. Eli, who had grown up around the aliens, recognized the sound for what it really was: a menace-filled growl. The sudden, slight twitching of the alien's right ear confirmed

Eli's initial reaction to the growl. His actions on the march had obviously raised his sergeant's ire—and it wasn't a slight raise, either. The Minith was—in his father's words—royally pissed off. He took a slow breath and mentally prepared himself for whatever might come next. He was meant to feel fear, but didn't. Unlike most of his kind, he'd been raised around Minith. There was none of the inherent fright of them that they no doubt expected—and received—from his fellow human recruits. They could try to intimidate him all they wanted, but it wouldn't work out as they wanted. He once again reminded himself that they were the conquered race; he represented the victors. Besides, he'd done nothing he regretted, or wouldn't do again, in the same circumstances.

"How did these sheep ever defeat us, Twigg?"

The question was posed in a near-whisper, meant only for the other sergeant, but Eli had no problem making out the words even though they were issued in the low, growling-grunt rasp that distinguished the Minith language. The muscles in Eli's stomach tightened, and he struggled against balling his hands into fists. Not only were the two going against established regulations by talking in their native tongue, they were blatantly disparaging him and his race. He doubted they would be so open with their ridicule if they knew he understood what they were saying. It confirmed his decision to keep that piece of information to himself. Instead, he clinched his jaw tightly, swallowed the need to respond to Brek's slur, and remained facing stoically forward.

"At ease, Private Jayson," Twigg commanded. Jayson immediately spread his feet shoulder width apart while clasping his hands behind him at the small of his back. It was a more relaxed, but still somewhat formal position. The major benefit was the position allowed his head and eyes to follow the two sergeants instead of having to focus directly forward. It also allowed him a better view of the map behind the two Minith. It was of the Telgoran landscape, the coloration revealing an area located in the livable band, though slightly more on the sun-side than the cold. The Minith markings and notes on the map indicated military unit locations. One of the units was his.

Eli waited for the training sergeant to begin. He didn't have to wait long.

"Why did you assist the less-abled recruits on yesterday's march?"

There was no way he could tell the two Minith that he did it to spite them—to show that humans weren't soft-willed sheep, as they obviously believed. He couldn't tell them that he had overheard their conversation, or that he felt they weren't playing fair with the soldiers that had been placed under their tutelage, or that he had given up his place at the front of the march for one reason: to help his fellow humans stick it to the Minith who wanted to see them gone. No, they wouldn't take those admissions lightly.

So, instead of telling them the truth, he said, "I don't know, Sergeant Twigg. It just seemed like a good idea at the time."

"The march is an individual test, Private. It is designed to separate the weak from the strong. You cheated the test and spoiled the results."

Eli was shocked. How could you cheat a forced march? The rules were simple. As long as you didn't take a shortcut, or get a ride on a carrier vehicle, all you had to do was cross the finish line in front of the pacer. It couldn't get any simpler.

"With all due respect, Sergeant, no one cheated," Eli stated calmly, though he felt the kernel of anger that had formed in his chest grow hotter. He was a stickler for rules, always had been. He had never cheated at any test, game, or challenge in his life. Push the boundaries of the rules, or think outside the box of accepted norms? Certainly. That was his nature, and one of his strengths. But to disregard the boundaries to win or get ahead? Never. "Everyone finished ahead of the pacer within the time allotted."

"True, Private," Brek growled. "But you carried another's burden. And you were carried over the last segment of the course. Neither of these facts is acceptable. Corrective actions must be taken."

The threat was evident in the statement and in the manner in which it was delivered. These two Minith were considering removing him, and anyone else who received help, from training. He bit down on the spray of angry words that threatened to spill forth, took a deep breath, and gathered his thoughts before replying.

"The rules of the march as they were explained by Sergeant Twigg to my unit were very clear," he replied, enunciating so that his words wouldn't be misunderstood. "'Finish ahead of the pacer within the time allowed.' To my knowledge, Sergeant Twigg, nor any other training sergeant, issued any further rules or limitations regarding the march. Am I mistaken? Perhaps a review panel should be assembled?"

The two Minith soldiers exchanged looks. Brek's right ear twitched and Twigg released another of those purr-growls. Eli had touched a nerve with the assertion and, in doing so, had quietly issued his own indirect threat. Despite how much the two might want him and others gone, they had to justify every washout to a formal review panel made up of Telgoran, human, and Minith overseers. In most cases, the review was a formality—a rubber stamp placed on the scores of washout cases that passed their desks each month. On the other hand, an occasional case was challenged by a recruit and overturned. Based on his knowledge of the Minith—and of his sergeants, in particular—he had no doubt that they'd do whatever was needed to avoid scrutiny by their superiors. As such, the mere hint of a challenge—and a justifiable one, at that—would probably be enough to dissuade them from taking action.

After a minute of quiet contemplation, Twigg finally spoke.

"No. You are not mistaken. No further limitations were issued."

The giant alien soldier's massive hands clenched into large fists and both ears quivered. If the sergeant was royally pissed before, he was thoroughly beside himself with rage now, and Eli knew he had made an enemy—if not for life, then at least as long as he was in this training detachment.

"Thank you for reminding us of the criteria. Going forward, we will be clearer on specifics."

The urge to say "you're welcome" was strong, but Eli resisted—this time. His understanding of the need to keep his mouth shut at inappropriate times was often overridden by his inability to do so. But he was learning. Besides, he was in enough hot water already with these two without pressing his luck.

* * *

Even now, two days after the meeting in Twigg's office, Eli remained cautious. He knew he had barely escaped the confrontation with the two sergeants by the slimmest of margins. He couldn't imagine returning to Waa as a washout. The humiliation and disgrace—in his own eyes, if no one else's—would have been too much to take. For as long as he could recall, his entire life had been focused on an eventual life in the military. When other children were outside playing, he spent his time—thousands of hours—studying military history. He knew more about ancient battles and campaigns, both human and Minith, than most people knew about the most recent war.

As the son of the greatest military mind in the Shiale Alliance, he had had the best weapons, fighters, and trainers at his disposal, and he had taken full advantage of the unique opportunities he was given. He balanced his mental training with an intensive, well-balanced regimen of exercise, running, and martial arts. Those efforts, when combined with the genes of his parents, had given him the toned, well-muscled physique and the knowledge of a well-trained soldier. Albeit, an unproven, inexperienced soldier.

After the tense meeting, Eli had tried to refocus his efforts on remaining in the background, but it was no use. The opportunity for keeping a low profile had evaporated. Despite trying to recapture his place as just one more human among a platoon of humans, the eyes of the Minith sergeants always seemed to search him out and study him. He could be standing in the chow line, marching in formation, or working through the next training assignment with his fellow recruits. Whenever he looked their way, they seemed to be looking back.

Like now.

Eli stood inside the fighting ring. Sweat dripped from his body. His arms were beginning to tire, and the welt across his chest—the result of a well-timed strike from his last opponent—was beginning to throb. The ever-present sun and wind beat against his bare torso, and he needed a drink of water badly. But the rules were clear. If you won, you remained in the ring and fought.

In his right hand, he loosely held a wooden sparring staff. At nearly two-and-a-half meters in length, and five centimeters in diameter, the Minith weapon was meant for much larger hands than his. The weight of the thing called for larger muscles as well. Nevertheless, the hours upon hours of sparring with his Minith teachers on Waa had made him an expert in its use. The recruit he faced, a large, rough-looking private from Third Platoon named Crimsa, seemed less sure. Crimsa hefted the weapon in his right hand, testing its weight and balance just like the previous six foes Eli had already bested.

The remaining recruits in their battalion—nearly 150 in all—formed a large, human circle around the two fighters. Many were armed with their own staffs and given instructions to contain the two fighters to the ring. Eli had learned the hard way to remain well away from the outer ring. Some of his peers from the other two platoons took their responsibility a little too seriously. Several of their blows to his back and legs would no doubt leave ugly bruises for the next few days.

Sergeant Brek stood beyond the circle, his large head and ears clearly visible over the heads of the much-shorter humans. He waited patiently for the two contestants to signal their readiness to begin. Eli had already nodded in Brek's direction and waited for Crimsa to do the same.

Apparently satisfied with his inspection of the staff, Crimsa finally nodded his own readiness to Brek. The sergeant clapped his hands, signaling the start of the match.

Eli stood his ground and waited for the other man to make the first move.

He didn't have to wait long. Crimsa lifted the Minith staff over his head, held it at the center with both hands, and began to twirl it slowly. Eli grinned. The movement was a standard two-handed spin that was a key technique of the Minith when battling with the staffs. Crimsa had been trained at some point in the past. Eli immediately raised his own staff and began his own two-handed spin, matching his opponent. Crimsa's spin picked up speed as he charged.

For a fraction of a second, Eli considered allowing the other man to land a blow. If he ended up on the ground, the match would be over, and he could leave the ring. But he discounted the notion just as quickly as it entered his mind. It wasn't in his nature to voluntarily cede a match, regardless of how sore, tired, or thirsty he was. If he was going to leave the ring, it would be because he had given it his all and been fairly beaten.

He watched Crimsa approach at a near-run. He was at the halfway point now, and Eli increased the speed of his own staff. He waited. Watched. Waited.

Crimsa was within ten feet when he made the move Eli was anticipating. It was a classic strike-from-spin attack, and one of the first offensive maneuvers taught to fighters. Using the momentum created by his forward movement and the spinning of his staff, Crimsa released his hold on the staff slightly. The release caused the staff to slip away from the man until, with a well-practiced grasp that Eli couldn't help but admire, the weapon was caught in his right hand. And that hand directed the staff in a well-timed strike aimed at Eli's head.

Eli stopped the spin of his staff a fraction of a second before Crimsa's blow landed and dropped. From his crouched position, he heard the other man's staff whistle over his head as his momentum continued to carry his toward Eli. Eli twisted his crouched body to the left and whipped his own weapon around, completing a full, counter-clockwise spin. As he intended, the staff caught the other man behind the knees, and Eli put all of his strength into the sweep. The force of the blow ran up both his arms, but Eli pushed through, completing the maneuver. A grunted *whoosh* of air left Crimsa's lungs as he slammed heavily to the dirt on his back.

The match was over, and like a blanket being lifted, the world outside the ring came back into focus for Eli. He heard several comments and a scattering of shouts from the recruits manning the ring. Eli glanced at Brek saw the expected scowl. He could almost hear the growl that probably accompanied it. He put the Minith sergeant out of his mind and rushed to his fallen opponent, who was trying to push himself from the ground.

"Hold up, Crimsa," Eli instructed as he reached down to help the other man to his knees. "Are you okay?"

"Thought I . . . had you." Crimsa struggled to his feet with Eli's help.

"Yeah. You almost did," Eli replied. "I suppose I got lucky."

Crimsa turned his head, fixed his eyes on Eli, and shook his head. “Don’t even try that with me, Jayson. I’ve been in enough matches to know luck when I see it. And skill.”

“Well, we can discuss it later.” Eli spied Adrienne at the ring and, with a tip of his head, called her over. She trotted into the ring at once.

“This one’s yours, I believe?”

She dropped her eyes to the ground and offered a slight nod. She then gripped Crimsa’s right arm and led him slowly from the ring. She looked back at Eli briefly as she led her fellow recruit away, and Eli thought there may have been a hint of recognition in her eyes. He wondered briefly if his anonymity was still intact, then filed it away for later consideration. If so, there was nothing he could do about it, but he made a mental note to speak with her soon. If she really did know who he was, perhaps she could be convinced to keep it to herself.

Eli turned to face Brek again and noticed that he had been joined by Sergeant Twigg. The two were quietly conversing, and as Eli watched, seemed to come to a conclusion. Twigg approached the ring and passed through the line of recruits. Most of his peers still held the aliens in a type of fearful dread, and they moved quickly aside to make way for the sergeant’s bulk.

Twigg closed the distance quickly and stopped directly in front of Eli. Eli had to crane his head upward to look into the sergeant’s eyes, a situation that Twigg had no doubt created on purpose. The need to intimidate and threaten, especially by a supposed superior to an inferior, was as natural to a Minith as sleeping was to a human. Eli refused to be cowed, though, and returned the sergeant’s stare.

"Sergeant Brek says that you fight well enough. For a human." Twigg kept his voice low, his words meant only for the two of them. Eli chose to ignore the "for a human" comment. He didn't know what response was expected, so merely waited for the Minith to continue. "Perhaps you'd like more . . . *serious* competition?"

Eli was intrigued but suspicious. "What did you have in mind, Sergeant?"

The Minith's lip curled, and his ears flattened slightly. He was enjoying this.

"I haven't sparred with the staff in a very long time. Perhaps you would like to meet me in the ring?" Eli's internal alarms started going off. He didn't see any good coming from a match with his training sergeant. Unfortunately, he also couldn't see any way out of the match without sounding like a coward. "Just a friendly match, little one."

Little one.

The very first Minith he had ever met, Treel, had called him Little One. From Treel, one of his most trusted friends, the name was an endearment—a nickname earned as a five-year-old learning to play chess. From Sergeant Twigg, it was an affront, and felt rotten. At that moment, he wanted nothing more than to hand the sergeant's ego to him on the end of a staff. But that was a dangerous emotion, especially when going up against someone like Twigg. Eli thought about Treel's son, Arok, his best friend since the age of seven. He had sparred against Arok, and numerous other Minith over the years, many of whom were experts with the staff, but none of them had wanted to do him serious harm. He wasn't sure that was the case with Twigg. He had no doubt the sergeant wanted to get even for their earlier confrontation in his office.

Regardless, even if he had really wanted to, Eli couldn't think of any way to get out of the match. So he set his mind to winning the contest instead. There were two good approaches he had discovered for gaining an advantage over a Minith fighter. The first was to downplay your own abilities from the start and lull the alien into a false sense of superiority. This often caused them to take chances that they normally wouldn't or to make a move that they wouldn't typically make against a better opponent. In other words, the trick was to get them to play down to the suspected level of their competitor.

The second approach relied on taking advantage of their tendency to anger easily. It was a much more dangerous game, but Eli had found that if he could anger his Minith opponent from the beginning, they usually responded with a fighting style that relied more on wild aggression and less on solid reasoning and technique.

Eli suspected Sergeant Twigg would be more susceptible to the latter method. He was emotional and seemed to be someone who angered easily. On the other hand, except for the last fight with Crimsa, Eli hadn't revealed much actual staff-fighting technique. The Minith sergeants had no idea of his experience level, and he could use that to his advantage.

Unsure if he was making the correct choice, he decided to flatter his opponent while downplaying his own abilities.

"Of course, Sergeant." He tore his eyes away from Twigg, bowed his head and stared down at the ground as he replied. If he was going to act like an unworthy adversary, he might as well go all the way. "I'm probably no match for a Minith, but I'll try my best."

"Excellent. Let us begin."

* * *

The men and woman that formed the ring around the human and Minith combatants buzzed with curiosity and excitement. Word was passed around the circle of what was taking place, and when Sergeant Twigg picked up the staff and spun it quickly and expertly above his head, all eyes turned his way. A few of his platoon-mates offered whispered words of encouragement as Eli took his place and waited for the contest to begin.

In Twigg's large hand, the lengthy weapon looked much smaller than its true size—like a human twirling a mop handle. But Eli knew that to be an illusion caused by his opponent's size. It was a simple matter of scale. In contrast, the staff he held in his hands suddenly seemed heavier and more awkward.

The young fighter struggled to prepare in the few moments before the match started. This was his eighth match with no rest, and he had no doubt that it would be the toughest by far. He rolled his head and neck in a circle and forced the buzz of the spectators out of his mind. He twisted his torso side-to-side in an attempt to loosen the accumulated soreness and fatigue from his back and shoulders.

He took a deep breath, held it, exhaled slowly.

As ready as he could be, he nodded to Brek. Then he turned his focus to the large alien standing on the far side of the ring. He watched Twigg nod his own readiness. He heard the clap, and moved forward to meet the battle.

Twigg walked directly, and with purpose, to the

center of the ring, his long legs covering the distance quickly. He flicked his weapon sideways and gripped the end of the stick with his large, right hand. The entire length extended away from his body in a horizontal position. It wasn't a standard opening move, and Eli swallowed a smile. It appeared the Minith sergeant thought he could play around with his human opponent. Not wanting to reveal his expertise with the weapon so early in the contest, Eli resisted the urge to close the distance and strike right away. He might land a stinging blow easily enough, but—while that would be extremely satisfying—it wouldn't put the other fighter on the ground. The Minith were tough, aggressive fighters who could take a lot of punishment before going down. Eli didn't want a long, drawn-out contest if he could avoid it. That path could be painful and dangerous. Ideally, he wanted to surprise Twigg with a trip maneuver similar to the one he had dished out to Crimsa.

Instead, of going for the strike that Twigg had invited him to take, Eli halted his forward movement just outside the reach of the other's staff.

"What now, Sergeant?"

"I'm offering you an opening, human," Twigg growled. "You should take it."

Eli watched the chain of events take place in his head, as Twigg no doubt envisioned them playing out. He would step forward swinging his staff at the Minith's head or chest. Once his swing was committed, Twigg would step backward, letting the blow pass, then swing his own weapon in an arcing move toward Eli's body—or worse, his head. On most humans, who had little or no training, the move would probably work. But Eli had no intention of stepping into the trap. Instead, he put his mind to making the trap work for him.

"I think I will," he said, then stepped forward and began a two-handed swing of the staff. The rod moved quickly toward the Minith's head and Eli waited for the reaction. As expected, just before the blow landed, Twigg took a step backward, waited for the tip of the staff to pass his face, then stepped forward and began his counter-swing.

As soon as the sergeant began his movement, Eli initiated his own counter. Instead of finishing his swing naturally on two feet, as most would do, he relaxed his knees and allowed the forward energy of the swing to propel his body downward and toward his opponent. He dropped his right shoulder to the ground and rolled inside the arc of Twigg's weapon. The roll returned him to his knees as the wooden pole whistled over his head. Twigg was now standing to his immediate right. He was off-balance from his swing and no doubt just coming to terms with the fact that his target had evaded what should have been a maiming, perhaps killing, blow.

"What—" That's all Twigg managed to say before the tip of Eli's weapon caught him under the jaw with a powerful, upward thrust. Unwilling to let up now that he had gained the advantage, Eli spun clockwise and inserted his staff between Twigg's legs from the rear. Using a move he had practiced hundreds of times, he jammed the tip of the staff into the dirt at the outside of the sergeant's right ankle and levered the middle of his staff into the back of the Minith's left knee. At that point, it was just a matter of exerting enough pressure until the large alien toppled sideways.

It was a perfectly executed move that had never failed Eli over dozens of attempts.

Only this time, it did.

Twigg twisted his body in the air as he fell. Instead of landing on his back as Eli expected, he landed facedown. Facedown should have been fine, but for one thing: except for his hands and feet, the alien's body never touched the ground. He landed in a classic push-up pose that—as Eli watched in amazement—Twigg quickly turned into a standing position.

Eli tried to roll away from the giant towering over him, but knew he was doomed. The Minith had the advantage and wouldn't mess up a second opportunity.

The slap of the heavy wooden staff as it connected with the top of his head dropped him to the ground.

As the darkness rushed in, Eli's only thought was that maybe he should have gone with the anger approach.

CHAPTER 6

How old are these vids? Grant asked, pushing himself up from his chair.

Sixteen earth days, Sha'n answered. The nonverbal response entered Grant's mind like a cool wind, and Grant frowned at his aide. The Waa had added a calming undertone to her last message.

"Knock it off, Sha'n," Grant replied. The spoken words surprised her—caused her large, dark eyes to blink twice rapidly. They rarely spoke out loud, but Grant wanted to make this point clear. "I'm a big boy. I don't need or want you to dampen my emotions."

Mind-speak was extremely powerful, and had many advantages over verbal-speak. But Grant also recognized the potential dangers. He relied on his natural feelings, gut reactions, and experience to help him make decisions. He couldn't allow his aide to stifle his reactions with mind-speak, even if she thought it was for his own benefit.

Despite their years together, they were still in a learning mode on a lot of cultural issues. What was second nature to one of them—like Sha'n's natural desire to ease his emotional pain—was often strange, unpredictable, or downright repulsive to the other.

Welcome to the new reality, Grant thought. *I guess we call them* aliens *for a reason.*

Sha'n's dark orbs blinked purposefully once. Twice.

Grant realized she had "heard" his mental sidebar

and was letting him know in her own way that she understood and did not resent his concerns. In fact, she shared them. He sent a conscious flow of warmth in her direction and was rewarded with a return of warmth and understanding.

In less than a second, their thoughts-motivations-understanding regained calibration, and they moved forward.

Grant blocked his thoughts from Sha'n—a skill he was coming to master—and thought, *If only it was that easy with Avery*. It wouldn't be so easy with his wife—or any other human, Minith, or Telgoran—when it came to forgiving and forgetting. They were limited to verbal communication.

The man refocused on the vid screen before him. What he had observed filled him with the mixed emotions of anger, pride, and confusion.

The images were captured by the floating orbs that followed every training unit on Telgora. What Eli and the rest of the recruits knew as "the pacer" was actually a multi-purpose device used by the Shiale Defense Force to assist training efforts. In addition to keeping the pace on marches, it recorded video, tracked statistics, and monitored the location of each recruit. If a soldier was having trouble hitting targets during weapons training, the device communicated the fact to the appropriate sergeants so they could work with the soldier on improving his or her score. If a recruit didn't complete a required task within the allotted time, the orb recognized, reported, and tracked the deficit. When a recruit's biometric data—tracked through an electronic chip implanted in each person's right arm prior to training—showed life-threatening readings, medical personnel were immediately notified.

Most soldiers in the defense forces never experienced a single incident that would trigger a medical alert. In less than three weeks of training, Eli's chip had already been triggered twice. The first time his chip was sparked into alert mode, Eli had overheated due to exertion and had collapsed near the end of a forced march. His temperature quickly came back into normal range and the call for medical attention had been canceled almost as soon as it was sent. Grant had watched the replay of the entire march and watched in proud silence at Eli's decision to forgo his normal position at the head of the march and help his peers who were in danger of falling behind. Grant's analytical mind reviewed the scene and—although he was proud to see Eli had taken a leadership role in the march—recognized his son's failure. He should have rallied others to his mission and generated consensus of action. Instead, his son had acted alone. It was a decision that almost resulted in his being bounced from training. Fortunately for Eli, it worked out in the end when several of his fellows helped him cross the finish just ahead of the pacer.

The second medical call was more serious, and had kept him out of training for two days. Eli was fine now, and back with his unit, but that knowledge didn't prevent Grant from reviewing the scenes of Eli's bouts with the staff closely. The pride he felt at his son's performance in the ring was tempered by anger at a Minith sergeant thinking it was somehow appropriate to face off against a recruit—any recruit—unless it was to teach them, or to spar with constraint. Full-out contests weren't allowed, and for good reason. Most recruits were straight from Earth. They possessed limited training and had no chance in the ring against a fully trained Minith warrior. While that didn't apply to Eli, the sergeant, Twigg, could not have known that. And that's what angered and confused Grant. Sergeant Twigg had broken standard protocol. The first question that bothered him was "why?" The second question he wanted to answer was "what was being done about it on Telgora?" Unfortunately, his hands were firmly tied. He couldn't easily explain why he had a personal interest in events taking place in a single, relatively unimportant training unit. All he could do was sit back and observe. For now.

* * *

Eli and his unit were back on the training field and for the first time, the Telgoran weather didn't bother them. The new armor suits they had just been issued solved that problem.

Entering the armor for the first time was trying. It took fifteen minutes, and a pair of robotic assistants, to help him with aligning the pieces to his body. But when the helmet was lowered and the suit's systems were finally activated, Eli was in awe. The inside of the suit, where it met all the parts of his body, was both yielding and firm at the same time. Molded especially for his frame, the agsel-wrought body shield felt like a second skin.

Developed by the military research and development teams on Waa, the newly developed fighting suit had been created for humans in the defense forces for use in all climates and atmospheres—even deep space. The soldiers in Eli's training cycle were the first to wear the suits, and it was the primary reason why he had waited six months past his eligibility date to join the Shiale Defense Force. He was a techno-file, and the lure of being the first to wear the armor outweighed the need to become a soldier right away. He owed his knowledge of the new technological development, and the timing of its delivery, to this recruit training unit, to his father. Although he didn't want his dad's position to influence his training or have any effect on his peers or his superiors, he felt comfortable using that influence to put him in this unit, at this particular time.

The technical name for the armor was a mouthful, and could be directly attributed to his father's sense of irony, practicality, and ancient love for military acronyms. Realizing the need to appease the peace-loving citizens of Earth, while also needing to accurately describe the armor for the proud men and women who would wear it, he had christened the human body armor with the name Personal Enhanced Atmospheric Combat Environment. Or PEACE Armor, for short. Like most military acronyms from ancient earth, the name was descriptively appropriate, somewhat forced, and just hokey enough to induce a fair amount of eye rolling.

Eli ignored the data flashing across the upper right of his face screen—external temp, biometrics, oxygen level, weapon status, and a hundred other items—and focused on the feel of his new body. He lifted his right arm, spread his fingers, and flexed the muscles of his forearm. Good. He lifted his right leg, tapped the knee with his hand, then repeated the move with the left leg. Though the PEACE armor weighed roughly four times his own body weight, his movements felt easy, natural, and fluid.

Within minutes of donning the suit, it felt like

home. For the first time since landing on Telgora, he could stand comfortably under the Telgoran sky. The armor protected him from the scorching, ever-present heat and negated the irritating cyclonelike wind with its relentless sand-bites. The background smells of sulfur, sweat, and cooking grease were masked with the familiar, mundane scent of recycled oxygen. The suit was a soothing salve against the cruel harshness of the Telgoran environment, and Eli felt a growing appreciation for the native race for their ability to evolve—and, in many ways, thrive—on this hostile planet.

He had always respected the Telgorans for their contributions against the Minith during the Peace War, but until now had never given the mostly silent race much thought. Where he had a nativelike understanding of the Minith due to his first-hand interactions, most of what he knew of the tall, gray-skinned Telgorans was learned through conversations overheard during training or around the dinner table. He knew they were mind-talkers who shared a common, hivelike awareness, and according to his father, had steellike muscles and quick reflexes that made them fearsome fighters in hand-to-hand situations. Once they made a decision through *shiale*—their name for reaching collective agreement—their resolve was steady, unshakable. Every human above the age of six knew the Shiale Alliance was named in honor of that concept.

Despite being on Telgora for more than a month already, Eli had yet to see one of the locals. That wasn't unusual since they were primarily underground dwellers, and tended to shy away from areas where the Minith lived. But still, entrances to their underground communities dotted the landscape and it would have been interesting to engage with them. His sole interactions growing up had been limited to a couple of passing glimpses. Unlike the other three races in the Alliance, the Telgorans had no permanent presence on Waa. They visited the planet rarely and seemed content to allow the other members to do as they wished as long as they weren't directly affected.

It was a strange way to live, Eli thought as he continued to explore his new armor.

He squatted, bounced on his haunches for a few seconds, then shot his body upward into a vertical leap, arms reaching for the sky. When he realized he was a dozen feet above the surface, a flash of panic caused him to windmill his arms, but he fought the fear and barely managed to land on both feet. He smiled in wonder as the mechanically assisted joints absorbed the impact without issue. He repeated the jump, testing the mechanics of the move. He rose to a height of about ten feet before landing with a softness that belied the solid *thump* and puff of dust that surrounded him as his feet hit the Telgoran surface. With a howl of glee, he jumped again, this time giving it everything his muscles and the suit had to give. He estimated his apex at fifteen feet and observed the top of the barracks buildings surrounding him with a sense of wonder. He landed easily and looked around at his fellow soldiers, who were also getting their first taste of the suits. Most were standing in place, moving their limbs, or stretching. A few ran back and forth along the hard path, apparently testing their new legs. The speed they managed was impressive, and Eli immediately wanted to test his own speed. A few weren't moving at all, and Eli wondered if their armor wasn't functioning.

Using the enhancement feature built into his face

screen, he amplified the view of one still trooper's chest plate and read the name. Private A. Tenney.

"Private channel. Tenney," Eli spoke into his helmet. The communication display on his screen changed colors as a private channel was opened between himself and Tenney. "Tenney, you okay over there?"

He saw her helmet jerk up and scan the crowd for a few seconds before settling in his direction.

"Fine, Private Jayson," Adrienne replied calmly. "Just running through the command and control sequences to make sure everything's in order before I start throwing my body around like the rest of these newbs. I'd hate to discover something inoperable or a bug in a system when I'm fifteen feet in the air."

The delight Eli had felt only moments before evaporated instantly, replaced by a cold realization of his own foolishness. He should have thought to check his own systems before giving his body over to the armor. He noted the lesson and filed it away for the future. It was a mistake he wouldn't make again.

"Good thinking, Tenney."

"I thought so." A hint of humor came through the comm system. "But those high jumps of yours certainly looked like a lot of fun."

Eli ground his teeth and shelved the desire to sprint. Turning his focus to the armor's info display, he began the less-thrilling—but much more salient—task of checking the automated systems and processes designed to assist his survival.

* * *

The next seven days were spent acclimatizing the

recruits to their new armor. Eli and his peers spent all of their waking hours in the suits. The Minith sergeants watched silently from the sidelines as a team of human and Waa scientists, machinists and engineers—the folks responsible for creating the new outfits—walked their recruits through every component and system. Over time, each soldier became much more adept at donning and shedding the various components that made up the armor. By day seven, every member of Eli's platoon could strip down and re-armor in under a minute without assistance or even giving the process their full attention. In the barracks, they shuttered the windows, turned out the lights, and practiced in the dark.

Two things quickly became apparent to Eli.

The first and most obvious was the armor did exactly what it was designed to do. It greatly enhanced each soldier's ability to perform the tasks that were put in front of them. They were stronger, ran faster, jumped higher, and performed physical feats that wouldn't have been possible without the agsel-enhanced suits. The internal computer systems facilitated communications, provided an awareness of every other recruit's location and health, assisted with weapons targeting, and provided a more-than-adequate system of chameleonlike camouflage.

After a week in the suit, Eli couldn't imagine a more efficient way for a human soldier to enter battle.

The second realization Eli had regarding the suit wasn't as positive as the first. And it directly affected his unit's ability to successfully perform the second-most important task of any soldier: the ability to wait. As his dad was fond of saying, roughly 10 percent of a soldier's life was spent in productive action. The remaining 90 percent was equally divided between "hurry up" and "wait." It was an adage Eli had immediately validated upon arriving at the training base. Day after day was filled with real-life examples of the hurry up and wait domain in which they existed. Rush to get dressed in the morning only to stand at attention for an hour for the sergeants to begin the day's training. Dash to the chow hall, then wait in a long, slow line for your turn to be fed. Scarf your meal under the harried urging of the Minith sergeants, scamper outside, then stand in formation yet again. March at top speed to the firing range, then stand silently while waiting for your turn to knock down targets.

Hurry up and wait, hurry up and wait, hurry up and wait.

Hurrying was now easier for the recruits. Their new armor was designed for movement. It encouraged action.

Unfortunately, it wasn't designed to accommodate all of the waiting that was required.

While the suit initially felt like a second skin, it soon became apparent that it didn't stay that way. Standing still for longer than thirty minutes became an exercise in pain toleration. As the body settled into the suit, most recruits noticed areas that became uncomfortable, areas where the unforgiving metal didn't always mesh perfectly with the body. Although it varied from person to person, the feet, crotch and armpit areas were the primary places where the body's weight settled roughly against the suit.

To help alleviate the discomfort, Eli began jumping up and down in place when the unit was in any sort of stand-by situation. Through experimentation, he discovered that bounces of eighteen to twenty-four inches were adequate to provide relief. His actions were soon mimicked by those around him. Now, it was rare to see anyone standing or sitting motionless unless they were assembled in formation. To an outsider, their group might have looked like a hundred bouncing, overeager robots, unable to stand still. But to the recruits, movement meant comfort, and bouncing was movement.

After their allotted seven days, the human research and development team thanked their human test subjects and left. They took with them a list of tweaks to be made and improvements to incorporate into the next version of the armor. They also accepted suggestions from the soldiers, and Eli submitted a few recommendations. Needless to say, long-term comfort while not in motion was at the top of everyone's "must have" list.

Less than six weeks remained in the training cycle. Eli knew they'd be deployed with the current armor at the end of that time, or it would be shelved pending arrival of an improved version. He hoped for the former. Even with the flaw, the suits provided a significant advantage for troops deployed to a hostile environment like Telgora.

* * *

The Zrthn race flourished for millennium beneath the warm, oily seas that covered 80 percent of their home world. As the unchallenged pinnacle of the underwater food chain, the sentient species hunted, thrived, and grew. They reached out tentacles to new and unexplored territories as their population exploded, and each new discovery brought migration and further growth. As their population grew, so did their knowledge. Science, architecture, and engineering evolved and helped foster and support their ongoing expansion. Eventually, their domination covered every corner of their underwater world.

As domination over their portion of the world grew, so did their appetite for food, resources, and areas to explore and conquer. Like many races, they lived for the present, often at the expense of the long-term well-being of their kind. As a collective unit, they recognized and understood the growing danger of their excesses. Their scientists and leaders railed about the need to change their hunting behavior, to adapt to the diminishing pools of prey and resources. But as individuals, none were willing to curb their own desires or limit their own excesses. As a result, their hunting and their expansion continued unabated. Food was available *now*, which meant it would be available tomorrow. And the next day. And the day after.

And it was.

Until—suddenly—it wasn't.

The ancient Zrthns nearly went extinct as a result.

It was the need for food that first drove them from the waves onto the dry, arid land that existed above. At first, they could only live for a short period out of the water, but it was enough time to hunt for food. When the food near the water's shores disappeared, they reached out tentacles farther inland, and the process of growth repeated itself. This expansion was aided by evolution, and in time, the Zrthn eventually left their barren, watery existence behind for good.

Eventually, the ever-present hunger for expansion required the race to turn their attention to the stars, because space was the only truly boundless expanse that could meet their need to hunt, consume, and grow. Their initial forays beyond their home planet revealed other worlds, worlds with great reserves of resources that were important for continued growth. Finding food was no longer a need, but that didn't lessen their appetite for excess, which drove them forward and outward.

As they encountered other species, they quickly realized they weren't the strongest, quickest, or most intelligent race. They were adaptable, though, which led them to develop methods for gaining what they needed with the least amount of effort. Somewhere along their journeys, they learned the principles of the barter system and quickly discovered the benefits of growth through nonviolent means. Within a generation, they established a culture centered on achievement of goals through trade, contracts, and negotiations. They still used force and violence when needed, but it became a secondary tactic, something to fall back on when the ideals of commerce failed.

It is common knowledge among sentient races that successful trade relies on the principles of supply and demand. Resources, goods, and services that are in high demand, yet are limited in supply, fetch the greatest prices. Controlling high demand items provides leverage in negotiations and can often be used to influence agreements or dictate favorable contractual terms.

For space-faring races, one thing is cherished above all others: agsel. The ore makes faster than light space travel possible.

CHAPTER 7

"How did this race ever defeat us, Brek?"

Sergeant Twigg received only a bored grunt for a reply. Hadn't expected much more. The view outside the watch tower showed the same flat, sand and rock-covered terrain that they had been staring at for years. The inside of the tower was stark, with two desks and the monitoring equipment that would provide updates on the humans they were tasked with watching over. Neither of them really cared to monitor the pale beings, though. There was no need really. They had never been surprised by anything the sheep ever did on this particular exercise.

Cycle after cycle of training the human sheep had sapped their energy. Each day was a repeat of the drudgery, monotony, and boredom that had become their companions. They were Minith. They were born to fight, conquer, and subjugate lesser races. Yet, here they sat. Babysitters, relegated to a foreign world, without the possibility of a battle or the satisfaction of victory. Twigg recalled what life had been like before the home world had been destroyed and their mighty race conquered by such weak specimens as humans. They had once ruled the worlds that now belonged to the so-called "Shiale Alliance." His spirit longed for a return to those days. What little satisfaction he now received came on days like this. And little satisfaction it was.

"Which group is up next?" Twigg asked Brek.

It was the other sergeant's responsibility to track the recruits on the vid screen and report on their positions.

Although they couldn't see the humans in the distance, electronic monitoring of their location was accomplished via a pacer device, and projected onto a holo-screen that sat atop the desk where Brek sat. As Twigg watched, Brek straightened in his chair to view the data. A sudden spark of life flashed in the other sergeant's eyes, and before the words left his snout, Twigg knew which group was preparing to initiate the training exercise.

Jayson.

"The young human who nearly bested you in the ring is in this grouping," Brek confirmed.

The twitch of ear that accompanied the remark informed Twigg that his fellow warrior was having fun at his expense. He growled menacingly in reply, which caused the other's ears to twitch even faster. The heat rising in his chest nearly caused him to jump the table where Brek sat and beat the twitch from those ears, but he pushed back against the rage and angrily swallowed the desire.

"Careful, Brek," he cautioned. "Your humor won't last longer than the reach of my boot."

"Perhaps," Brek responded. "But I have boots as well."

The two Minith giants stared at each other for several seconds, each waiting to see if the other's words were more than an idle threat. After years of jostling for position and supremacy, they had never really tangled to determine who the true alpha was. But each knew it was simply a matter of time.

With a final growl, Twigg turned away and looked out the viewing window of the watch tower, his gaze fixed on the landscape ahead. It was a barren land. Sun-bleached sand and rock covered every inch of the rolling, hilly terrain. If he stared east or west, he could pretend the entire planet was covered by similar land. A casual look to the north or south, however, and the differences became quickly apparent. To the south lay the ever-present sun. If you moved far enough in that direction, you would eventually find yourself walking across lakes of baked sand, flat and smooth as glass, or skirting a pool of melted rock and agsel. To the north, it was the opposite. The lack of sun in that direction turned the landscape into a frozen wasteland of ice. Either direction carried death to those that ventured too far from the equator.

He could not see his human charges in the distance. The five kilometers that separated them was simply too far. But he knew they'd arrive soon enough. The exercise they were conducting guaranteed it. Sometimes they arrived in formation, sometimes at a run, other times creeping slowly from rock-to-rock. Regardless of how they approached, though, he and his warriors always saw them. Saw them, and "killed" them. The killing was electronic in nature. Twigg, Brek, and the dozen Minith soldiers arranged in a semicircle at the foot of the tower were outfitted with pulse weapons that were *mostly* harmless. The electronic pulses incapacitated targets with nonlethal—albeit excruciatingly painful—jolts of electricity that temporarily stunned and paralyzed.

No human had ever made it within half a kilometer of the tower. They weren't meant to make it. This was a test of their mental make-up, a way to assess how the humans acted when faced with an unwinnable scenario. The pacer monitored the planning processes used and assessed each recruit's actions as a way to determine their motivations and understand their tendencies. Would they be aggressive? Tentative? Cautious or careless? Would they sacrifice people to help accomplish their mission, or would they try to ensure everyone's safety? There was no pass-fail criterion. It was more of a mental measurement exercise, with the results entered into their records as a way to help their future superiors predict future performance.

"Any movement, Brek?"

"Nothing yet. They are still at the demarcation point."

This was the fourth grouping today, and Twigg had been pleased to learn that the humans' new fighting armor actually helped monitor their location. In addition to the feedback being sent from the pacer, the suits' built-in mapping systems were actively pinging their positions to Brek's screen. They would know when Jayson and his team moved out and be able to track their movements. The new armor made a simple task even easier.

Twigg smiled at the thought of hitting Jayson with multiple pulses. The human had become an outlet for the anger, contempt, and frustration he felt for humans. The pale, puny Earthling deserved whatever punishment he could mete out. He wondered how many electronic jolts he could realistically deliver without raising unwanted attention, finally deciding four or five would be reasonable.

He fingered his weapon and felt his ears quiver with anticipation. It was just a matter of time.

* * *

He was known among the Family as Alone.

It wasn't his name—he had never been granted a

true name by his kind. It was simply a classification, a statement—a truth not worthy of further consideration. It was the way in which his people acknowledged his existence, while simultaneously noting his lack of presence.

He was *from* the Family. But he was not *of* the Family.

His mother and father were of the Family. His siblings were of the Family. His birth mirrored those that came before him, and those that came after. His outward appearance was unremarkable as far as his kind went. He was strong, fast, and as physically capable as any other.

In all aspects except the most important one, he was like any other Telgoran. He was incapable of sharing the mass mind that connected his people into a single, cohesive entity—the Family. His consciousness resided outside the familial circle. The thoughts in his head were his own, not those of the Family. He did not link with the others, did not know what they thought or why. He had never held *shiale*.

Although he was pitied—looked upon as something less by the Family—he was rarely uncomfortable in his solitude. It was all he had ever known. Joining together in mass thought was as foreign a concept to him as . . . flying. You cannot regret the loss of something you never had. Instead, he reveled in the ownership of something that only he possessed. Individuality and self-direction.

Titan, the human emissary that spent his existence with the Family, had once shared an Earth-word for how he existed: freedom. Since that day, the man had taken to calling him "Free" whenever he encountered him in the tunnels and caverns. The Telgoran hungrily latched onto the name. Claimed it for himself.

Among the Family, he was Alone. But to himself, he was Free.

Free lay inside the mouth of the cave and looked down the slope at the humans below. Over the past few years, he had spent hundreds of hours quietly observing the strange behavior of the Earthlings as they trained to become soldiers.

The dozen small, pale humans were arranged in a loose line, sheltered behind large boulders that were obviously meant to hide their location from some unseen "enemy" in the distance. He looked out across the sun-scorched terrain to see if he could detect their opponents, but as usual, he saw nothing moving in the distance. He had seen this scenario play out numerous times over the years: the humans were dropped here, waited for an hour or so, then moved out toward some distant target or foe. Two hours later, another group would take their place. Two hours after that, yet another group would assemble. This often went on for two or three days, as different groups took their turn assaulting whatever lay in the distance. He had never followed any of the soldiers to determine their destination, or learn what waited for them in the distance. He had been instructed by the Family not to engage the human soldiers or—Family forbid—the Minith warriors who sometimes accompanied them.

Like all of his people, he neither trusted nor liked the Minith who still occupied Telgora. At the urging of the general—the great human warrior who had released their world from the Minith years earlier—they had reached *shiale* on an alliance, but it was a tenuous arrangement where the Minith were concerned. The Family allowed their continued presence on Telgora but only in limited numbers, and only because the evil aliens had been conquered through the combined efforts of Telgoran and human forces.

It took a moment for Free to notice, but the soldiers below were outfitted in a manner that he had never seen before. They were still short, stocky creatures, but their clothing seemed . . . different, bulkier and more rigid than usual.

He crawled closer to the cave opening for a better view.

* * *

Eli had been elected team leader by the members of his squad, and he wore the responsibility with the seriousness that it deserved. As a life-long student of all things soldier-related, and the son of the man who had designed this training regimen, he understood the situation he and his team currently faced. He knew the purpose of this exercise and struggled with the knowledge that they weren't expected to succeed in their mission of reaching the tower that stood five kilometers away. No one had ever reached it because they weren't meant to reach it. It was a mental test, designed to measure individual tendencies, strategic planning, and abstract thinking.

He knew they were expected to fail. And that knowledge pissed him off.

Why give them a mission they couldn't achieve? Why set them up to fail just so someone could monitor their thought processes or try to interpret their possible future actions? He stared across the terrain. He couldn't see it, but knew a tower stood in the distance. It was a real target. One that held a contingent of real Minith fighters. Minith fighters who waited, ready to cut the humans down before they could get within range and bring their own weapons to bear.

He snarled in frustration and struggled to solve what was designed to be unsolvable.

Adrienne Tenney had led her own team toward that goal earlier in the day without success. He had questioned her at length on what she had seen and experienced, quizzed her regarding the tactics she had employed. Nothing she offered proved helpful to cracking the code. Her team hadn't come close to the tower before being dispatched by the long-range weapons its defenders were using. She was clear on one thing though: the shock of being hit with those weapons was no joke. She described the experience as "like being hit with a bolt of lightning." The shudder in her voice reiterated the discomfort she had felt. The subsequent gleam in her eye told Eli she couldn't wait for him to feel it for himself.

There was one thing she said that tugged at his mind, though. Tenney relayed how her team used their suits' cover and concealment systems to approach the tower, but it hadn't mattered. The suits were designed to be near-invisible, and could match the terrain as they passed across it. That should have supported their attack, offered an advantage. But it hadn't. When they reached a point that put them in range of the defenders, they were picked off easily, one-by-one, as soon as they moved to advance. She described her own experience clearly: She was concealed behind a large boulder, protected from any possible shot. She identified her next position and prepared to move up. She hadn't taken a single step before being taken down by a blast. It was like the tower defenders knew exactly where they were at all times. In other words, they were being tracked in some fashion—probably electronically.

To Eli, that was cheating, and he struggled for a way to overcome the disadvantage.

"What are we going to do, Jayson," Benson asked his bunkmate? His voice rang inside Eli's helmet like an accusation, but that was an unfair assessment, he knew. His frustration was merely coloring his friend's innocent question. The other recruit had begun relying more and more on Eli to get them through the grueling cycle of training. The fact that Eli was now his squad leader lent credibility to the query. It was his job to come up with a plan. He noted with a resigned sigh that all of the faces in his team were turned to him.

"I'm thinking," he answered, making eye contact with each recruit in turn. "And I'm open to suggestions."

"Speed," Ellison offered from the far right of their line. "Use this nice, new armor and just rush them before they can react."

Eli accepted the suggestion with a nod, filed it away as a possibility, but knew it wasn't the key to the puzzle. Other units had tried that. Their new armor might help, but racing to contact would just speed up the inevitable, especially if they were being tracked electronically.

"Other ideas?"

"What if we circle to the north or south, try to get around them that way?" Benson suggested. "This armor should protect us from the extreme temps, don't you think?"

The suggestion was intriguing. He had considered that himself. It was unlikely that the Minith would expect them to approach from the south or the north. The terrain in both directions was just too hostile. Unarmored, no one in their right mind would enter those regions. Their new armor would protect them from the elements, but if they were being tracked, it still wouldn't matter in the long run. Again, the proposed tactic didn't solve the puzzle. He relayed his thoughts to the group. Several nodded in agreement, obviously relieved not to put their PEACE armor to that particular test.

"Maybe we should ask the Telgorans for help," Benson tossed out flippantly. The offhand manner in which he made the comment suggested sarcasm. However, for some reason, the idea resonated with Eli. He was willing to grasp any straw that might help solve this riddle, despite how ridiculous it might seem.

Ask the Telgorans for help.

Being so caught up with the day-to-day struggles associated with training, it was easy to forget where they were. Or who else occupied this inhospitable marble of a planet as it rolled around the sun. *This is Telgora*, Eli reminded himself. A race of people resided beneath the surface of this planet. They were hidden away from the daily grind through which he and his fellow recruits dragged themselves, but they were there nonetheless. Perhaps most importantly, the Telgorans had little, if any, regard for the Minith that had once enslaved their world, and killed their people with regularity. They had agreed to join the Shiale Alliance , but it was well-known to the Alliance leaders on Waa that they would have preferred to cast their large, green foes out into the stars, given the choice. It was only a result of their allegiance to, and regard for, the humans who had come to their planet, and led them in the defeat their enemies, that they conceded to join the union. But the distrust and the dislike remained.

Eli turned that reality over in his mind, looking for any clues that might help solve the puzzle he had been handed. With a gasp, he recalled a key detail from the battle for Telgora that had been waged more than a dozen years before. The Telgorans had used a series of underground tunnels to surprise the Minith in their mining bases. The attack from below had taken the defenders by surprise and helped secure the combined human and Telgoran victory over the Minith here on this planet. Not for the first time, he thanked his own curiosity and his father's insistence that he study history. Perhaps looking to the past would help solve the present.

For the first time, he took his eyes from the direction of their target and scanned the entire landscape that surrounded them. He quickly spied what he was looking for on the hillside at their rear. It was one of the dark entrances to the Telgoran underground. Benson's flippant comment became a fleeting notion, which became an idea. The idea quickly grew into the outline of a plan.

You've got to be kidding me, he thought, surprised by his apparent willingness to even consider such a reckless scheme. There were so many holes in the plan, so many intangibles that could cause failure, that he felt compelled to abandon it immediately. And yet… what was there to lose? *A lot*, he replied, the internal debate now fully engaged. They could lose their way, for one. He could lose his recruit status for another. This was thinking outside the box—perhaps too far outside. If the move caused any backlash, he'd have to fall on his sword and make sure everyone knew it was his idea, his plan and no one else's. Then there were the Telgorans. They held no animosity or distrust of humans, he knew, but what would their group tell those they passed? Don't mind us, we're just passing through? Despite the uncertainties, those were all things he could handle. It was the potential loss of dignity, respect and the ability to look his father in the eye that made him pause.

Despite the potential downfalls, Eli didn't see another way through this task that offered any hope of success. He struggled with the choice, and noted the others looking at him expectantly as he did so. Play things safe and suffer failure, or risk it all on the slim hope that success was possible? His father often spoke about the need for weighing the risks of an action against the potential rewards that action could offer. One of his favorite sayings was, "You've got to go out on a limb sometimes. That's where the fruit is." One thing was certain: there was no fruit to be had by crossing the plain in front of them.

Limb it is, he decided with a heavy sigh and shake of his head.

"Okay, everyone," he announced to the team. "Take off your armor down to your boots, but leave it powered up. Except for you, Ellison. I have a task for you."

The members of his team shared looks, obviously uncertain of the order they had been given.

"Let's go folks. You heard the man," Benson urged as he began shedding his new skin. With some scattered murmuring, the others quickly followed his lead.

Eli pulled Ellison aside and instructed him on what he wanted. The other recruit asked a few clarifying questions, but quickly grasped the concept of what he was being asked to do.

Satisfied that his orders would be closely followed, Eli began stripping down to the black, one-piece garment they all wore under their armor. It was elastic in nature to ensure a snug fit, and left little to the imagination. But it would have to do.

He surveyed his team. Dressed in black, form fitting skins and armored boots, they were an odd sight to behold. The pulse weapons they carried rounded out their strange ensemble. It would have to do. They weren't going down without a fight, and he now had a plan that might somehow work. If they were lucky.

"Here's what we're going to do . . ."

* * *

Free hopped to his feet, retreated into the darkness and placed his back against the cavern wall. The armed humans were climbing the hill and seemed to be headed directly for his location. He didn't think they had spotted him yet, and he wondered what he should do. Should he retreat or stand his ground?

For one of the only times in his life, he wished he could reach out to the Family with his mind. He needed guidance and direction.

* * *

"Jayson, we've got company."

Eli looked to where Benson was pointing and noted with some trepidation that the ever-present pacer was hovering along ten meters behind their column as they double-timed up the hill. Apparently, the floating orb had elected to track them versus staying with Ellison. He wondered briefly if it would relay their location to the Minith at the tower, and briefly considered shooting it down. He dismissed that idea almost immediately. Going off the grid to accomplish a training mission was one thing, destroying Alliance property in the process was something else entirely.

"We'll have to live with it," he replied with a shrug. They were fully committed to this course of action. Either his plan would work, or it wouldn't. The presence of the pacer was a factor beyond their control. All they could do was continue forward. He just hoped the orb wasn't the manner with which the Minith tracked their location.

The mouth of the cavern loomed ahead, and Eli pushed his pace, anxious to reach the entrance to the Telgoran underground. He had heard stories of what lay beneath from his father and from the man called Titan, who was Earth's Emissary to the Telgoran people. His excitement at seeing this strange world for himself was muted only by his worry of how their presence would be met. Although they were allies, it wasn't every day that a group of armed humans was permitted to enter their world. The fact that their weapons weren't capable of lethal force probably wouldn't matter much to the native population.

Eli crossed the final few meters and slowed as he approached the cavern entrance. Although speed was paramount to their plan, he didn't know what to expect inside and opted for caution.

It was a good call on his part as it gave him the fraction of a second that was needed for his training to kick in. He noticed a blur of motion and instinctively twisted his torso to the right. The lighting-fast thrust of the agsel staff missed by centimeters. Without thinking, he grasped the staff with his left hand and pulled, trying to disarm the thin, gray-skinned figure that wielded the weapon. His effort yielded zero results. His strength could not match the Telgoran's. The sticklike arms held muscles like steel, and the alien used those muscles and Eli's grip to yank him forward. Eli gave himself up to the movement and used the momentum of being yanked to leave his feet and twist his body to the left. He landed neatly beside the Telgoran, lifted the weapon he held in his right hand, and fired.

Eli was surprised by the agony that suddenly coursed through his body.

Not the welcome I was hoping for, he thought as he and the Telgoran collapsed to the ground.

* * *

In business or in war, the process is the same, even if the methods are a bit different, Oinoo thought.

Approach undetected. Observe in silence. When the time is right, prod for weakness, then retreat and assess. Repeat the cycle, using increasingly forceful prods, until you've determined whether your opponent is weak or strong. When you find weakness, you initiate steps to consume and absorb. If you find an opponent who is too tough to digest, you move on.

As the leader of the Zrthn force moving against Telgora, it was his responsibility to assess the situation and develop the strategy they would follow. He considered their initial prodding forays against the Shiale Alliance's defenses. Weakness had been revealed.

It was time to take the first real bite.

CHAPTER 8

Eli came to slowly. His head pounded and his body ached from the electrical pulse that he had sent into the Telgoran—and which had obviously traveled through the agsel staff and into his own body.

Stupid.

"You okay, Jayson?" Eli opened his eyes to find Benson standing over him.

"Yeah," he croaked. "How long have I been out?"

"Not long. A minute or so."

Eli pushed himself into a sitting position and looked around. The Telgoran was still out. He lay a couple of meters away, surrounded by three of the team. All had weapons pointed.

Two of the team were keeping watch at the cave entrance. The remaining four were spread out in a defensive line ten meters down the tunnel.

Good.

He shook his head against the throbbing, stood slowly, and approached the gray figure. Eli had met Telgorans before, but it had been years since his last encounter. His dad had once shown him a picture of giant stone carvings from an island on Earth that closely resembled the natives of this world. This one looked like what he remembered. Even prone, it was clear he was taller than a man. He had a head that seemed too large for his thin, reedlike body. He had just learned firsthand that the strength in those deceptively thin arms and legs lived up to everything he had been told.

Eli looked at the darkened cave beyond their position. He noticed the floor dropped noticeably downward as the tunnel descended beneath the planet's surface. He expected company at any moment and marveled at the idiocy of his thinking. What had seemed like a good idea only minutes before now seemed like the largest blunder of his life. He considered abandoning the cave before additional Telgorans arrived—and they would. An attack on one was an attack on all. That was a benefit of having a mental link. But he wouldn't leave. That was a coward's way out, and he resigned himself to standing firm and taking accountability for his actions.

He rubbed his eyes and exhaled. Failure was a tough pill to swallow, but he reconciled himself to proceed as best as he could.

"Saunders, Sanchez, Perot, Childes," he called out to the four men guarding the tunnel. They turned in his direction. "Lower your weapons and step back to the tunnel entrance."

"What's going on?" Benson asked.

"I messed up," Eli confessed. "We're going to put our weapons down so we don't pose a threat to the other Telgorans when they show up. That goes for everyone. Weapons on the ground and retreat to the entrance."

Without complaint or further questions, everyone did as they were instructed. Weapons were piled up next to the Telgoran on the cave floor and they moved to the entrance and sat down.

All they could do now was wait.

* * *

Free awoke with a start and jumped to his feet. He

still held the staff and swung it in a circle as he looked around.

What he saw was both confusing and comforting. The humans were seated at the cave entrance, hands on top of their heads. Their weapons were piled at his feet.

"What is this?" he asked.

One of the humans—it looked to be the one he had fought—stood up.

"We . . . friends," the man answered in a rough, but passable, version of Telgoran.

* * *

"Don't tell me you speak Telgoran too."

Eli shook his head at Benson and gave him a hard look. Hopefully, the other recruit got the message. *Not now*.

Eli turned back to the Telgoran and held his hands open, out at his sides.

"You have our weapons," he said, pointing to the pile. "We mean no harm."

Unlike his mastery of Minith, Eli's Telgoran was rudimentary. He had spent hundreds of hours learning the basics of the language, but not having a native speaker to practice with limited his abilities. Again, he thanked his father for his foresight in suggesting he study all the languages of the Shiale Alliance—not just the two he had grown up around, Earth Standard and Minith.

"Why did you enter our cavern?" The Telgoran's voice was high in pitch, but clearly understandable. He debated on how best to answer the question, decided on the truth.

"Long story," he began.

* * *

Free listened to the story, only stopping the man when necessary to ensure he understood what was being communicated. The human's speech patterns were halting, and he used the wrong tenses and words on occasion, but for the most part, he got his message across.

As he listened, understanding filtered down upon Free's mind. Gaps were filled in and bridges of knowledge were built. He finally knew why the human soldiers gathered on the plain below and where they went when they departed. He was surprised to learn that Minith waited in the distance with weapons, and that no human force had ever managed to reach them, much less defeat them. The story reminded him of his own people's failed attempts at defeating the Minith in the years before the humans had arrived and showed them a new way.

By the time the human, who called himself "Eli," finished, Free understood their need. He knew of the tower that stood alone in the desert. An entrance to their underground home was nearby. He agreed to help them in the same way that the emissary, Titan, had helped his own people years earlier.

He only had one condition.

* * *

"His name is Free and he's agreed to lead us to the tower," Eli relayed to the team. The announcement was greeted with muted cheers and smiles all around. "Everyone grab your weapons and get ready to move. We don't have much time. Ellison should already be moving by now."

"What's he doing anyway?" Benson asked. "We didn't have time to discuss that earlier."

Eli smiled. "He's making sure the Minith think we're still playing their game."

"Okay. Whatever that means," the other man ceded as he picked up his rifle and slung it over his shoulder. "I still can't get my mind around how you speak both Minith and Telgoran. You'll probably tell me next that you speak Waa also."

"Not likely," Eli replied. He grabbed his own weapon from the pile and clapped Benson on the shoulder. "They don't share their language with the likes of us lowly humans. They all speak Earth Standard, though, so there aren't any language barriers."

"Oh . . . yeah. I forgot."

Once everyone was set, Eli nodded to Free.

"We're ready."

"Try to keep up," the Telgoran announced. He then turned and sped off into the tunnel without a single glance backward.

Damn, he's fast, Eli thought as he rushed to catch up. He had told Free that speed was important and that they needed to hurry. He hoped his team could maintain the pace and chanced a quick glance behind. So far, so good. Everyone was keeping up.

He also noted the pacer floating along in its normal position, ten meters behind the last soldier. He had no doubt *it* could keep the pace.

CHAPTER 9

"These pings are getting more intense, Major." Shawn Tinson, the corporal in charge of monitoring the deep-space probes for the Rhino-3 station focused his attention on the screen at the front of his stations and adjusted the buds seated firmly in his ears. "There's something out there, but I can't tell what—or exactly where—it is."

"I'm not surprised," Major Stevens replied, looking over Corporal Tinson's shoulder. As commander of the monitoring station, it was Stevens's job to receive information, analyze it, and make the appropriate decision on how to respond. He was trying to do that now, but the incomplete data was making him both anxious and more than a bit irritated. "Despite what they tell us, these sensors aren't good at picking out hard targets beyond the outer edge of the system."

They had been receiving ghostlike pings for the past two hours, but nothing definitive had shown itself. He sincerely hoped it was a glitch, but his gut and experience told him otherwise. He'd have been certain the system was acting up only three days earlier, before they'd lost contact with Rhino-2. That station was located in the next closest solar system, which was virtually right next door, less than three day's travel by mothership. As the outermost ring of the Shiale Alliance defenses, it was up to stations like theirs to monitor space traffic, watch for unexpected incursions into their territory, and report back to Waa on anything out of the ordinary. Not that it would do them any good if they were attacked. It took three days for messages to reach the nearest mothership and another week for them to be relayed to Waa. Designed primarily as a remote listening outpost, their on-ground forces were minimal—less than a thousand soldiers, most of who were trained in communications. The 350 Minith posted to the tiny planet made up the core of their infantry force. They were truly the outermost line of the Shiale Alliance.

Stevens turned to the sergeant on his right.

"Send word to the mothership that we've got potential targets on the outer horizon. Then alert the Minith commander and the rest of our forces to stand ready. It's probably nothing, but I'd rather be prepared than not."

"Yes, Major," the sergeant replied. He swallowed before continuing. "The mothership is probably just entering range of Rhino-1 and hasn't yet received our message about Rhino-2 going silent. By the time they receive this transmission, they will likely be en route to that location."

"I'm aware of the timing issues, Sergeant Bloom. But there's not a lot we can do about it."

It was obvious the mothership, with its load of five thousand soldiers and hundreds of fighting vehicles, was chasing ghosts of its own. If someone was playing cat and mouse with them, they were cleverly staying one step ahead of the Alliance cavalry.

The support mothership was normally stationed an equal distance from the three outposts that made up the Rhino sector. Its job was to provide backup and support to the three stations if and when needed. That was the idea, anyway. Unfortunately, the three-day comm lag had turned into a week when the ship moved out to support Rhino-1, who had been the first to report the ghost pings that Stevens and his team were now seeing.

The week delay in communications, coupled with the four-days of travel time once the mothership received the message, meant help was a long way off for Rhino-3, should it be needed.

"Contact!" The single word from the corporal interrupted Major Steven's thoughts like the alarm it was. "Zrthn battle carrier just crossed into the outer fringe of the solar system. Looks like . . . at least a half dozen support ships in attendance."

"Bloom, get a message out to the mothership and another to Waa!"

"Already on—" the sergeant began, then snapped his jaws shut. He worked furiously at the controls before him before reaching his right hand up to wipe his brow. Stevens wondered what the man was doing and was about to demand a response when the man spoke. "Um. Sir?"

"Spit it out, Bloom. What's going on?"

"Um. It looks as if the incoming ships are blocking our transmissions," the suddenly nervous sergeant answered. "I'm getting nothing on the trans-beam. Just noise."

"They're jamming our comms?" Stevens asked, but already knew the answer. That explained why they hadn't received a final transmission from Rhino-2 before they went silent. They hadn't been able to break through the jamming.

"Yes, sir."

"Keep trying," Stevens ordered before taking a moment to consider the situation. "Do we still have local comms?"

"Negative, Major. All systems are nonfunctional."

"Flock me," he swore under his breath. The urge to shout the accepted military profanity was strong, but the lifelong demand for peace that had been instilled by his parents since childhood kicked in, and he held back. He swallowed the anger that threatened to explode from his chest and took a deep breath. "Sergeant?"

"Yes, sir."

"Can you run to the Minith barracks and alert Major Grinnt of our situation? He'll know what to do to prepare our forces to receive the Zrthn force headed our way."

"Um. Of course, sir."

Major Stevens watched the young soldier exit the command center at a sprint, then turned to the corporal at the console. "How long until they reach us, Corporal?"

"They can land on the planet in . . . approximately twenty-six hours, sir."

"Well, keep trying to get our comms operational," Stevens sighed. He knew it would probably prove useless, but what could they do except keep trying? For all intents and purposes, they were on their own against whatever the Zrthns were planning. If the continued silence from Rhino-2 was any indication, whatever they were planning couldn't be good.

* * *

"They've begun their approach," Brek stated, looking up from the monitor that reported on the location of the humans in their charge.

"What method have they chosen?" Twigg asked.

Not that it would matter.

"It's very . . . unusual," the Minith sergeant replied. "They aren't moving as a team. There are . . . five moving out in a direct line for the tower. The rest are still at the jump-off point."

Twigg growled. This was the human called Jayson's attempt at strategy, no doubt. He was clever, that was for certain. No matter. Cleverness could not overcome the certainty of meeting the tower and its superior weapons. Their ability to track the exact location of each human also helped, of course. The human could delay the inevitable, but the end result would be the same.

The urge to teach the human a lesson, as well as those who had elected him as their leader, grew stronger with each passing moment.

"Pass word to the warriors below," Twigg instructed the private that assisted them in the tower. "Each human receives a minimum of two pulses."

"Yes, Sergeant," the private replied with a smile and an ear twitch. "A *minimum* of two."

* * *

Ellison waited fifteen minutes before beginning, just as he had been instructed.

Now, he jogged forward at a steady pace. Under each arm, he carried two of the PEACE suits that had been abandoned by Jayson and the others. His own armor provided enough strength to make the task a relatively simple one. His heads-up display alerted him when he reached a point exactly half a kilometer from their starting point, and he halted. After a quick scan of his surroundings, he deposited each of the suits behind a large rock. Satisfied with their placement, he turned around and jogged back to retrieve the next four. Three trips in this leg to bring all eleven suits forward. Three trips in the next.

With luck on their side, Jayson and the rest of the team would reach the tower and complete their mission before a third leg was needed. If it took longer, no problem. He had plenty of trips to make before he would reach the point where he'd be in range of the Minith weapons pointed in his direction.

* * *

Although the tower where the Minith waited was only five kilometers from their drop-off point, the tunnels the team traveled weren't set out in a straight line. Because of the winding path they followed, the distance they traveled before reaching their final destination was significantly longer. Eli estimated they had traveled nearly eight kilometers by the time they arrived at the cave opening that was closest to their goal. Everyone was covered in sweat and breathing in ragged gasps when Free finally stopped running. Unlike the humans, he didn't seem tired at all.

They had not lost anyone along the way, though it had been touch and go in a few spots. They were given one brief reprieve early on when they encountered their first Telgoran. To Eli's surprise, Free stopped when he met the other native—a female—and he took his time explaining in some detail the reason why he was leading a group of armed humans through their territory. When she heard of their mission and noted that an attack on a group of Minith waited at the far end of their journey, she stood still for nearly a minute before nodding. Only after receiving the nod, did Free begin running again. Eli wondered if he had just had his first experience with the decision-making ritual that was known as *Shiale*.

After that initial encounter, they did not stop for any other Telgorans, although they passed dozens more along the way. As they progressed through the caverns, the number of Telgorans steadily increased. By the end of their trek, the tunnel walls were lined with hundreds of the planet's native inhabitants. Apparently, they wanted to witness the unexpected human procession first hand. It was both a strange and marvelous experience for Eli, and he scanned his team for how they were handling this turn of events as he fought to find his breath. For the most part, what he saw on the faces around him seemed to mirror his own thoughts. Wonder. Uncertainty. Relief. Exhaustion.

He estimated that the entire journey, from the time they left their armor lying in the dirt, to the time they reached the exit point, took them just under ninety minutes. Not bad considering everything that had happened since then, but not great. They were behind schedule and needed to hurry. Ellison had to be nearing the halfway point to the tower by now, even at his slower speed.

Eli took another deep breath and stood straight before announcing, "Get ready. We move out in five minutes."

* * *

"They've reached the midway point."

"But why so slow? And why the unusual

approach, Brek? What purpose could that serve?"

"There's no purpose in it, Twigg," Brek responded. The boredom was evident in his voice. "The humans are being overly cautious. That's all."

"Hmmm." Twigg pondered the situation. The human, Jayson, had shown aggression and intelligence in the past. Caution, especially caution to this degree, was out of character. Something did not feel right. "Do we have a link with the pacer attached to the unit?"

Brek issued a grunt and casually entered the command sequence for the pacer into the keypad behind which he lazed. He waited several seconds, then repeated the commands, this time with a bit more urgency. Twigg watched with increased interest.

"The pacer attached to this unit isn't responding."

"Check it again."

"I've checked it three times. It is either damaged or out of range." Alarms began going off in Twigg's head at the news.

"Send another pacer out immediately," he instructed the other sergeant. "Private, pass word to the soldiers below to remain alert. The enemy is still on track for a direct frontal approach. We're tracking them on our monitor, but we've lost our visual link."

"Yes, Sergeant."

"Let me know when we have the replacement pacer on target, Brek, and bring up the visual on your monitor."

"Fifteen minutes," Brek replied with disinterest.

* * *

The tower sat two hundred meters to the southwest

of the cave opening, which was perfect. They were behind the tower, hidden from the Minith's line of sight. The pacer that had followed them into the Telgoran underground was at the rear of their line, still well back from the cave entrance, and Eli hoped its signal wouldn't give their position away. Nothing at the tower indicated they had been detected. At least not yet.

From his vantage point at the mouth of the cave, Eli noted the dozen Minith warriors were arranged on a semicircular platform that fronted the tower. While the tower itself rose five meters or so from the desert floor, the platform where the Minith waited was only three meters high. The height provided the defenders with a clear view and unobstructed firing lanes. The platform had a defensive barrier on the west-facing side that offered protection from a random shot that might come their way. Fortunately, Eli noted with excitement, the back of the platform—the side where his team would approach—was unprotected.

He took a few moments to envision in his mind's eye how he wanted this to play out, then crawled backward slowly from the opening. When he reached a safe point, he stood up and turned to face his team. And Free.

"Okay, listen up," he began. "Our target is two hundred meters southwest. We're going to exit the tunnel and proceed due south. Then we're going to turn west and approach from the rear of the tower in a side-by-side line formation.

"You'll notice this as soon as you exit the tunnel, but there's a raised platform on the far side of the tower with a dozen Minith. They're facing west and their attention will probably remain in that direction since that's where they expect us to be. We're going to move quietly, but we also need to move quickly. I'll move out first, so just follow my lead. With luck, they won't know we're there until we start firing."

Benson raised a hand, asked, "What if they spot us sooner?"

"If they see us, don't hesitate to light them up. We're well within weapons range now."

He took time to look at each member of his team. Received affirmation from each that they understood.

He then turned to Free and handed him his pulse rifle. The Telgoran took it and handed Eli his agsel staff in return.

"What are you doing, Jayson?"

Eli held up a "just a minute" hand to Benson while he relayed instructions to Free. He told him to follow behind the last human and also gave the Telgoran a quick, thirty-second lesson on how to aim and fire the pulse weapon. Like all of their weapons on this exercise, it was set to a nonlethal pulse, so the risk of him causing any real damage to the Minith—or to the humans with whom he traveled—was minimal. When he finished, he turned to his team.

"It was a condition I agreed to earlier. In exchange for his help, he wanted a chance to shoot some Minith." Eli grinned and hefted the agsel staff, testing its weight. "It seemed like a reasonable enough request. How could I refuse?"

"So, you're going to charge a tower of armed Minith carrying an agsel staff?"

"Why not? The Telgorans did it for years before we came along," Eli replied. "They charged Minith defenders who wielded *real* weapons. They did it knowing it was suicide, but that never stopped them. He's earned the right to shoot some volts into one or two of the guards waiting for us outside."

"I suppose you're right," Benson admitted. "Besides, I've seen how well you handle a staff."

"All right then. Everyone ready?"

Eli got nods all around. He spun the staff slowly, getting a feel for the weapon, and walked to the cavern entrance. He looked over his shoulder, saw the others taking their positions. He hoped they wouldn't be disqualified for enlisting Free in the upcoming attack, but there was nothing he would change. The Telgoran had helped them reach this point. He had earned his place with their group.

He took a deep breath and concentrated on settling his thoughts, focusing on what needed to be accomplished in the next few minutes. He settled into a semi-calm state and allowed his body and mind to relax. He was as ready as he would ever be.

Without a conscious thought, he was out the entrance and running south, almost at full speed. To his surprise, it felt good to be moving again. The earlier sprint through the caverns hadn't drained all of his strength. His muscles were loose, his legs were still strong, and he was eager to cover the ground ahead.

He kept his attention divided between the ground and the tower that was at his right-front. The two o'clock position, his dad would have said. He spotted no problems and quickly found himself with the tower at the three o'clock position. He turned toward the rear of their target and slowed to a determined walk. He looked to his right and noted with satisfaction that his team was exactly where they should be—in a line next to him, weapons trained on the Minith backs a hundred meters ahead. Free was positioned on the far end of the line, his weapon also pointed exactly where it should be.

None of the Minith turned in their direction as they approached the tower.

When they reached a point only twenty meters from their objective, Eli slowed . . . halted . . . dropped to one knee. His team followed suit, but kept their weapons aimed firmly on the broad backs that were conveniently arranged in a line just ahead. The purple fabric that was incorporated into their battle uniforms made the Minith excellent targets. Eli knew they could easily take out every one of them now without suffering any casualties of their own.

But the door to the tower grabbed his attention.

The initial plan had only focused on the Minith aligned along the platform ahead. The doorway leading into the tower now called out to him like a siren's song. Sergeant Twigg was probably up there.

Eli quickly revised the plan.

* * *

"The second pacer is coming up on the humans," Brek called out. Twigg turned away from the viewing window and approached the monitor where Brek sat.

"Bring up the visual."

Brek didn't answer. He merely entered the appropriate commands into the system and watched as the screen filled with a view of the desert floor rushing past. The pacer raced from the west at a height of ten meters as it approached. Twigg watched over his peer's shoulder as the humans came into focus. The small blobs aligned on the desert floor quickly grew in size as the pacer neared.

“Is he . . . carrying them?” Brek’s question confirmed what his own eyes saw, though it didn’t help the sight make any more sense. The human carried two other humans under his left arm and had a third tucked under his right. The pacer slowed as it arrived and the visual honed in on the scene.

That was when Twigg saw the reality of the situation.

The suits being carried by the human were empty.

Twigg rocked back, stunned. Where were the humans?

“Pacer one is back online!”

“Show the visual! Now!” The order was unnecessary, he knew. Brek had seen what he had seen, was already bringing the view onto the screen. But the rage and concern that flooded him needed release, could not be restrained.

When the view came onto the screen, Twigg was confused. It showed three humans, dressed in the black garment they wore under their new armor. Two held weapons, the third—Jayson, he noted—carried only a staff. They were standing outside a door. Jayson was in the process of opening it.

Recognition flooded into Twigg’s brain at the same moment as he heard the door below them being thrown open. The sound from below mirrored the actions he observed on Brek’s screen.

The humans had somehow reached the tower. *Impossible!*

He heard the sound of weapons being fired outside. He heard the sound of boots racing up the steps that led to the top of the tower—where he and Brek waited. Somehow, what Twigg had previously considered impossible had just become reality.

The Minith sergeant snarled in frustration and slammed a fist into the desktop. His next move was to grab the pulse rifle that he had leaned against the wall earlier—the rifle he had never needed to use when overseeing this particular exercise. The overwhelming desire to pull a trigger and inflict pain on another being had never been stronger.

* * *

Jayson rushed up the circular stairway, intent on reaching the top as quickly as possible. He heard his team firing on the Minith outside as they had been instructed. He wanted to take the tower, but taking out the soldiers on the platform was paramount. That was their primary objective.

They were a third of the way up the stairs when they met a Minith private headed down. The look of surprise on the private's face lasted only moments—just long enough for Benson to fire his weapon. They stepped over the twitching form and continued upward.

Eli reached the doorway at the top of the staircase and paused. By now, those inside would have been alerted to their presence; would have had time to prepare.

He looked at Benson and Childes. Both held their weapons up, ready for the door to swing open so they could pour volts into the room beyond.

"I'm going in low and to the right," Eli whispered. He was apprehensive about what waited for them on the other side of the door, but also eager to find out. He had no doubt that the team below had taken out their targets—

they were too large and easy to miss. Now, he, Benson and Childes just had to finish the job. "Be prepared for shots headed out when the door opens."

Both men nodded, took up positions on either side of the door.

Eli crouched, twisted the door handle, and pushed. The door swung freely, and he followed its path, rolling into the room and to the right. As he expected, a shot passed immediately over his head. He continued moving forward and scanned the room for movement. He noticed Twigg directly in front of him. The Minith sergeant looked his way briefly, but kept his weapon aimed at the doorway. Brek was seated in front of a computer. He did not appear to be armed.

"The two of you outside the door," Twigg called out, his weapon still aimed in that direction. "Put down your weapons immediately!"

In reply, Childes dodged around the frame and released a wild shot that passed over Twigg's head. Twigg's return fire was immediate and on target. Childes collapsed to the floor, his body twitching wildly as a result of the volts passing through his system.

That's what I must have looked like earlier, Eli thought. The thought angered him.

"That's one," Twigg called out. His weapon was still aimed at the doorway. "I know there's one more out there. Drop your weapon now and you'll avoid a similar fate."

Twigg glanced briefly at Eli and spat, "You'll get yours in just a moment." The Minith's ears were laid back and his voice was a growl.

Eli was crouched on the floor, the staff held out in front of him. He wondered briefly how Benson would respond to the order from the Minith Sergeant, then realized he didn't care. His emotions boiled as the scenario played out. He waited anxiously for whatever opportunity presented itself.

He didn't have to wait long. Mirroring his own entrance into the room just moments before, his roommate rolled in low and fast. He was raising his weapon to fire, but Twigg was ready and got his shot off first. The pulse found its mark and Benson dropped, but the distraction gave Eli the opening he needed.

He struck forward with the butt of the staff and landed a solid blow to Twigg's chest. The strike pushed the Minith backward and Eli darted ahead, landing a second thrusting strike to the sergeant's chin. Not daring to give the larger opponent a moment to recover, he spun to his right and twirled the staff over his head, building up momentum and power. At the height of his spin, he delivered a backhand strike that connected with the side of Twigg's head, just under his ear. It was an especially sensitive spot for Minith, Eli knew.

The Minith growled in pain and anger, dropped his weapon, and reached for the injury. Eli rolled and snatched the pulse pistol before it could hit the floor. He twisted left, swung the barrel of the weapon around and filled his sight with the sergeant's broad chest. With a sense of enraged satisfaction, born from weeks of torment, he pulled the trigger.

The Minith warrior dropped like a stone . . . a twitching, mewling, pain-riddled stone.

Eli considered his next move for less than a second, before redirecting the barrel of the pistol toward Brek. The Minith was just beginning to rise from his seat.

With a determined grin etched across his face, Eli

added a second Minith sergeant to the pile of twitching bodies that covered the floor.

CHAPTER 10

He's created quite a stir.

Yes, apparently he has, Sha'n, Grant replied. The video of Eli's latest brush with authority had just finished playing. Eli had involved the Telgorans in his latest activities. Enlisting their support against the Minith was rarely a good thing. Regardless of the alliance they shared, there were too many tensions still bubbling between the two races. Like two bullies who loved to fight, it was usually best to keep them at separate ends of the playground. Still, Eli had overcome a problem that wasn't designed to be solved.

You are proud of him.

Grant waved the comment away. His feelings on the matter weren't important. But she was correct.

"The Telgoran Alliance Council is assembling a formal review panel. There are some serious charges being cited by the Minith contingent."

Yet, you will not become involved.

"No," he conceded. "Eli was very clear. He wanted to succeed or fail on his own merit. What kind of message would I be sending—to him, or to the council—if I stepped in now? Besides, I have faith in the system we've put in place. Whatever justice they've meted out has already taken place. My involvement would only be after the fact."

You think they will clear him.

You can read my thoughts, Sha'n. You know what I think. And what I fear.

The fact was Grant firmly believed Eli's actions, while unconventional, were justified. His reasoning was sound. His problem-solving abilities were off the charts. But pitting the Telgorans against the Minith? That was the wild card. He didn't know how things would play out—had already played out, he amended, recalling the comms' delay—but whatever happened would take place without his interference or influence.

You are getting better at concealing your thoughts. You've been practicing.

That's what you'd have me believe.

The truth was that he could block his thoughts from being read only with intense concentration, and only for short periods. The Waa were a patient people. If Sha'n or any other Waa wanted to know what was in is head, it was just a matter of time. He couldn't focus on blocking them forever—an hour or two, at best.

"So, what else is on the agenda this morning?"

Sha'n paused before replying. When she did respond, her unease was evident in her thoughts.

We have lost contact with Rhino-3.

Grant dropped into his seat and placed his hands on top of his desk. Rhino-3 was a small but important defensive outpost the Alliance had established on a planet called Song. Song was in a solar system located at the outermost boundary of their relatively small sphere of influence. The purpose of the units stationed on Rhino-3 was to patrol the edges of their territory for threats and to make known the Alliance's claim on the region. Now, it was the second outpost in the last two weeks that had gone quiet. Reports had yet to come back on the status of the first, and he cursed his lack of intel.

It was no secret that powerful entities outside the

Alliance coveted the agsel mines on Telgora. The Zrthns were the most likely, and best prepared, to make a move, but there were other races out there who knew where they were and what they owned. Grant could envision a time when one or more of those entities might make a move against the Alliance. If so, they were as prepared as they could be. There was still work to be accomplished, and additional defenses to put in place, but the twelve years that had passed since the end of the Minith wars were good ones for the Shiale Alliance. They were prosperous and peaceful, and much of what had been destroyed on Earth, Telgora, and Waa had been rebuilt. And because of Grant's insistence, the years had also allowed them time to build a strong army and amass a formidable armada of spaceships.

He wondered if the time had finally arrived to put those forces into play.

* * *

"Do you understand the reason for this inquiry, Private Jayson?"

The question was posed by a Minith wearing the rank of an Alliance Defense Force colonel. He sat in the center of the main table. As the ranking military member at the table, he apparently headed up the review panel.

Eli considered the question and looked around the large room at the individuals that were assembled for the review. He had to force his right leg to be still. The nervous uncertainty of the situation made his body want to move, but a jittery, bouncing leg might send the wrong message to those who were here to judge him. He reminded himself that he had done nothing wrong, so had little to worry about. The mental reminder did little to quell his unease, though.

The setup reminded him of an ancient courtroom on Earth. The panel of six reviewers—two Minith, three human, and one Telgoran—sat facing him from behind a long, raised table.

One of the humans he knew well. Ambassador Titan was a long-time friend of his family and was the permanent human emissary to the Telgorans. On Earth, the man was shunned as a Violent, while here he was revered as a warrior. He was highly respected by the planet's native race, having led them in battle against the Minith twelve years earlier. Although human, and a good friend of his father, Eli knew the ambassador was as loyal to the Telgorans as much as he was to his own race.

The other members of the panel were strangers. With the exception of Ambassador Titan and the Telgoran delegate, all were dressed in Shiale Alliance Defense uniforms. The colonel was joined by another Minith, a captain. The two humans both wore the rank of major.

As the subject of the inquiry, Eli sat alone at a much smaller table. His table was centered before the review panel, and surrounded by three meters of open space on all sides. He was a veritable island, seated alone and surrounded in the crowded room.

Behind his table, separated by a short pony wall, sat a mass of onlookers and witnesses. Most were Minith, but he noticed a scattering of his fellow recruits and the only other Telgoran in the large hall—Free.

Forming the right border of his personal space was a similar, small table like his own. That table was reserved for whatever witnesses would be called to provide statements and testimony. He suspected that some would speak in his favor, while others would not. He'd never been witness to a formal inquiry, so could only guess as to what was to come. He swallowed in an attempt to clear the growing lump from his throat and put his right hand on his thigh to quell a renewed round of jitter-bounce.

"Private Jayson . . ."

"Um. Sorry. Yes, sir, I believe so."

"You believe so?" the Minith officer repeated. Eli could tell the colonel wasn't looking down his greenish, apelike nose at him with respect. The repeated flaring of the nostrils, the flattened ears, the slight turn of the lips. All pointed to feelings of disdain and contempt flowing from the officer. As easily as Eli could pick up on the cues, he doubted that any of the other humans present noted anything other than the standard sense of grouchiness that the Minith usually displayed.

"Allow me to state the reasons we are here, Private." The colonel glanced at the ceiling where a pacer recorded the proceedings and picked up a printed page from which he read. "For the record, you are charged with one count of failure to follow orders. One count of trespass. Eleven counts of abuse of authority. And fifteen counts of unlawful assault on ranking members of the Shiale Alliance Defense Forces."

The colonel dropped the page onto the table top and refocused his attention on Eli.

"How do you respond to these charges?"

"They're complete nonsense," Eli stated simply. Despite his nervousness, he refused to cower before the panel or to admit his actions were anything other than appropriate. A chatter of various voices and exclamations arose from the gallery behind Eli. He couldn't make out any specifics, but his assessment of the charges had gotten the attention of more than a few of the assembled. He experienced a brief moment of déjà vu and thought back on his previous meeting with Twigg in his office. He doubted this audience would be so quick to dismiss their charges as the Minith sergeant had been. He no longer had the leverage of involving a review panel to support his position.

The Minith colonel didn't seem pleased with his reply; however, the slight grin Eli noted on Titan's face before he covered his mouth with his hand indicated he had at least one ally at the long table. Eli paused a moment to let the din subside, then pushed ahead.

"My orders were very specific: Move to contact with the tower. Assault the defenders located there. I mean no disrespect, Colonel, but that's exactly what we did."

The Minith colonel issued a low growl and placed both hands on the table.

"You were expected to attack the tower from a direct approach, Private. That did not happen. Instead, you trespassed through Telgoran territory and launched a . . . less than courageous . . . attack from the rear."

The rage was immediate and hot. Eli wanted to spit an angry response at the colonel, but—for one of the few times in his young life—he held his tongue. Nothing that issued forth from his lips at this particular moment would be good, either for his present or his future. Instead, he clenched his jaws in a steely bite and stared directly into the dark, angry eyes of the Minith. The two locked gazes for seconds that felt like hours, each refusing to cede. Then, with a burst of clarity and understanding,

Eli realized something important. The Minith colonel was pushing him toward a cliff and hoping—yes, there was a glint of expectation and hope in the other's eyes—that Eli would take the bait. Jump at the taunt and chase it over the precipice to his doom. It didn't matter what had happened during the training exercise if he failed here. He could be exonerated of all charges for what happened *then*. But if he acted out *now*, against a senior officer, in front of dozens of witnesses . . . there would be no exoneration for that insubordination.

Eli knew the Minith people, understood their culture, their tendencies, and their motivations. No Minith would sit quietly while another, regardless of rank, openly questioned their courage. To a Minith, bravery and aggression were the lifeblood of their core, crucial to their being and sense of self-worth. It was one of the key differences between their race and humans. Humans could sometimes interject rational thinking into the decision-making process, even when angry.

He refused to take the bait. The crushing sense of rage that had threatened to overtake his body and mind only moments before lifted. A knowing smile replaced the clenched-teeth grimace that he hadn't realized was on his face until it was released. He took a deep breath, relaxed back into his seat, and winked—actually *winked*—at the colonel.

The colonel snarled and inhaled sharply. Before he could reply, Titan spoke up from the far right of the table.

"Colonel Drah," he began. So, the colonel had a name. "As the Telgoran ambassador for the Shiale Alliance, I have been asked by the Telgoran people to speak on their behalf."

Drah's angry glare left Eli's face with reluctance

and slid sideways down the table toward Titan.

“Yes?”

“Colonel, the Telgorans do not agree to the charge of trespass,” the ambassador stated. “The private and his team requested permission to enter the underground caverns and were granted permission. The Telgoran’s reached *shiale* on that decision. As a result, that charge should be removed from the scope of this panel review.”

The Telgoran seated next to Titan was nodding his large, elongated head up and down in a slow, systematic fashion. Eli had no doubt he was relaying events to the rest of the Family and that they were in agreement with Titan’s statement. Drah must have also noted the words and the nodding motion of the Telgoran. He grimaced at the announcement, but had no option but to nod as well.

“Very well, Ambassador. The charge of trespass will be removed,” the colonel acceded. He then refocused attention on Eli. “We will focus on the remaining charges. Let’s begin with the charges surrounding your abuse of authority.”

The next sixty minutes passed quickly. One by one, the five members of Eli’s squad who had been requested to attend the panel review took their place at the small table on the right side of the room. Each relayed the same basic facts, and provided similar testimony.

They had overwhelmingly elected Eli as their squad leader. They had done so because he had proved himself to be capable and competent, and over the weeks leading up to the exercise, had earned the respect and trust of every recruit in their unit. All denied that he abused his authority. No one had been forced to follow him or to act in any manner that they had not been in full agreement with. He had requested their input and suggestions when forming their strategy for completing their assigned mission. Without exception, all of them had agreed with the plan and given their approval to proceed.

"I jokingly suggested that we ask the Telgorans for help" Private Gale Benson proudly stated when asked how Eli had come up with the plan. "Eli took that idea, mulled it over for a minute, and then ran with it. We all thought it was a bit crazy at first, but what did we have to lose? We knew that no unit had ever launched a successful attack on the tower. This at least gave us a shot of succeeding and kicking some Minith butt. Um . . . no offense intended, Colonel."

The two Minith officers grimaced and their ears flattened against their heads. In contrast, Eli noted that Titan and the two human majors stifled grins at Benson's less-than-tactful comment. The reactions highlighted the divisions that still ran deep between the two cultures. Humans had won the Peace War and forged the Alliance, but the Minith still rankled at the defeat.

Despite the minor faux pas by Benson, Eli felt his team presented the human viewpoint very well. They were given an unwinnable mission and had managed to come out the victors. He was proud to have led them and hoped he would get a chance to stay with them and complete their training.

Still, it was the Minith version of events that would hold sway with the colonel. When Twigg was called forward, Eli shuddered. The sergeant was not a friend. Just the opposite. He had displayed his intense dislike of Eli—all humans, really—on multiple occasions. Of all the speakers, it was his testimony that would command the attention of Colonel Drah and perhaps dictate the outcome of the review.

The eight-foot-tall warrior made his way to the witness table without looking in Eli's direction. When his bulk settled into the chair, it issued a groan that had not been evident when the previous human occupants had sat down. Dressed in full battle gear, he was an impressive figure, even for a Minith.

"Sergeant Twigg," the colonel began. "Can you tell us how you know Private Jayson?"

For the first time, the sergeant looked at Eli.

As the dark brown eyes searched his face, Eli was surprised that he couldn't tell what the Minith was feeling, had no clue as to what he might be thinking. Over a lifetime spent with the aliens, he had become adept at translating their tics, movements, and expressions. They weren't known for hiding their inner thoughts, but that's what he found when he looked at Twigg.

"I have known Private Jayson for ten weeks," Twigg answered. "He is a recruit in the training company that I lead here on Telgora."

"Can you describe your interactions with the private, Sergeant? Has he been a model recruit?"

"Not even close," Twigg replied, still hiding his emotions.

"Elaborate please, Sergeant."

"Private Jayson is not like most humans recruits. He doesn't follow directions in the same fashion. He doesn't think only about his position, or how he can get himself through the tasks he is assigned. He thinks . . . differently." Twigg's right ear dipped, and his shoulders hunched in the distinctive Minith way that displayed confusion or bewilderment. It was clear to Eli—as well as to the Minith in the room, he had no doubt—that the sergeant was stumped by Eli's behavior.

"I'm not sure I follow, Sergeant. How has he acted that makes him a poor recruit? What has he done that would dictate his removal from the Alliance Defense forces?"

For the first time, Eli noted a real emotion. Twigg was smiling at the colonel.

"He is a natural leader," the sergeant replied. "One who leads through example. Not through threats or by creating fear. In the past ten weeks, he has displayed a remarkable ability to win allegiance and support from his men."

"Exactly!"

"That's right."

"Yeah!"

Eli recognized the calls from the team members seated behind him as he sat immobile, stunned by the sergeant's unexpected admission.

"Silence!" Drah slammed his fist on the table and looked across the room. The shouts died out quickly. Having silenced the humans, the colonel refocused his attention on the Minith sergeant.

"This is not what we discussed," Drah spoke quietly in Minith. The sudden switch from Earth Standard language drew curious looks from the humans seated at the table. *"This human must be taught a lesson."*

"It may not be what we discussed, Colonel," Twigg replied in his native language. *"But it is the truth. The human should not be expelled. He should be promoted."*

Promoted? The surprises just kept on coming. For the first time since Eli sat down, his leg didn't feel the urge to bounce. The jittery nervousness he had previously felt had been replaced by surprise and relief. The sergeant was actually speaking up on his behalf—something Eli never would have expected. That realization was quickly replaced by another, more startling awareness as Colonel Drah's features morphed from alarmed disbelief to angered resignation. The look the two Minith exchanged was clear for anyone who understood Minith expressions. By going against Colonel Drah's wishes, Sergeant Twigg had just saved the career of a lowly, anonymous private and, in so doing, had sacrificed his own.

"Colonel, please stop speaking Minith and address the witness in Earth Standard," the major seated on the left spoke for the first time. He drew an angry, sideways glare from the ranking officer but did not look away. It was obvious he knew the protocol for these reviews and wouldn't let the colonel run over the proceedings.

"I apologize," the colonel acquiesced, switching back to Standard. The look of disdain disappeared and was quickly replaced with a stoic, respectful smile that Eli couldn't help but recognize as forced. "I was merely clarifying a point with the sergeant."

"Pardon me for the intrusion, Colonel Drah," Eli interjected in Minith. The look of surprise on the colonel's face at hearing his native language being spoken by a human was the fourth separate and distinct reaction to grace the colonel's face in the past ten seconds. Eli found that fact pleasingly humorous, in a ruthless sort of way. He didn't hesitate to amplify the colonel's sudden discomfort another notch. *"Perhaps you can explain to the panel how teaching me a lesson is the same as clarifying a point?"*

The room was suddenly filled with gasps and cries of surprise. Of the members of the review panel, only Titan seemed unmoved at hearing Eli speak Minith.

Colonel Drah scowled at Eli from across the space that separated them. The look contained a heated mixture of angry promises and raw emotions. His dad was fond of an ancient saying that seemed to fit this situation: *If looks could kill*. Eli wondered how anyone, knowledgeable of Minith mannerisms or not, could miss the blatant hostility in Drah's countenance.

The colonel quickly recovered, though, and erased the threatening glare from his face. As before, he replaced the negative reaction with another fake smile. He then slowly turned his head until his attention was back on Sergeant Twigg.

"Please continue, Sergeant," the colonel commanded in an even voice that belied the storm Eli knew was still brewing beneath the suddenly calm exterior. "You were praising Private Jayson's leadership abilities, I believe."

"Thank you, Colonel," Twigg smiled in the Minith way, with a twitch of ear and upturned lips. Eli recognized that Twigg was enjoying himself. He also reveled in the fact that it wasn't at his expense this time. He wondered what the sergeant's future might hold. Angering a Minith colonel was not something a lowly sergeant accomplished with any degree of success. By speaking out against his superior, Twigg was clearly on borrowed time. The sacrifice wasn't something that Eli would quickly forget. For better or worse, he was now indebted to the alien sergeant. "As I was saying. Jayson is a natural leader. But he has substantial abilities in other areas. He is a skilled fighter with every weapon we've trained with, as an example."

Twigg paused for questions, but received only nods to continue from the panel. He did so.

"And he is clever. His problem solving abilities are unique."

"Can you give us an example, Sergeant?" the second human major asked.

"Of course. Do we have the capability to view pacer video from the tower exercise?" He received nods from the panel. "I believe watching his actions on that occasion will provide adequate explanation."

It took several minutes for support staff to find the footage, but once found, a nod from Drah kicked it off. Eli watched along with everyone else in the room as he and his team came into focus on a large vid-screen located on the left wall of the chamber. They were at the demarcation point, discussing options. The look of defeat was evident on all of their faces as they prepared to launch an attack that was bound to fail. Then, Benson's comment of, "Maybe we should ask the Telgorans for help" was heard by everyone and looks were exchanged by the panel members. On the screen, the emotions of the team began to change as they discussed their plan and hope for potential success began to emerge.

The video showed Eli giving directions to Ellison on how, when, and where to move the team's armor, then followed the rest of team into the cavern. There was a tense moment when the altercation between Free and Jayson was shown, but Titan quickly announced that the Telgorans would not hold Eli accountable for the attack since it was obviously self-defense on his part. The dash through the caverns was played in spurts, showing only the occasional frame to save time. The assembled Telgorans at the end of the journey were seen, then Eli's comments to the team as they prepared for their attack were heard. Eli flinched mentally when the video showed the exchange of his pulse rifle for Free's agsel staff. If there was any charge that might be valid, it would be him giving his weapon to a noncombatant. Oh well, it was what it was, and a casual look at the panel showed no concerns on any of the faces seated at the table. Maybe he had dodged that particular bullet.

Finally, the attack itself played out on the large screen and Eli watched their advance from a distance some ten meters to their rear where the pacer tracked them. He watched as they stopped their advance, already clearly in firing range of the Minith who were positioned on the platforms ahead. It was also clear that the defenders were completely unaware of their presence. Their focus was to the front, where they believed the attackers to be.

The pacer remained outside when he, Benson, and Childes entered the tower. Eli sat up and watched as the team, supported by Free from the far right, began taking out the Minith, not ten meters away. It was like shooting at still targets on the range, only easier because they were so close. He watched with pride as they made quick work of the defenders. Within ten seconds, all twelve of the Minith soldiers were twitching away. Eli noticed that Free managed to score hits on two different Minith. The Telgoran seemed like a natural, at least from close in.

The video then showed Eli exiting the tower. He took a moment to check on the team, then made his way over to Free, where he retrieved his weapon and returned the staff.

When the video ended, no one said anything for several seconds. Then Twigg filled the silence.

"We've been conducting this tower exercise for years. In that time, no one—Minith or human—has ever found a way to accomplish the mission that is given. It was designed as an exercise that couldn't be beaten. We track each recruit's movements so we know exactly where they are at all times. When they are in range of our weapons, we shoot them. End of exercise.

"The charges of failing to follow orders and the assault of ranking soldiers that have been levied against Private Jayson are laughable. The orders given were simple and clear: attack the tower, defeat the defenders. "

Twigg paused briefly to look at Colonel Drah. Drah avoided eye contact, looking down at the table top.

"The video we just watched shows that Private Jayson did exactly what he was ordered to do. He attacked the tower and he defeated its defenders. The fact that he was *supposed* to fail, but managed to succeed, should not be held against him."

* * *

The panel review wound down quickly after Sergeant Twigg's testimony, and the proceedings took on an air of finality and completion. Eli didn't follow much of what transpired in the final stages—his surprise and shock at being defended by Twigg clouded his thoughts—but the comments Drah made regarding a private review by the panel and a final determination of Eli's eventual status managed to sink in. His fate was now in the hands of the individuals seated at the long table.

He was surprised to find he didn't really care what judgment they might come back with. He had done what was required and, given the chance, would do it all again in the exact same fashion. Well . . . with one possible exception. His initial encounter with Free hadn't been particularly enjoyable. Given another opportunity he'd prefer an introduction that didn't involve thousands of volts coursing through their bodies. He smiled with the recollection.

"Private Jayson," Colonel Drah's direct address brought Eli back to the here and now.

"Yes, sir."

"Return back to your barracks and remain there. You will be informed when we have concluded our review. Do you have any questions?"

"No, sir," Eli replied. He noted the colonel had taken a cue from Twigg and was now effectively concealing his emotions. Learning that the human seated before him understood and spoke Minith probably had some influence.

"Very well. You are dismissed," he informed the private. He pushed himself from his seat and announced to the assembly, "This panel is adjourned."

Eli sat unmoving and watched the panel members rise and make their way to the private doorway located behind their table. As befitting such a formal occasion, each member of the panel appeared stoic and resolute. None looked in his direction.

Except for Ambassador Titan.

Titan stood, waited for the other panel members to exit, then raised a finger, indicating he wanted a word. Eli simply nodded, stood. The bustle and murmurs of the crowd behind him let him know that the observers and witnesses were making their own, noisy exit through the doors at the rear.

Eli marveled at the man's size as he approached. He wasn't as large as a Minith, but standing at nearly seven feet tall and weighing almost three hundred pounds—still muscle, even at his age—he was the largest man Eli had ever met. He was also one of the most important. Not only was he the human emissary here on Telgora, but after Eli's father, Titan was the person most responsible for the defeat of the Minith twelve years earlier. He had destroyed the Minith home planet and led Free's people in a successful underground assault against the Minith bases here on Telgora. That attack, which led to the freeing of Telgora from Minith domination, had been the inspiration for Eli's tower assault only a few days earlier.

"Ah, Eli," Titan greeted the younger man. He gave Eli a solid handshake, then pulled him into a crushing embrace. Fortunately, it lasted only a second or two. "It's been too long, son."

"Two years, give or take a couple of months," Eli agreed, rolling his shoulders in an effort to dispel the pain from the unexpected hug. He also glanced over his shoulder to see who might have observed the greeting. Most of the crowd had already left, and the few remaining were walking away from them. Only Free was left, still seated. The young Telgoran was watching.

"Don't worry," Titan said, lowering his voice. "Your secret is safe with me. You father filled me in on your situation and asked me to respect your request for anonymity. Not sure why you'd take that route, but who am I to question it?"

Eli considered citing his reasons but quickly decided not to bother. It was a complex thing, growing up as the only son of the most popular man alive—not to mention, the greatest warrior in human history. On one hand, he had advantages that were beyond compare—superior educational opportunities, advanced military and physical training, knowledge of how the Alliance was formed, how it operated and managed to survive. He couldn't imagine not having access to these privileges and did his best to use them as a way to improve and prepare for the future—a future he was convinced resided within the Alliance Defense Force.

"Thanks for understanding."

"General Treel has been briefed also should you run into him," Titan said.

"Treel? Treel's here on Telgora?" When Eli was three, his father introduced him to the Minith soldier, who was a prisoner on Earth at the time. Treel and Eli spent a lot of time together and formed a strong bond that continued until the Peace Wars ended. When the war ended, and his father moved them to Waa, Treel's son, Arok, became Eli's closest friend.

"Yes, I thought you knew," Titan explained. "He's here to observe Arok's graduation."

"Of course," Eli exclaimed. He had been so caught up in his training, he had little time to consider that Arok was going through the Minith version of basic on the other side of the planet. He wondered how Arok had performed for his human sergeants but knew without asking that the Minith had excelled, as usual. Since the age of seven, Eli and his alien friend had been put through most of the same training. The only major differences involved their spare time. Eli preferred studying military history and scouring libraries for insights into ancient battles and tactics. Arok devoted his discretionary time to additional combat and weapons training. Their individual tendencies usually revealed themselves when the two sparred, which was daily. Arok was a beast who could fight all day and then some. He usually got the better of

Eli, except for those times when Eli was able to pick up on the other's most current fighting style and use it to his advantage. When that happened, Eli described what he had uncovered and how he used it against Arok. Once explained, Arok promptly corrected the pattern, or concealed it well enough to once again get the better of his human foe. It was an ongoing, circular process that made them both better.

"Yes, and unlike you, Arok's not hiding who his father is. Which makes it possible for Treel to visit."

Eli didn't rise to the bait. He looked around and noted that only Free remained in the room with them. He nodded to the Telgoran, who returned the gesture.

"Ah, yes," Titan stated, seeing the interaction. "Our good friend, Free. That's what I wanted to speak to you about."

"About Free?"

"Yes," Titan acknowledged. He tilted his head down and looked into Eli's eyes. "Thanks to you, it appears our independent thinker has taken a liking to the warrior lifestyle. He wants to know how he can join the Defense Force."

"What?" Eli was confused. Telgorans didn't join the alliance forces. Despite being members of the Shiale Alliance, they kept to themselves in their underground caverns where they didn't have to interact with outsiders, especially the still-hated Minith. They had existed in relative seclusion for . . . well, forever. Forays above-ground, even for alliance business and meetings were rare. At their insistence, Titan generally spoke for them and represented their decisions and interests. It was a responsibility that Titan took seriously. He was adamant in representing them in a manner that protected them in all ways. Eli's dad often joked that his old friend was more Telgoran than human, and Eli respected the large man for his dedication. "How's that possible? Doesn't he need the comfort of the Family mind to survive?"

"Usually, but Free is an anomaly among the Family," Titan explained. "He can't access the mass mind. He's a one-of-a-kind specimen, who's been living on the fringe of the Telgoran community since he was born. He hasn't been shunned. The Family doesn't do that. But he's a loner in a world that doesn't understand the concept. Do you know what the Family calls him?"

"They don't call him Free?"

Titan laughed. It was a hearty sound that started in the gut and filled the room.

"No, no. The word they use to describe him equates more to 'loner' or 'alone.' 'Free' is the name I gave him, kind of by accident," the large man stated. "Although he's Telgoran, he and I are very much the same. We're outsiders among our own kind. He's an outsider because he can't tap into the mass consciousness that defines his people. I'm an outsider because the people of Earth don't know how to deal with me."

"That's not true," Eli argued. "The people on Earth consider you a hero."

"Spoken like a human who's lived more than half his life—and all of his adult life—on the distant planet of Waa," Titan replied, with a shake of his head. "For a smart young man, who knows more about the Minith than probably any other human, you don't know a whole lot about your fellow humans. Ninety-nine point nine percent of the people on Earth are glad I'm on Telgora and not on their planet. When was the last time you were on Earth?"

"You know I haven't been back since I was six,

almost seven," Eli answered.

"Well, you probably don't remember much, but it hasn't really changed. Earth is still populated by billions and billions of peace-loving citizens, who tremble at the very thought of having an argument with their neighbor, much less wielding a rifle. They certainly don't enjoy my company—a person who wiped out the lives of billions of sentient, though aggressive and murderous, beings." Eli, like all humans, knew the ambassador was almost single-handedly responsible for destroying the Minith home planet. Though that act had saved humanity, and allowed the Minith to be defeated, it hadn't gone over well on Earth.

Titan's voice remained low, but it carried an undercurrent of distaste. It was distaste for how most of humanity, the majority of the people on Earth, felt about aggression and fighting. He sometimes heard the same tone in his father's voice when he talked about Earth's citizenry. "If it weren't for those few, like your father, who understand that war is sometimes the only pathway to peace, we'd still be slaves, getting crunched into the dirt under a Minith boot. That's why ninety percent of the Alliance's current fighters are Minith. Even now, a dozen years after the war ended, Earth still can't supply enough recruits who are able and willing to pick up a weapon to defend its freedom. Instead, we have to rely on the Minith culture-ism that requires them to bow down before a conqueror."

Titan's words struck a chord with Eli. He thought back to what he knew of the Minith. One of their binding culture principles was the requirement to cede supremacy to anyone who defeated them in battle. It was why they now served under the flag of the human-led Shiale

Alliance. They had been beaten by humanity, therefore humanity had won their subordination. He wondered for a moment how long that subordination could last, but then immediately thought of something else.

Like a cloud parting before the sun, the shadow of confusion lifted and Eli suddenly realized why Sergeant Twigg had spoken out on his behalf. Eli and his team had defeated the Minith at the tower. Eli had shot Twigg and dropped him to the ground in the process. By Minith standards, that meant Twigg had to cede supremacy to Eli.

Things suddenly made sense, at least when considered from the Minith perspective.

"That would explain why Twigg spoke up on my behalf, wouldn't it?" he asked Titan, anxious to gain his insight.

"Try to keep up, Eli. Of course that's why he spoke for you," Titan confirmed, albeit in a not-too-sympathetic manner. That's one of the things Eli liked about the giant. He said what he felt and thought with few filters. "The point I'm trying to make is that Free and I are both outsiders, who are more at home with each other than with our own kind. And, here's the important thing: so are you. Even if you don't know it yet. You're human, but you're not an Earthlike human. Most of those peace-loving citizens wouldn't know how to act around you, and definitely wouldn't want you hanging around. No. They want you exactly where you are. They want me where I am, and they damn sure want your father where he is. On a far-away planet, doing the work they're too scared to do themselves."

Eli thought about it for a moment and had to agree. Despite the ambassador's assertion to the contrary, he remembered what it had been like before he left Earth. Even living on a military compound as they did, it was impossible to ignore the fear and uncertainty that surrounded their existence. Not everyone, obviously. Many were fighters who were training to fight the Minith. But those in support roles—the cooks, supply personnel, drivers, and the like—they spoke little and kept to themselves, and Eli recognized it as fear that drove them. Beyond the limits of the training base, it had to have been ten times worse.

"So, what do you suggest?"

"I'm not suggesting anything," Titan replied. He put a large hand on Eli's shoulder and squeezed. It didn't hurt *too* much. "We just keep on doing what we're doing and hope things work out."

Keep doing what we're doing, Eli thought. It sounded so easy, and he supposed it was. After all, what else could they do but give their best despite what came their way?

"Is it done?" Free asked from behind in Telgoran. He had walked to within a meter without Eli noticing. *"I can fight now? Like Eli?"*

Eli looked at Titan with a questioning frown.

"I told you. He wants to join the Defense Force."

"Well, good luck with that," Eli replied with a shrug. He liked Free and wished he could help, but he was just a lowly private. "Maybe Treel or . . . my dad can help. Either way, I have to get back to my barracks before Colonel Drah sends out a search party."

"I wouldn't worry too much about Drah, Eli," Titan stated. "Twigg's speaking up on your behalf pretty much assures there will be no consequences. Plus, I'm a voting member of the panel, and I possess a significant amount of sway. Despite Drah's personal preferences on this issue, I don't envision any problems."

"I can fight now? Yes?"

Eli looked at Free, then back to Titan. He reached out and shook his hero's hand, then turned to leave.

"I think your problem might be standing right there, Ambassador."

"Good luck, my friend," he offered to Free as he passed.

* * *

Eli was allowed to stew for twenty-four hours before being summoned back before the panel. Despite the assurances that he received from his peers as they passed his bunk, or the parting comments that Titan had made regarding his not needing to worry, all he could do was wonder what he would do if the review didn't go in his favor. He had prepared for a life in the Defense Force. It was his entire life, and he couldn't imagine doing anything else. If relieved from duty, how would his father react? How would Arok or Treel treat him going forward? For the first time, he felt a sliver of doubt over his decision to enter training as someone other than Eli Justice, his father's only son. It was a fleeting thought, though. Even if the decision came back as the worst case, he wouldn't have done anything differently. Failing on his own merit was preferable to succeeding on his father's reputation.

Now, once again, he sat alone, facing the long table where the review panel was just being seated. Eli noted with surprise that neither Titan nor the Telgoran representative were present—only the Minith and human military representatives. Except for Sergeant Twigg, who had accompanied him from the barracks, the rows of seats behind him were empty. Visitors had been prohibited from this portion of the proceedings by an unexpected decree from Colonel Drah.

He sat straight and unmoving as the four officers arranged themselves before him. Colonel Drah did not speak, but stared coldly in his direction.

"Private Jayson," one of the human majors read from a single page that he held before him. "The review panel has weighed the testimony put before us and has unanimously agreed that the charges levied against you as a result of your actions during the tower exercise were without merit. To the contrary, this panel believes that your actions demonstrated exemplary leadership skills and remarkable problem-solving abilities. Upon the recommendation of your training leader, Sergeant Twigg, you will be entered into the Sift where you will have additional opportunity to demonstrate and develop these attributes."

The major paused and looked down at Eli. Eli struggled to keep his seat. He felt like shouting out his excitement, but knew it wouldn't be tolerated, so he bit down on his tongue and fought to keep his face as passive as possible. Despite his best efforts, he couldn't hold back the grin that insisted on making an extended and gleeful appearance.

"Private, do you have any questions to ask, or comments you'd like to make, before we close this case and adjourn?"

"No, sir," Eli replied. He shouldn't have been surprised. He knew he was on solid ground, and the assurances from Titan seemed sincere. Still, the relief at finally hearing the verdict being granted in his favor was a sweet, sweet feeling.

"Very well. You are dismissed, and we wish you the best."

Without another word, the four officers stood and made their way to the door behind the long table. Drah paused before walking out and turned back. He glared for a moment at Twigg, then turned an indignant gaze toward Eli.

The young private translated the unspoken look without difficulty.

As unlikely at it might have seemed a few days earlier, he and the sergeant now shared a common enemy.

CHAPTER 11

Grant received word of Eli's entry into the Sift and felt a surge of paternal pride. He settled back into his seat and turned to view the city skyline outside his office window.

He was getting old; there was no denying the hands of the clock. Even the oldest and strongest soldier couldn't defeat that particular march. But the knowledge didn't alarm or concern him. His son was growing into a man, and that pleased him. The passing of the torch always took place; the old always gave way to the young. It was nature at its most basic, and he welcomed the eventuality.

Creating an army on a world where peace was cherished above all other things was one of Grant Justice's major accomplishments. Second to using that army to defeat the Minith, it was also his greatest challenge. When Grant began his work, Earth had no experienced cadre of soldiers standing ready to train new recruits. There was no preexisting corps of officers, commissioned or otherwise, to lead those few who volunteered to exchange their lives of peace for the burden of defending their world. There was no military defense industry cranking out tanks, planes, or rifles.

With humanity's existence in the balance, Grant was handed a void and was asked to fill it. In hindsight, his success at being able to meet the challenge with which he had been presented was both monumental and historic. At the time, however, the work seemed impossible and nearly crushed him under an inescapable weight of obligation and responsibility.

In addition to committing every fiber of his being to his task, Grant had the backing of Earth's Leadership Council. As a result, all the resources of the planet were at his disposal, including the brightest human thinkers, scientists, and builders. He was supported by a small, but dedicated core of believers—those humans who staunchly believed that preparing for battle was the only way they could survive and defeat the aliens who had enslaved their world. He also had the love and support of his wife, Avery, who bore him a son and helped him persevere when the dark weight of his burden threatened to overwhelm his being. Together, over a span of only six short years, they built, equipped, and trained an army. From nothing, a force capable of defending humanity and eventually defeating the Minith was created.

One of the more important systems Grant implemented was the method by which officers and NCOs were chosen. Without an existing hierarchy in place, the need to identify and promote individuals into key leadership roles was imperative. With no other alternative for filling the ranks, Grant developed a competition-based process that was built on peer evaluation, willingness to fight, and demonstrated ability. In short, leaders were selected based on a competition that pitted the highest-performing recruits against one another in a series of tests and trials.

In the early days, Grant selected the candidates, and the competitions—which had been collectively named "the Sift"—commenced.

Now, more than a dozen years later, the Sift still existed, but with a few modifications. The training sergeants now selected those recruits they felt had performed best throughout the training cycle and entered their names for sifting. In addition, each training platoon selected candidates from within their ranks who they felt could best lead them. Allowing the recruits to put forth their own candidates was critical to the process. With few exceptions, units of the Shiale Defense Force remained intact upon completion of basic training. This meant leaders were selected from within each unit and elevated to leadership positions. A person who was your peer today could be your sergeant or your lieutenant tomorrow if they did well in the competition.

Finally, the Sift was open to all on a self-selection basis. Individuals not selected by their sergeants or by their units, but who felt they could lead, could nominate themselves for a place to compete.

The system wasn't without problems or shortcomings, but it filled the leadership vacancies in an objective manner that offered everyone a chance, and rewarded good performance.

Grant turned away from the window and settled back into his work. He tried to put Eli and the Sift out of his mind for now, telling himself there was nothing he could do for his son. It helped, though, knowing that the good ones always did well in the trials.

* * *

Two weeks after Eli received the all-clear from the review panel, elections for the Sift were formally announced by Twigg. The announcements were made, without preamble, at the first formation of the day, and took Eli by surprise. They were coming up on the final weeks of training, so it shouldn't have been unexpected, but he had been so engaged with the panel inquiry, and the training that followed, that he hadn't given the process a moment's thought. He also hadn't made any peer selections. He could only assume that they had all been made while he was sitting in the review chamber. Not that one vote would have made much of a difference when all was said and done, but still . . . he felt as though he had missed an opportunity. There were several of his platoon-mates that he would have selected for the honor.

Although the announcement was nice to hear, he wasn't completely surprised when his name was the first to be called by Sergeant Twigg. The panel's commendation at the end of the hearing—barring the unspoken *condemnation* of Drah—had been an indicator that the Sift was in his future. Eli also had no disillusion regarding his performance over the past months. The last ten years of his life had been preparing him for the life of a soldier. He had performed well in nearly every aspect of their training. He would never say it to those around him, but in many ways, the training he did here on Telgora was less grueling than what his tutors on Waa subjected him to.

As instructed, Eli fell out of formation and ran to the front where he stood next to the Minith sergeant.

"Private Jayson is both a selection of the cadre and of his peers," Twigg announced to the platoon in the low, gravelly voice that was common to his race. There was a brief scattering of applause and a few hoots that immediately ceased when Twigg stepped menacingly toward the group, curled his upper lip into a sneer, and issued a single, threatening growl. The message was clear. Despite the platoon's approval of the selection, the recruits were still standing in formation and were expected to act like it. Though properly chastised by their sergeant, the smiles that dotted the faces in front of Eli showed that few, if any, seemed truly cowed by the Minith. It was a telling sign that the platoon had matured since they arrived on Telgora. On day one, the unspoken threat by Twigg would have had many of his peers quaking in their boots. In recognition of their metamorphosis, Eli offered his own smile and a quick nod of acknowledgment to the men and women standing before him.

Having restored a semblance of order, Twigg promptly announced the next Sift candidate for Second Platoon.

"Private Ellison is a selection of his peers," the sergeant rumbled. He took half a step toward the platoon and curled his lip. The slight movement was a silent warning to the assembled recruits that another outburst would not be tolerated. It had the desired effect. None of the humans called out or clapped. The smiles on their faces told Eli all he needed to know, though. It was a good selection. If Eli had voted, Ellison would have been his choice as well. He was popular and had proved he could handle whatever task he was given. The diversion he created by moving the PEACE suits across the plain while Eli and the rest of the team attacked the tower had been instrumental in their success.

Ellison joined Eli and Sergeant Twigg at the front of the formation and Eli clapped him on the shoulder.

Out of the corner of his right eye, Eli noticed Private Tenney running to the front of Third Platoon, where a similar process was taking place. She glanced in his direction as she made her way to the front, and they shared a silent nod of encouragement. He had known the girl from his past life was destined to make the Sift. She was simply too good not to get selected. She took her place next to—surprise—Private Sims, the recruit Eli had saved from the pacer on the second forced march. Apparently, the man had done well in the rest of their training, and Eli felt pleased that he had helped in his small way to keep the soldier from washing out.

Eli glanced to his left at First Platoon. As expected, Private Johnson was standing in front of his peers. Another recruit, whose name Eli couldn't remember stood next to him.

When the cadre and peer selections for all three platoons were complete, there were six candidates for the Sift standing in front, next to their sergeants. Sergeant Twigg nodded to his fellow Minith Sergeants, Beck and Krrp. The sergeants said something to their candidates that Eli couldn't make out, but the four immediately left their platoons and made their way to the center of the company to join Eli and Ellison. The six shared nods and smiles as they lined up behind Sergeant Twigg.

"Recruits," Twigg called out, his gravel-filled voice straining to be heard by the entire company. "These six have been selected by the training cadre and by their peers as the candidates to represent your unit in the Sift."

A single individual in Third Platoon clapped, and the action was quickly followed by other claps. Then more. Cheers quickly followed until the entire company joined into the congratulatory movement. Second Platoon, having been previously chastised, was hesitant to join in at first, but soon joined the fray. Twigg stood resolute and unmoving, apparently resigned to the humans having their moment to celebrate their own. Eli took the opportunity to congratulate the five recruits standing with him. It was a great moment, and he could tell the others were just as proud as he was to be standing there. The thought that they were reaching the end of their time in training struck him like a hammer, and he mentally reeled at the fact that this phase of his life was almost at an end. It hadn't been easy, despite his life-long preparations. In fact, he thought his path might have been made more difficult as a result of them.

The applause died down, and Twigg raised his hands to bring the noise to a halt. When silence was restored, he continued.

"In addition to these selections, the Sift is open to any recruit who wishes to join the competition," he rasped. "Is there anyone who wants to be entered into the Sift? If so, please step forward and join these six."

"Here we go," Tenney muttered just loudly enough for Eli to hear. He wondered what she meant, but did not have time to dwell. A series of groans echoed from the direction of Third Platoon and Eli looked over to see Crimsa stepping out of the formation. The man who had showed his experience in the sparring ring weeks earlier was making his way forward. From the groans and looks being shared by the men and women in his platoon, Eli surmised the man's decision to join the Sift was not a popular one among his peers.

Crimsa jogged to the line of six and took his place at the end. He looked down the line, and catching Eli's eye, gave a slight nod. The tight smile fixed to his face seemed to acknowledge the fact that his fellow recruits didn't approve, but that he was pressing on anyway. Eli gave him points for that.

Eli then looked to his own platoon to see if anyone

was stepping forward. His gaze landed on Benson, his bunkmate. If anyone else deserved to step forward, it would be him. Benson seemed undecided, however. His body leaned forward as if he wanted to move, but his feet remained firmly planted. The look on his face hinted at the internal struggle that Eli knew was taking place. They had discussed this once a few weeks back—whether either of them would self-select if not chosen for the Sift. Eli had quickly announced his intention to do so. Benson hadn't committed. Apparently, he still wasn't ready to commit. Which was a mistake.

"Benson," Eli called out, knowing he wasn't allowed to speak but unable to stop himself.

"Silence!" Twigg commanded and looked back over his shoulder. He scanned the seven candidates, apparently unsure of which one had spoken. His gaze lingered on Eli a moment longer than the others, though. He had to know the two men were close, which made him the obvious choice. Eli faced forward innocently and studiously ignored the sergeant's look. The alien turned back to the company. "Anyone else?"

The action paid off. When Eli turned to look again, Benson was looking in his direction. Eli nodded once, sending a clear message. *You can do this.* Benson grinned and immediately stepped out of line. A few moments later, he was standing at the end, next to Crimsa.

Eight recruits were entered into the Sift.

CHAPTER 12

Eli grabbed his tray and looked around the mess hall for an empty seat. He spied Ellison seated alone at a table near the rear of the large room. He jabbed an elbow into Benson's side and pointed his chin at their lone platoon-mate.

"Go ahead," Benson looked to where Eli indicated, and nodded. "I'll be over in a minute."

"Just go with the green slop," Eli said with a grin. His bunkmate was notorious for taking his time when making his food choices. Ever since the second forced march incident in week three, no one in their unit touched *chakka* again, despite its flavorful nature. Instead, they went with the duller but infinitely safer choices that remained.

Benson claimed each food had unique flavor profiles that improved or degraded depending on how the food was prepared and how long it had been sitting. He insisted much of it was not only edible, but delicious under the right conditions, and he took his time evaluating each dish before dropping it onto his plate. To Eli's unrefined palate, the processed patties, nuggets, and mushy lumps of starches and proteins were all more or less the same. The primary difference between one selection and the next was the unique colors they were given. Each color was meant to help the recruits identify the underlying taste profile of the food, but all seemed lifeless and drab.

For Eli, the stuff was consumed for one reason

only—sustenance. The joy of a good meal was what he missed most about his home on Waa. They grew real food there. Many of Earth's native vegetables, fruits, and animals had been successfully transplanted to the new planet. Unfortunately, the terrain of Telgora was not quite so hospitable, and the logistics required to transport food to Telgora were enormous. As a result, 95 percent of their meals were a scientifically sustaining combination of processed nutrients, proteins, and thickening agents that were collectively referred to by the soldiers on Telgora as "slop."

Eli shook his head and began winding his way between tables.

"Enjoying the daily lunch menu?" he asked as he dropped his tray next to Ellison. Ellison gave him a withered look and shoveled a significant forkful of the green muck into his mouth.

"I swear," Ellison replied, speaking around the large bite, "if Earth told potential recruits about this slop, no one would join the defense forces."

Eli chuckled. "I dunno. Benson seems to love the stuff."

"Yeah, but he's a certified freak."

"Well, there is that," Eli agreed as he took his first bite of the off-white patty that was meant to taste like potato. He didn't taste potato, but the slightly bitter stickiness identified it as being from the starch family. He swallowed the bite and moved on to the green mush that the defense force substituted for green beans. All he could taste was slop.

"Mind if we join you second platoon geeks?"

Eli looked up to see Adrienne Tenney standing beside him. Standing behind her was Private Sims, the other Sift nominee from Third Platoon. He looked to Ellison, received an indifferent shrug, so he nodded and pointed to the seat next to him.

"Sure, have a seat."

The two settled in at the table and silence filled the space as the four concentrated on the slop in front of them.

"What, are we hanging out with the competition now?" Benson's arrival broke the silence as he dropped his tray on the table in the space across from Tenney.

"Is that what we are? Competition?" Tenney calmly placed her fork on her plate and focused her attention on the man across from her. Eli could sense the tension ratchet up a notch.

"Of course," Benson said, seemingly unaware that he was suddenly under Tenney's internal microscope. "You're in the Sift. We're in the Sift. There's only one commanding officer position available. We can't all win it. Some of you guys will have to be my underlings."

"And you think a self-select has a chance at the CO position?" The question was posed in a calm tone, but it was meant to get a rise out of Benson. He hadn't been nominated for the Sift by his peers or by the cadre, he had put himself into the mix. Eli watched the exchange and saw Benson's face flushed suddenly with anger. Tenney's words had struck their mark. Eli didn't wait for Benson to reply.

"Everyone has a chance," he announced, anxious to defuse the mounting tension. "A large percentage of self-selects achieve top position, actually."

"Really?" Tenney and Benson asked at the same time. Benson seemed surprised, while Tenney seemed dubious of the announcement.

"About one in four," Eli stated in a matter-of-fact tone. "Apparently, those who possess the confidence to volunteer often possess the qualities that make them excellent leaders." Eli did not add that it was just as likely to make them terrible candidates for the Sift. Statistically, a fourth of those who self-selected outperformed their peers. Another fourth did well enough to gain officer positions. The other half usually failed one or more of the selection criteria.

Benson smiled and sat up straighter at the news. Tenney offered little more than a doubtful, muttered "huh."

"How is it that you know so much about the Sift, Jayson?" Sims asked from his position on the other side of Tenney.

"Our good man, EJ, knows everything about the Alliance Defense Forces." Benson's overenthusiastic response launched tiny flecks of greenish paste across the table. One of the larger flecks landed just in front of Tenney's plate, and she stared at the offending particle of slop for two seconds before redirecting her stare at Benson. "Oops. Sorry," he offered meekly before continuing. "He's a walking tree of knowledge when it comes to the military."

The table fell silent as all heads turned in Eli's direction. Instead of meeting the looks, he put his head down and focused on the brown protein patty that was supposed to taste like beef. He carved a bite of the offending substance and popped it in his mouth. *No way does this taste like beef.*

"I've been wondering about that," a voice cut into the silence from behind Jayson.

Crimsa.

The self-select from Tenney's platoon ambled around the table and claimed the last seat on the far side of Benson.

Eli heard Sims, who was directly across from Crimsa, groan. Crimsa heard it as well, but just offered a slight smile to his peer before turning his attention back to Eli. Eli had the distinct impression Sims had just been acknowledged, then summarily dismissed from the other man's consideration. *Rude*.

"How is it that an orphan from Earth knows so much about this place? Or how is it that you always seem to know what the sergeants are going to do next? Or how is it that you can speak Minith? Huh? Can you tell me that, *Private* Jayson? Oh, and while you're at it, maybe you can fill us in on where you obtained your weapons training? There's more to you than what's on the surface and I, for one, would like some answers. Who are you? Where are you from, and—most importantly—what secrets are you hiding?"

Eli was surprised at the man's garish audacity, and from the looks on the faces around him, the rest of the table felt the same. Although the recruits here had all—well, almost all—been raised as orphans, destined to enter the Defense Forces from the time they were small children, they were still from Earth. And Earth was still by and large a peace-loving world where most of the population lived in strict communities that prohibited all forms of violence and aggression. Twenty years earlier, Eli knew, a confrontation like the one Crimsa was fostering now would have classified him as someone to watch, a potential Violent. But not now. Things were beginning to change, and Eli felt somehow comforted by that fact. If they were to build an effective army, they needed to cast off the old chains that came with the unrelenting mantra of peace-above-all-else, and learn to defend themselves as a race. It was a struggle that had started with his father, and he had sworn years ago to carry the torch forward. Now was his time. And the time of those around him.

He lifted his head from his "beef" and turned toward the man at the other end of the table. He looked directly into Crimsa's eyes. "My secrets are my own, Crimsa," he announced in a calm, steady voice that did not falter, did not waver. A cool rush of confidence and control swept through him as he locked eyes with the other man. "You'll get answers if and when I decide to give them to you."

Eli looked at each of the recruits seated at the table, making eye contact with each in turn.

"You all will. Until then, the best advice I can offer is to stay focused on the task in front of you. The Sift begins tomorrow, and make no mistake, we *are* competitors. But we aren't competing *against* one another. We are competing *for* one another. Regardless of how we place in the Sift, we can't move forward as individuals. We have to move forward as a team—a team that the rest of our company looks to for leadership."

Eli noted that all of their eyes were on him. Some were nodding, others just stared. They seemed to be taking in his words and weighing them for merit, which was all he could hope for at this moment. He didn't know how they felt about their fellow soldiers, what they considered their chances were in the Sift, or how they might react should they win top position. All he knew was how he felt, and he did his best to express his thoughts. He lifted his chin and pointed to other, non-Sifted recruits seated around them.

"They deserve the best leadership we can offer, so do your best in the days ahead. Regardless of how our positions land when the Sift is done, you all have my word that I will support you to the best of my abilities. If one of you becomes my CO, I'll give you a hundred percent every day, and on every mission that comes our way. I will do so gladly, and without complaint. Hopefully, you'll do the same for me if we find ourselves in those positions."

Eli returned his gaze to Crimsa so there was no question to whom his final words were directed.

"But if you don't—if you can't—I won't hesitate to put you in line, or put you out the door."

Without waiting for comment, Eli stood up and grabbed his tray. He dropped it on the recycle belt as he passed, and exited the mess hall. He had one thought on his mind as he left the others behind.

Time to prepare.

* * *

Twigg paced the boundary of his office with an anger-fueled anxiousness he struggled to contain. The compulsive need to move when pondering serious issues was a trait of his race. Pacing served to increase the flow of purple blood across the brain, which in turn, triggered synaptic vesicles to release specific neurotransmitters that facilitated thought and planning. Not that anyone cared about the physiology of the process. For the most part, pacing was merely an unbidden instinctual need that couldn't be ignored. For the Minith sergeant, the urge to pace was combined with a similarly strong desire to release the rage that had built up inside. He was compelled to pound something, and for the most part, it didn't matter what. The walls, his desk, his fellow soldiers—they all seemed like potential targets. More than anything, though, he felt the overwhelming desire to search out and pummel Colonel Drah—the witless oaf who had lured him into the web of deceit where he now found himself hopelessly mired. For the past year, the highest ranking Minith on the planet had led him down a path of treachery and underhanded maneuvering that—at the time—had seemed almost reasonable. Keep as many humans out of the Defense Forces as possible. Fewer human soldiers meant a reduction of human power and influence. Over time, that reduction in power and influence would then lead to their being overthrown as the accepted leaders of the Shiale Alliance.

But Twigg knew now that it had been a fool's plan, destined to fail. Humans weren't lesser beings, destined to one day fall to Minith domination. They had proved themselves time and again to be worthy soldiers and competent adversaries, deserving of a place beside the Minith. That had become evident twelve years earlier when they defeated the Minith on Earth, on Telgora, and on Waa.

Twigg had been a soldier on Waa at the time and had seen firsthand how close the small human invading force had come to breaking through their lines to reach the governor's palace. The tenacious aggression with which the outnumbered humans had fought, combined with their superior tactical maneuvering and equipment, had almost won the day.

Drah, on the other hand, had been posted to some distant planet that hadn't been engaged in any battles. It was one reason why the colonel had risen in the Minith chain of command while others, who had fought and lost—like Twigg—had not. His personal record had not been stained by a loss. That lack of stain was what fed Drah's beliefs. He hadn't faced humans and didn't know their strengths. He saw only their weaknesses and likely still believed what all Minith had once believed . . . that humans were weak, nothing more than two-legged sheep, who belonged in a Minith-controlled flock.

The sergeant thought about Private Jayson and wondered how Drah would fare against that particular "sheep" in the fighting ring. His lip curled into a smile at the thought. He had no doubt the colonel might rethink his stance after such an encounter. He recalled his own bout. The human, though smaller, was quick and well trained. He was the better fighter with a staff and Twigg held no illusion over what had happened during that bout. He had gotten lucky. Ninety-nine times out of a hundred, the blow he had received from the human would have landed him in the dirt, with a definite notch in the loss column. Somehow, he had managed to save himself and the win. He doubted he could do it again, the young human was that good. Then there was Jayson's performance in the tower exercise . . .

Twigg shook his head and stopped pacing. Despite Drah's continued ranting to destroy Jayson in the Sift, Twigg knew that he could not. And he would have to prevent Brek and Krrp from following their instructions to do the same. It would mean an end to his career and his aspirations—Drah would see to that. But he had no choice. He was a Minith warrior. As such, he was driven by the established mores and ethos that accompanied that particular life-culture.

The human had bested him. He had earned his respect, won his subordination. It was beyond his culture, beyond his honor as a Minith, to offer anything less than complete deference to the young private.

CHAPTER 13

The fourth day of the Sift trials began with a surprise for Eli. He and Tenney were neck-and-neck for top ranking, with him leading by only three points. His lead had been more than fifteen points the previous morning, which meant he had lost ground as a result of the military knowledge testing. It was a surprise because he had considered that area of the trials to be one of his primary strengths. He wondered briefly if the last second switch of the tests by Sergeant Brek had anything to do with the results, and made a mental note to speak with Tenney or one of the others about their tests at morning chow. Although he considered himself an expert at military history and weapons, many of the questions he had been required to answer were so obscure, he doubted anyone without access to a data-link could have done better than average. It was interesting, to say the least.

He turned away from the results—which the sergeants always posted while the recruits slept—just as two other recruits stepped forward to review them. He heard one mutter something about Crimsa and detected a hint of disappointment. Crimsa was doing well, just a few points behind Tenney, in third place. Apparently, those in third platoon who knew him weren't exactly pleased. He made another mental note to ask Tenney or Sims about that as well. His own interactions with Crimsa hadn't been overly positive, but the guy seemed to know his stuff, which Eli respected.

The short trek to the mess hall took less than five

minutes, and he fell into line. He looked across the room as he waited for the morning's offering to be plopped onto his tray. He noted that Benson, Tenney, and Sims were already seated at the table that had become "theirs." Ever since being entered into the Sift, the group—with the exception of Crimsa, who preferred his own company—gathered at the same table for each meal. It seemed that the other non-Sift recruits preferred the separation as much as they did, and he noted, not for the first time, that the separation of the company's eventual officers from the enlisted had already commenced.

"Good morning," he announced to the table as he took his usual seat across from Ellison and beside Tenney.

"We were just talking about you, EJ," Benson replied jovially. "Have you seen the postings yet?"

"Of course," Eli answered. For the past four days, the ranking sheet was the last thing he looked at before leaving the barracks. He turned to Tenney. "Congratulations on your performance yesterday. Impressive."

She cast him a sideways glance and placed her mug of coffee on the table. "Thanks," she replied. "I'd have thought you would have aced that test, Jayson. It was the easiest thing we've been handed so far. What happened?"

The comment caused him to pause. It validated his previous concerns. He knew they received different versions of the exam, but each version was intended to cover similar content as the others, and they should have been relatively identical in perceived difficulty. Brek had obviously slipped him a more difficult test than the others.

"Just had an off day, I guess."

"Crud," Benson challenged, pointing to his

bunkmate. "You know this stuff inside and out. There's no way you couldn't have passed that test with anything but a perfect score. Tell us. What gives?"

Eli sighed and debated for only a moment before answering. "I'm not sure what types of questions were on your test but mine were a bit . . . obscure."

"Obscure?" Tenney turned in her chair to face Eli. As usual, he felt his face grow hot in response to her sudden attention. "The questions I had were pretty straightforward. Ninety percent of the recruits in my platoon could have scored a perfect." Sims and Benson nodded and added brief comments that confirmed they had received similar tests. If there had been any doubt about receiving a different exam than his peers before, it was now gone.

"So . . . no questions on Waterloo, Battle of the Bulge, or the type of cartridge fired by an ancient weapon called an AK-47?"

The other three shared confused looks.

"Sorry, buddy," Benson replied. "You're speaking a language I've never heard. What's a waterloo?"

"It's not a what, but a where," Eli answered. He realized that all of his previous studying of ancient battles and tactics had probably saved him from complete disaster. "I even had a few questions about some arcane Minith battles that took place over a hundred years ago. I assume you didn't have any of that stuff, either?"

"Ha," Benson snorted. "You're joking, right?"

Eli just shook his head. "It appears as though our Minith leaders don't want me doing well in the Sift."

"Why would they care?" Benson asked. "It's not like you'll be leading *them* into battle."

"No, it makes sense," Tenney interjected. "Think

about it. Jayson's been a thorn in their side from the moment he turned around to help our fellow recruits on that forced march in week three. Nearly dropping Twigg in the ring was another blow to their supposed superiority. Then he beats the tower exercise—not to mention the squad of Minith defending the tower—and two sergeants. Then getting absolved by the inquiry panel. Let's be honest. You haven't endeared yourself to our large, green allies, Jayson. Apparently, they've decided to conspire against you."

Eli knew she was right, but didn't know what, if anything, he could do to prevent it or evade it. Fortunately, the Sift didn't include many opportunities, like the recent test, to actively alter or influence a score. He'd just have to be vigilant and perform to his potential. All he could do was his best, despite what they sent his way.

He shrugged off the negative emotions threatening to boil over and reminded himself that he was still leading the competition. Even if he didn't win the Sift, life would go on, and he would be okay in the greater scheme of things. At worst case, he would be reporting to one of his peers and that wasn't bad. They were all good, competent soldiers, who he'd gladly follow. Except for perhaps Crimsa. He still didn't know that guy's story.

"It is what it is. All I can do is my best, the same as you guys," he said.

"Yeah, but if they fooled with the test, it isn't exactly fair," Sims remarked from the other side of Tenney.

Eli smiled. "My dad had a saying for situations like this: 'Life isn't fair. Get used to it.' Seems like good advice right now."

"You remember your dad?"

Oops. Although he had never said as much, Eli had allowed the others to believe he was an orphan like nearly every human recruit to the Defense Forces. It made keeping his identity a secret that much easier.

"It's a long story that I'll tell you about one of these days," Eli dodged. He turned to Tenney and promptly altered the course of the discussion. "What's up with your guy, Crimsa? He seems like he has . . . issues."

The question caused Tenney to choke on the bite in her mouth. Eli thought she might spit the mouthful out, but she forced it down while glaring at him. With the obstruction removed, she asked, "What do you mean 'my guy'? He's his own person, and I stay as far from him as possible. Or haven't you noticed?"

"Sorry," Eli offered timidly, hands up in surrender. "I only meant that he's in Third Platoon, and I automatically think of everyone in Third Platoon as being yours."

Sims leaned forward over the table and glared at Eli over Tenney's tray. Of course. He was also in Third Platoon.

"Um. No offense, Sims." Sims just shook his head, offered a thin smile, and sat back in his seat. Eli turned back to Tenney. "The guy is obviously competent, but he doesn't seem very popular with the platoon. What gives?"

"The guy's a crud monkey," Simms offered through a mouth of egg paste. He didn't elaborate, so Eli looked to Tenney with raised eyebrows. Tenney took a swallow of coffee, and Eli could tell she was pondering her response carefully.

"He's competent, all right. He knows his stuff and

catches on to new things quickly. The problem is that he has no patience with those who don't catch on just as quickly. He has zero tolerance for anyone who doesn't meet his personal expectations, and he doesn't hesitate to let them know in a way that could best be described as rude, aggressive, in-your-face. He could be a great soldier, but Sims is right. The guy's a crud monkey."

"Well," Eli replied. "That would explain the groans coming out of Third Platoon when he self-selected for the Sift."

* * *

The carrier vehicle hovered three meters above the frozen landscape that made up the northern face of Telgora. Eli peered through the tiny window set into the carrier's rear door and tried to make out details of what might be waiting below. The PEACE armor's optic sensors couldn't pick up anything through the metal door or the thick glass window, so it was a wasted exercise. Unable to see the ground below, he turned his focus to what he *could* see—the five recruits that had been randomly assigned as his team for this stage of the Sift. He scanned the faces of the three men and two women standing behind him. Because they were on the dark side of Telgora, their visors were set to translucent. He knew Crimsa wouldn't have that opportunity. He and his team were preparing to jump onto the bright, sun-facing side of the planet. Their visors would be set for darkened mirrors to preserve their eyesight against the sun's glare.

But he'll be able to see the ground from his carrier.

He pushed the thought away, refusing to waste

time contemplating the advantages that came from maneuvering on the south side of the planet versus the north side. The frozen side had its own advantages: solid footing on frozen turf instead of shifting sand was the primary one. Besides, the armor's optic sensors should even the playing field somewhat where visibility was concerned. At least that was the idea. No one had ever really tested the principle before. In the past, this portion of the Sift had been conducted in the center, livable areas of Telgora, with the two competing teams dropped on opposite sides of the planet. Not so now. The introduction of the new armor had changed things up a bit. It allowed the training cadre to modify the test to include use of the suits and the enhanced capabilities they offered. It made sense, Eli knew. Employing the suits effectively to accomplish a mission was key to their ability to perform as individuals and, ultimately, to lead their teams.

The five-minute warning sounded and pulled Eli's thoughts back to the five soldiers standing with him. The faces in front of him told a silent story. The fear, uncertainty, and doubt that looked back at him were a problem, and he searched for a way to dispel the negative energy that filled the cabin of the carrier. As he often did, he asked himself what his dad would do in this situation. It usually helped calm his nerves and focus his thoughts, and this instance was no exception. His father was a true leader, and over the course of a lifetime observing the man's interactions with warriors of all races, Eli had adopted many of his habits and mannerisms. He doubted he could ever match his father's ability to lead troops, but that didn't mean he couldn't emulate the example he had been given, and put what he *had* learned about leadership into action.

Calm the team. Control what you can control. Focus on the mission.

"Okay, team," Eli began, speaking slowly and with confidence. He made a conscious effort to make eye contact with each of the men and women as he spoke. "This may be part of the Sift, but think of it as just another exercise. We're going to think before we act and take things one step at a time, exactly like we practiced. When the door opens, follow me to the ground and wait for my signal to move. While you wait, I want you to check all of your system inputs to ensure they're still working properly. It's only a short drop to the surface—nothing these suits can't handle with ease—but we're going to check systems regularly just to be safe. You should already have an alarm programmed to do so at five minute intervals. Correct?"

He looked to each of them in turn and received nods of confirmation all around.

"Very good," he continued. "Once we're on the ground, we're going to move quickly in single file to the first checkpoint. Keep proper distance between you and the person in front of you. We don't want unnecessary chatter, but if you encounter any issues, or even suspect that something might not be right, don't hesitate to speak up. Does anyone have any questions?"

No one had any.

"All right, then. Let's cut the interior lights and activate nighttime sensors."

He issued the appropriate commands into his suit and the view of the interior changed. Instead of the "normal" white light, the armored suit provided electronic-enabled visibility that had a reddish tint. Although tinted, the view was amazingly clear, and he marveled again at the engineering that had gone into the suit's design. Perhaps the disadvantage of being on the dark side of Telgora wouldn't be such a disadvantage after all.

He watched his team as their views came up and saw that they were equally impressed. He was also pleased to see that the faces that had previously displayed hints of fear and uncertainty were now showing signs of resolve and determination. He made eye contact with each of the five one last time before turning around to face the rear door.

At one minute from drop-time, the door lifted and the interior of the cabin was filled with swirling snow and ice particles. Though he couldn't feel it, the gauge on his interior visor showed a rapid decline in temperature, and he knew the suit's bio-system was actively working to counter the sudden change. By the time the "wait" light on his visor changed to "go" and he stepped off the deck of the carrier, the temperature had dropped to well below freezing.

Eli watched calmly as the frozen surface of Telgora reached up to greet him. He bent his knees and allowed the suit to work its magic. As expected, he hit the surface and felt an almost tender sway as the mechanical joints of the agsel-fighting suit absorbed the energy of impact. He'd had harder landings getting out of bed. The small cloud of dustlike snow that billowed around him was the landing's only real surprise.

The carrier had been moving slowly on a westerly track as the team exited. This allowed them to each step from the vehicle safely, without fear of landing on their fellow soldiers. Eli took care to observe the others' landings and noted that their spacing was correct and as predicted. When the last member of the squad, Private Turner, kicked up his own snow cloud without any visible issues, Eli asked for a situation report. All members of the team responded positively before performing the preplanned check of their systems.

Within moments of landing, Eli received the notification he had been expecting. It was an electronic message detailing the coordinates of their first objective. The mission was still a mystery, and he assumed he would find out what it entailed when they arrived. He waited until his systems check was completed, then quickly read the message that appeared on the upper right of his visor. Once he had the coordinates plugged into his system, he forwarded the message to the rest of the team and directed his suit to load the coordinates into the other suits.

Two minutes later, the team was headed west toward their first checkpoint.

* * *

The going was much slower for the team than Eli had anticipated. After more than an hour of movement, they had covered only two kilometers, which was only halfway to the first check point. His initial concern regarding limited visibility in the cold, dark terrain had been unnecessary. The optics package engineered into the armor was more than adequate—excellent even. The issue was the terrain. Though solid underfoot, the landscape was a series of tall, craggy mounds and towers of frozen ice. Interspersed between the mounds and towers were narrow, pathlike breaks that could be easily navigated, but didn't allow a direct line of march, and this exercise was basically a timed event. The team leaders were awarded Sift points in direct correlation to the time it took for their teams to complete the mission.

Because of the broken terrain, Eli had been presented with a choice: speed or caution. Speed was an enticing option. With their armored suits, they could jump over the obstacles that they encountered easily enough. The problem was in the landings. What if a canyon or some other unseen danger waited on the other side of their jump? Despite the lure of speed, Eli opted for caution. This was only an exercise after all, and he refused to put any of the soldiers assigned to his team in unnecessary danger. As a result, they wound back and forth among the plateaulike towers, weaving a pattern that took them in the general direction they needed to go. He silently hoped that Crimsa was having similar problems on the sun side of the planet, and was also using caution over speed. Not that it mattered. All Eli could do, he reminded himself, was the best that he could do.

Control what you can control. Focus on the mission.

The speaker in his helmet pinged softly to let him know the auto check he had programmed into his suit had been completed and everything was okay.

"Team, check in. Status?" He could see each person's position on the map that displayed on the bottom left of his visor. Everyone was exactly where they were supposed to be, but thirty minutes had passed since their last verbal exchange. Having them relay their status was a good way to keep them alert.

"Ming," the soldier in line behind him immediately replied. "All systems green."

"Aquino, all systems are green."

"Samna. All systems . . . are, uh . . . green?"

Eli stopped moving forward and listened as Wagner, the soldier in line behind Samna reported all systems green. He did not wait for Turner, who was the last in their line, to respond.

"Samna. Are you asking me or telling me? Confirm all systems are green."

"Um," the soldier replied. Eli thought he detected a waver in her voice. "They show green. But . . ."

"But what, Samna? Speak up. What's the issue?"

"Is anyone else c-c-cold? The bio-temp systems are reading green, but my suit f-f-feels . . . colder than it should."

Eli opened a hinge on his left forearm and tapped in the code that would allow him to access Samna's systems. While all of his personal systems were accessed by voice-, eye-, or body-control, he could only access another's systems by using a manual interface built into the keypad on his suit's left arm.

He pulled up her suit's readings and scanned them quickly. They all seemed normal, but if they were, why was she feeling cold? The quavering of her words indicated a very real, physical issue. It wasn't until he bypassed the automated systems and commanded the sensors in Samna's suit to take and report the current outside and inside temps that he saw the problem. The outside temperature reading matched the one his suit was reporting: negative ten degrees. The inside temp, though, while not immediately life-threatening, was barely above freezing. As he was considering what was happening in Samna's suit, and debating on what actions they should take, the temperature in the suit dropped another degree. He immediately initiated a diagnostic run of the suit's bio-systems. It was a deeper scan than the cursory checks they had been performing and would hopefully pinpoint the problem so they could fix it. A moment later, the suit lost another degree of warmth.

"Everyone. Initiate a full diagnostic run of your suit's bio-systems right away. Report in when they are complete."

Eli initiated his own diagnostic and then pulled up a map of the Telgoran landscape. As he was plotting a new course for the team, the results of Samna's diagnostic run popped up on his visor. As unlikely as it seemed, she had a hole somewhere in the agsel casing of her suit. Despite the suit's efforts to maintain a comfortable environment for its owner, it was only a matter of time before the temperate inside the PEACE armor mirrored the temperature on the outside. Which meant they only had one option. Get Samna to safety, as quickly as possible. He considered calling the carrier they had jumped from back to assist, but he doubted that would be allowed. There was also no good place for the carrier to land, which meant this problem had to be solved by the group.

"Samna's suit has been compromised. I'm sending new coordinates to each of you. We're changing direction and will be moving out to the south right away."

"Jayson, this is Turner. What about the mission?"

"We've got a new mission now, Turner. We're heading south toward the equator."

"But that's over ten kilometers away."

"Noted," Eli stated, struggling to keep his voice calm. "We're going to be picking up the pace, everyone. We can't continue weaving through these paths. It's time we went up and over these rock formations."

"Now we're talking," Aquino quipped. "Let's see what these suits can really do!"

"I'm pleased you're excited, Aquino," Eli replied. "I want you in the lead. We need to be quick, but safe. Think you can do that?"

"You know it, Jayson."

"Samna, you're behind Aquino. I'll be behind you. Then Ming, Wagner, and Turner." Eli didn't like the idea of putting someone else at the front of their line, but he needed to keep an eye on Samna. If she faltered or stumbled, he wanted to know it right way. She would probably be fine, but he had to make sure, and the best place to do that was from directly behind her. "Questions or comments, anyone?"

Again, no one had anything. "Okay then, let's move."

Aquino took a running start, then leaped to the top of a rock formation to their south. Eli watched Samna complete her own jump, then followed suit. He kept an eye on the three bringing up the rear to make sure they followed, then turned his attention to the recruit to his front. Samna seemed fine, for now. He checked her suit for the current temp and noted that it still remained a few degrees above freezing. Her shivering indicated she was already experiencing mild hypothermia and the sensors from her suit showed her core temp to be slightly lower than it should be. The movement from the faster pace should help her body retain its heat, but he knew she was in danger. Where caution had been required before, they now needed speed and movement. The potential danger to Samna's health justified the increased risk of a bad jump.

They covered the first kilometer slowly, with Aquino jumping onto each successive rock formation, then down into the arroyolike pathway on the far side, then up onto the next formation, then back down again. It wasn't until Aquino tried jumping across a particularly narrow arroyo to the next elevated plateau that they picked up the pace. Before long, they were completing jumps across all but the longest rifts and that's when they really began making good time.

An hour later, they reached a point near the equator where they turned off their night optics and began navigating in the twilightlike light of the sun. Five minutes later, they reached the point where the sun was just peeking above the horizon, and Eli called a halt. The external temperature was now reading a relatively balmy sixty-six degrees Fahrenheit, eighteen degrees Celsius.

"How you doing, Samna?" He read her internal body temperature and saw it had lost another degree in their journey, but was still above the danger point of severe hypothermia. They had dodged a bullet.

"Still c-c-cold. But it feels warmer already."

"You should get out of your suit. You'll get warmer quicker without the contact against your body." She didn't disagree and began the process of dismounting the armor. Soon, she stood before them in the uni-body fighting suit they all wore underneath. "Now, let's take a look and see if we can find the problem."

A quick search turned up a perfectly round hole, roughly the same diameter of a pea—*or a drill*, Eli thought—in the right underarm area of her suit. It looked too perfect to have been the result of an accident, and Eli's first thought involved big, green aliens with overlarge ears. He fumed silently. It was one thing to sabotage his performance, another to put his fellow recruit's life at risk.

"Will you be okay on your own, Samna?" He got a nod in return. "Good. Get warmer, then re-suit. I'll alert the unit to pick you up here as soon as they can. It shouldn't take long."

"You going back to complete the mission?"

"Oh yeah," he acknowledged. The longer he thought about this situation, the more difficult it became to keep the anger from his voice. He took a deep breath and tried to steady his thoughts.

Control what you can control. Focus on the mission.

"I'm leading from here on," he informed the rest of the team, then turned to the north. Fortunately, Aquino had showed them a better way to navigate the frozen terrain. Now they just had to make up for lost time. "I'm gonna be moving fast, so keep up."

* * *

They made good time over the now-familiar terrain. The over-the-top method that Aquino had discovered on their trek to the south was a much better method for traveling than the safe, but slow winding through the valleys below. Despite the improvement in speed, the detour they had been forced to take had put them behind schedule, and he wondered for just a moment how Crimsa was doing on the other side of the Telgoran habitable zone. The brief thought urged him into a faster pace, and he scanned his visor for the positions of his team. A quick glance told him they were keeping up just fine, so he kept pushing ahead at the new pace.

Finally, after what seemed like hours, Eli spotted a marker flag in the distance. He verified that the marker matched their course and destination and made his way toward it. Upon arriving, he noted the large black box at the base of the flag.

Eli wasted no time. He had the box emptied by the time Turner, bringing up the rear, arrived at the checkpoint.

Six defense force weapons were now carefully arranged around the marker flag: a Ninny sniper rifle, two standard issue plasma pulse rifles, two Ginny shotgunlike weapons, and a single, large Boomer antitank weapon.

A message announced its arrival with a ping and a flashing, red icon on Eli's visor. He keyed it open and read it quickly:

Mission: One shot, one kill

Objective: Eliminate each target using one of the weapons provided.

Rules of engagement: Each weapon has one round, so can only be fired once. Each team member will be assigned a weapon by the Team Leader and is responsible for destroying their designated target. Team members cannot be assigned multiple weapons/targets.

Scoring Parameters: Points will be awarded for successfully destroying an assigned target, using the following schema:

Target 1: 25-centimeter circle. Ninny Sniper Rifle. Distance 300 meters. 10 points.

Target 2: Tank silhouette. Boomer Antitank Weapon. Distance 300 meters. 5 points.

Target 3: Human silhouette. Pulse Rifle. Distance 100 meters. 3 points.

Target 4: Human silhouette. Pulse Rifle. Distance 100 meters. 3 points.

Target 5: Human silhouette. Ginny Shotgun. Distance 15 meters. 3 points.

Target 6: Human silhouette. Ginny Shotgun. Distance 15 meters. 3 points.

Success Criteria: Successfully hitting a target, with the assigned weapon receives the points described. Failure to hit a target, or hitting a target with the incorrect weapon receives zero points.

Time Constraints: None

"Orders received. Forwarding now," he announced, then keyed a command that sent the message to the rest of the team.

While they read the message, he pulled up the performance reports for each of his charges that had been downloaded into his system files at the start of this exercise. He scanned them quickly, focusing on the weapons scores each had received over the course of their training. It didn't take long to see the problem. Samna was the only one of the team who had scored better than "average" during Ninny training. She was ranked "expert" with the weapon, which Eli respected. The long-range, cartridge-fire rifle—what his dad called a "sniper" rifle—was difficult to master and required a high degree of patience and precision. Although skilled with most weapons, Eli hadn't fared well on the Ninny course four weeks earlier. As someone who was used to mastering any type of weapon, his inability to account for all of the environmental factors that went into being a good long range marksman had frustrated him.

He reread the mission objective again, wishing he had his father's wisdom and experience to help him decide how to proceed. But he had neither. Nor did he have the time. In addition to being awarded points for hitting targets, the overall exercise was timed. A more rapid completion resulted in a higher score, and they had already lost too much time.

He made his decision.

"Okay, listen up," Eli began. "You've all read the mission brief. Any questions?"

"There are only five of us," Turner replied. "Who's going to take out the sixth target?"

"No one," Eli answered. "We take out five and leave one on the table."

The team shared looks, and Eli continued, not waiting for further questions.

"Aquino, you'll take the Boomer. Ming and Wagner, you two take the pulser rifles. Turner, you take a Ginny." Eli looked to each person as he issued assignments and received understanding nods in response.

"I'll take the Ninny."

It was a gamble taking on the sniper target, but one he felt was worth taking because of the time the team had already lost. The seven additional points that the Ninny target offered might be the difference between him and his competitors, and he refused to leave the most important target uncontested.

"Grab your weapons and assume your positions. Aquino, we'll wait for you to take out the tank with the Boomer, then we'll fire on our targets."

The members of the mission team moved to the crate and picked up their assigned weapons, then moved into their designated positions. The Minith in charge of preparing the mission had clearly identified each target's firing lane so there was no confusion on where each of them needed to be. Eli picked up the Ninny and inspected it closely. The others followed his lead with their own weapons. Once he was satisfied, he nodded to the team and motioned for them to take their positions. He watched as each person settled into his or her firing lane and prepared their weapons. He then moved to his own lane.

A brief look downrange offered no sign of the plate-size target he would need to hit. He anticipated that would change once he activated the rifle—with its integrated magnification scope—into his armor's weapon control system. He passed his thumb over the sensor embedded into the rifle's stock to initiate the activation process. Two seconds later, he received the green flash and accompanying beep that indicated the pairing was successful. He lifted the weapon into position against his shoulder and said, "Ninny sight."

As expected, the right side of his face plate immediately lit up with the view as seen through the rifle's integrated scope. The left half remained in normal, nighttime mode. Using the left view as a guide, he pointed the weapon downrange in the anticipated direction of the target he had selected for himself—a 25 centimeter-size circle. He found it within seconds, a dinner plate-size oval that had a large “1” painted on its face. He keyed the trigger in nonfire mode to pin the target into his system’s memory.

Satisfied with locating the downrange target, he turned his attention to the area in front of his lane and noted the lack of a shooting table or any other type of support. Without the PEACE armor, a prone position with elevated support would have given him the best firing stance. However, because of the suit’s ability to lock in place on command, an unsupported, standing position provided just as much stability as lying prone with support. He added another mental check mark to the suit’s “benefits” column.

Once he felt ready to address his target, Eli asked for a status from the other members of the team. All replied back that they were also ready.

“Okay, Aquino. Whenever you’re ready, release the Boomer. Everyone else, once the Boomer goes off, engage your targets whenever you’re ready.”

Eli began the process of dialing in the Ninny onto his target. From this distance, the circle seemed tiny, even with the help of the weapon’s scope and the armor’s assistance. He made adjustments to the sighting picture using verbal commands that took distance, wind, and atmospheric pressure into consideration, and watched as the right side of his screen centered onto the target. Once he felt he had the weapon locked in as best as he could, he ordered the suit to freeze in position. He then waited for the explosion that would signal Aquino had fired on the tanklike silhouette. The Boomer was a shoulder-fired rocket designed to destroy armored vehicles and entrenched placements. The other soldier had shown proficiency with the weapon during training, and Eli had no concerns that the man would hit his target. The same went for the others on the team. He had no doubt they would all be successful. His ability with the Ninny was the only doubt he had. Once again, he wished that Samna was still with them.

Although it was expected, the explosion of the Boomer rocket's impact surprised Eli. He had forgotten just how loud the weapon's munition could be. He silently thanked himself for having the foresight to freeze his armor's position beforehand. Hopefully, the others had done so as well. If not, they would likely have to revisit their targeting process.

Eli quickly put those thoughts out of his mind and focused his attention downrange.

Control what you can control.

He double-checked his target, made a slight adjustment to the sight picture. Although it didn't affect his shot because of the armor he wore, he automatically reverted to his non-armor routine.

He took a deep breath, released half of the air from his lungs, then gently squeezed the trigger.

As with any good shot, he was surprised by the impact of the weapon's firing.

As with any missed shot, he was also surprised when the target downrange remained untouched.

* * *

Eli stopped on his way to the latrine and looked over the shoulders of the small group of recruits who were pointing at the latest Sift results. When they noticed him pause in the hallway, they silently moved aside to allow him a clear view. He felt their eyes scanning him as he took his turn at the list.

As was his routine, he placed his left hand over the list of names without looking. Then, starting at the bottom, he slowly moved his hand upward, uncovering each name in turn. He slowly and carefully read each name and noted their score before moving up to the next name on the list. The first names he read weren't a surprise. Private Tomas, the second choice from First Platoon had started the trials at the bottom of the pack, and hadn't moved up since. As Eli had come to expect, the man remained in eighth place after the final test. Next, in seventh, was Sims from Third Platoon. Next were his own platoon-mates, Ellison in sixth and Benson in fifth. Benson's performance throughout the trials had exceeded the man's own expectations, though not those of Eli who knew what the other man was capable of doing. Unfortunately, though, while Benson was fully competent in all of the tasks they were given, he was a true master at none. As a result, he was relegated to the middle of the pack.

Eli's first surprise came when he moved his hand upward to reveal the fourth spot. Instead of seeing Crimsa's name, he noted that Johnson, the top candidate from First Platoon had lost a spot in the rankings. Even more surprising was the name that now sat in the third slot: Adrienne Tenney.

Eli jerked his hand away, unable to wait a moment longer.

There, in black and white, sat the final two names: Eli Jayson and Renaldo Crimsa.

Side-by-side, in a tie for first place.

CHAPTER 14

Twigg trod the familiar path around his office as his mind gnawed over the problem at hand.

The Sift had been compromised, likely on multiple occasions, and he growled at the discovery. In the past, taking steps to prevent the most qualified humans from doing well, would have fallen to him. Now Brek or Krrp, probably both, were interfering with the trials and molding the results. He knew he shouldn't blame them. Their instructions came from the same source as his always did—Colonel Drah. But blame them he did. They were looking toward their next promotion, and had no issue crawling over his back in the process. That angered Twigg, made him want to lash out with claw and boot at his fellow sergeants. And at Drah.

His recent loss of preferred status soured his entire being. It affected his work, kept him awake at night, and impaired his ability to enjoy what little life he had outside of this pitiful job. Drah expected nothing less than absolute loyalty, and Twigg's inability to speak poorly of the human, Jayson, had summoned his downfall in the colonel's eyes. But what is a Minith to do? The man had defeated him on the field of battle. If not for a lucky break, he would have also defeated him in the ring. The human had earned both his respect and his loyalty. Which is more than Twigg could ever say for Drah. There was no respect for his superior officer, and what loyalty he had felt was due to the rank that the other held, nothing more.

The Minith sergeant paused his shambling gait as

he passed behind his desk. He turned, placed his leathery, green hands flat on the desk's top and counted to ten. He had once overheard humans discussing the counting trick as a way to banish anger from their thoughts. Upon reaching "ten" he felt no better, so he repeated the process. Again, no better.

Twigg raised his hands, curled them into fists and slammed them with all his strength onto the surface. The metal relented, leaving two shallow indentations. The combination of physical action, shooting pain, and damaged property left him in a much better place.

Count to ten? Ridiculous. Lash out and hit something if you want to feel better!

He looked down at the two depressions his fists created and came to a decision.

When this cycle was over, he would put in for a transfer. He wouldn't work for Drah another day, and he no longer had any desire to keep their human allies from succeeding.

Satisfied with his decision, he squared his shoulders and marched out of his office. He was still the senior sergeant over this training cycle. As such, he was determined to make things as right as possible while he still possessed authority and could influence the outcome of the Sift.

* * *

Eli slid his tray onto the table and lowered himself into his usual spot next to Adrienne Tenney. He looked across the table to Ellison, then to the right at Benson. He quickly scanned the rest of the room but didn't see Crimsa anywhere. He wondered briefly if Crimsa had already seen the results. He assumed that he had.

It was obvious from the quiet that had settled over the table, and from the shared looks of his peers, they had all seen the latest posting. He focused on the slop in front of him and waited for the first question. He knew it wouldn't take long, and his money was on Benson. His bunkmate had an irritating inability to let things lie.

"So, EJ," Benson began. Eli fought to keep his face an unresponsive mask as a grin fought to break through. He knew he could count on Benson to keep things on the level, and he appreciated the other man for it. "What happened out there? The rumors being pushed around are crazy."

"Well, I'm not sure what people are saying, but the truth is a bit crazy," Eli replied. "Someone drilled a hole into my Ninny-gunner's armor. We had to evacuate her to the temperate zone in the middle of the exercise."

"I told you," Sims offered from the other side of Adrienne Tenney. "Samna's in my squad. She's a solid trooper who knows what's up. There's no way she'd invent or exaggerate something like that."

"No one said she did," Ellison said quietly. "But how do we know someone drilled a hole into the suit? Maybe something she . . . I don't know . . . maybe fell or rubbed against something that pierced the armor."

"Really?" Benson challenged the question. "What could she have fallen against that would pierce agsel?"

"I'm just saying there might be another explanation. Who would purposely endanger a person like that?"

"It was a perfectly round hole," Eli clarified. "I don't see any explanation for how it got there except that someone put it there on purpose. With a drill." Eli was ready to lay out his suspicions about the Minith sergeants—suspicions that had only gotten stronger over the past week—to the soldiers seated at the table, when he saw Benson pointing at something behind him.

"Here comes Crimsa."

Eli turned and watched Crimsa approach. Instead of passing the assembled group with a smirk and a nod, as was his usual custom, the soldier from First Platoon stopped in front of the open space to Eli's left. Crimsa's face was an expressionless mask. He seemed hesitant, but Eli had the feeling from the way he stood that he was considering joining their group. Eli didn't wait for the other man to decide. Instead, he reached over and pulled the chair away from the table and nodded toward it.

"Have a seat, Crimsa."

The man exhaled loudly, nodded silent thanks, and plopped down. He stared at the tray in front of him, either unwilling or unable to meet the questioning looks being exchanged by the regulars. It was clear that something was on his mind, or he had something to say. Hoping to put the man at ease, Eli smiled. "Good morning, Crimsa. I'm glad you joined us. We were just talking about the Sift," he started, hoping to break the ice. "Congratulations on your performance yesterday. You and your team did a great job."

"You guys kicked my team's butt," Tenney offered. Her face was an unreadable mask of stoic indifference, though it sounded to Eli like the admission was a painful one. It was no secret that she held little affection for her platoon-mate.

Crimsa put his fork down and looked up at the faces staring at him. He met each person's eyes and stopped last on Eli.

"I heard what happened with Samna," he began. "She's a good trooper, and I'm glad you and your team made sure she was safe. I know it cost you in points."

"Hey, any of us would have done the same thing," Eli said.

"No. I don't think everyone *would* have done the same." Crimsa turned in his chair to face Eli directly. "I don't think *I* could have made the same decision in that situation, knowing it would cost me points. That's the difference between you and me, Jayson. I think about what's best for *me*. My decision-making process is based on that guiding principle. I know I'm not well liked because of it, but I can't help it. It's just the way I am. *You*, on the other hand. You think about what's best for the group. It makes me angry to admit it, but I know you're a better choice for commanding officer. I may want it, but you deserve it."

Eli was shocked into silence. He was pondering how to respond when Benson pointed again.

"Don't look now, but here comes Twiggy."

All heads turned to watch as the giant, green Minith sergeant stomped his way toward their table. He passed through the other recruits in the chow hall like a battle tank crushing through a field of wheat.

* * *

Twigg marched into the human feed center and scanned the pale recruits. He quickly spotted Jayson seated across the room with a group of his Sift opponents. He wondered briefly why anyone would choose to eat with adversaries, but dismissed the thought as just another foolish human trait. Who knew why these small creatures did half the things they did? If they wanted to graze with their enemies, it was no concern of his.

He strode quickly through the crowd of humans, brushing the occasional man or woman aside when they failed to notice his approach or denied him adequate space.

Upon reaching the table, he noticed the one called Crimsa seated next to Jayson. He growled silently. The thought of two rivals eating one beside the other sent a pain through his stomach. Despite his acceptance of Eli as a human worth following, he did not have to agree with every human trait, especially the ones that made no sense. A more natural setting for the two males would be a fighting ring, where they could battle against each other, like true warriors.

Despite his distaste for the situation, the other man's presence made his job easier, and he swallowed his unease.

He pointed at Eli and Crimsa.

"You and you, follow me."

Without waiting for a reply, Twigg turned on his heel and stomped from the room, confident that he would be obeyed. Unlike his entry, none of the humans failed to notice his departure. His exit went unencumbered and he lifted his lips with satisfaction.

He passed through the doorway of the mess hall, proceeded to the outside of the building, and moved to an open area on the right. The ever-present sun lit the area and the wind threw its sand in Twigg's face. After years on the planet, he had come to hate the daylight and ignore the tiny grains. Upon reaching the open area, where they could converse without being overhear, he turned around. As expected, the two were close behind, scurrying to catch up. He crossed his arms and waited for them to assume the human position of attention—bodies ramrod straight, heels together, hands and arms tucked neatly to their sides.

"Stand at ease, privates," he commanded. The two men relaxed into less formal positions and waited for him to continue.

"We've reached the end of the Sift trials," Twigg stated the obvious. "As you know, you two are tied for the lead. We've never had that happen in the history of our combined cultures, but there is a process to determine the winner."

"That won't be needed, Sergeant." Twigg looked at the one called Crimsa. "I'm ceding first place to Private Jayson."

Although Private Jayson seemed somewhat surprised, Twigg felt a pang of disgust at Crimsa's announcement. What kind of being would cede dominance that wasn't won through battle or competition? Despite his initial reaction, the Minith sergeant did not hesitate or ask questions. The sudden abdication coincided with his agenda and that was good enough for him.

"Very well. I will make the announcement at first formation. You are excused."

Twigg didn't delay another second. He left the two men standing in place and headed for his office. That had gone much easier than he could have hoped.

CHAPTER 15

Captain (0) Eli Jayson moved along at the side of the company formation. The five-kilometer trek between their training barracks and their new unit seemed to drag, despite the speed at which the first sergeant called out their cadence. The armor they wore could have handled an even quicker pace, but the top noncommissioned officer in the new company wasn't yet outfitted for the gear, so they were limited to his pace. Which wasn't slow, by any means. Without their armor, the humans would have struggled to keep up.

Eli shook his head at how things had developed since the Sift ended.

He had been prepared to name Crimsa the company's first sergeant when Twigg announced that he had requested—and been granted—a permanent transfer into the unit. Inserting a Minith warrior into a human unit wasn't an unknown occurrence, but it *was* extremely rare. It had also thrown a wrench into Eli's plans for assigning the leadership positions won through the Sift. Crimsa's personality as a loner, combined with his reputation for being a "no excuses" perfectionist, made him an ideal candidate for first sergeant. Where the commanding officer—Eli's role—acted as the brain and the voice of the company, the first sergeant acted as the backbone, and when needed, the backhand. It was his role to keep the troops in shape, in line, and on time.

There was really no choice, though. Once Twigg was assigned to the company, he became the obvious selection for the slot. Which meant Crimsa was shifted into the platoon leader slot for Third Platoon. Not really an ideal fit, but it would have to work. Eli and Adrienne Tenney, who he had named as the company executive officer—or XO—would have to monitor his efforts and mold him into the officer they needed him to be.

Crimsa seemed pleased with the assignment since it made him a lieutenant, which, technically speaking, was a higher rank than first sergeant. Eli wondered how Crimsa might have felt about the posting if he had known that first sergeant, although a lower rank, carried far more influence and responsibility than a platoon leader. Oh well. It was what it was.

Tenney was the obvious choice for XO. As his second-in-command, she was more than capable and was well liked by the men and women of the company. Also, unlike some of their company, she didn't seem prejudiced against the Minith, which was good since she would have to work closely with Twigg on a regular basis. Between the two of them, they would handle most of the day-to-day tasks that kept the unit operational and ready to fight.

The only potential problem Eli could see with her being his second-in-command was the growing knot of anxiety and rush of excitement he felt whenever she was nearby. It wouldn't do to let those feelings get in the way of their careers, or their need to work together every day. He examined the idea of getting to know her on a personal level for a few, brief moments before burying the strange thought into a deep, hidden corner at the back of his mind.

Never gonna happen, he chastised himself. *It can't.*

* * *

"Enter!"

Eli paused for a moment to make a final, hurried check of his uniform, then entered the office of his new commander. He moved to the front of the desk, snapped to attention, and saluted the Lieutenant Colonel seated on the other side.

"Captain Eli Jayson reporting as ordered, ma'am."

Colonel Conway sat back in her seat and frowned.

She offered a weak salute, so Eli lowered his.

He remained at attention, his back straight, arms locked firmly to his side. His eyes were fixed on a point directly to his front, and he found himself staring at a picture of a younger version of the woman seated at the desk before him. In the vid pic, she was receiving a medal from none other than General Grant Justice—his father. He tried not to fidget as his new boss looked him over. He felt like a bug under a microscope and had the distinct impression the eyes on him didn't like what they saw.

"Are you always so formal, Captain?"

"Um . . . ma'am?" Eli stuttered. Apparently, his normal, confident self had slipped out the door while he wasn't looking.

"At ease, for peace sake," she spat. "You're wound tighter than an agsel seal around a mothership bay door."

Eli relaxed in place and folded his hands behind his back. His eyes left the photo and dropped to meet the colonel's. He was caught off guard at the shocking hue of blue he found staring back at him. Most human eyes were brown, with the occasional, rare green or hazel. Blue eyes, at one time a fairly common trait among his race, he knew, had almost entirely disappeared over the past two hundred years. Yet here they were calmly appraising him. A corner of the colonel's mouth lifted in a smirk and Eli had the impression that she knew exactly what he was thinking. It was likely that she had the same, startling effect on most of the people she met for the first time.

"Um. No ma'am. Not usually," he replied. He took a breath and focused on regathering his thoughts and emotions. "I *am* extremely focused when the need arises, but I try to remain flexible to the events taking place around me and adapt accordingly."

Eli smiled inside. He felt pleased with the recovery.

Colonel Conway offered a wry smile. Again, he had the feeling that she knew what he was thinking. Her next words seemed to confirm those suspicions.

"I wouldn't be so pleased if I were you, Captain Zero," she stated. "I'm the one who will determine how focused and flexible you are, and you've got a long way to go to prove yourself to me."

The Captain-Zero comment referred to the number of years of experience he had in the Shiale Defense Forces. His formal rank was Captain (0). As a comparison, Twigg's formal rank was First Sergeant (13), which reflected thirteen years of military service—twelve with the Alliance Defense Forces and one as a warrior in the Minith Army. The colonel was effectively telling him he was but a small cog in the machine and reminding him that, despite how well prepared he thought he was for his position, he was still a newbie with a lot to learn. And a lot still to prove. She was correct, of course.

"Yes, ma'am."

"Let me be blunt here, Captain. I had to shift my

top-rated ranger company to another battalion to make room for your unit of armored Goliaths." She punctuated her statement with an angry stab of index finger to the desk top. "You and your troopers better be worth the loss. I've read the reports, and I've reviewed the pacer vids. I like what I see, but that doesn't change the fact that you and yours are new, new, new! I don't have time for new. When the shout hits the air, I need soldiers who can fight, not armored kids who need someone to hold their hand. Is that understood?"

Eli swallowed the lump that had grown in his throat and nodded. He was put off guard at the less-than-welcome reception and made a quick decision to say as little as possible and escape with as little of his ass chewed off as possible. "Yes, ma'am. Understood."

"Good. You and your unit are now Company A of the Shiale Rangers. I expect you to live up to the standards your predecessors have set." Like a passing breeze, her bad mood dissipated quickly and without a trace. It was replaced by the calm, professional attitude Eli had come to expect from senior defense officers. "I see you've got a Minnie assigned to you as first sergeant. How'd that happen?"

Eli paused at hearing the colonel refer to Sergeant Twigg as a "Minnie." It was obviously another term for a Minith, and he filed the info away. Using as few words as possible, he relayed the pertinent points of how Twigg came to be his first sergeant. He left out the part about the tower assault exercise and Twigg's subsequent backing of Eli's position over Drah's wishes. If she wanted to know the details, they were available in his records and on vid. In fact, she seemed like the type of leader who had likely already checked out her new captain and already knew the answer to her question. It reinforced Eli's decision to keep his response concise.

"Hmm," she pondered when he finished. "Normally, I'd insist on giving you an experienced top sergeant to help get your unit up to speed, but it looks like you've already got one." The practice of switching out experienced leaders for new ones who had been promoted through a Sift, was common in the Defense Forces. Eli and his leaders had already discussed and were prepared for the possibility. "What about the rest of your Sift leaders? Is there anyone you'd like to change out for someone with more experience? And before you answer that, know that I normally don't give captain zero's the option to decide this for themselves. It's usually a nonnegotiable requirement. But that PEACE-all armor you've been assigned and trained with makes things a bit more . . . unconventional. Anyone we move over would take months to train. But still, we could manage. In fact, it probably still makes sense, even with the delay."

Eli nodded and immediately thought of offering up Crimsa. Moving the man to another unit would eliminate potential issues. The man was competent, but the manner in which he treated others, especially his subordinates, was a concern. It would be the easiest way to solve the problem, but no. He couldn't see moving the new lieutenant, and those potential issues, to someone else. For better or worse, Crimsa was his soldier, just like the rest of the soldiers in his company.

"No, ma'am. If it's all the same to you, I think we are fine in our present configuration."

"Very well. Lieutenant Crimsa is your cross to bear."

Eli blinked. Lieutenant Colonel Conway grinned.

He was beginning to wonder if his new superior *could* read his mind.

"I can't read minds, Captain Zero," she quipped knowingly. "I've just been around soldiers long enough to know how they think. There's not a lot that you're going through that I haven't been through or seen others go through. To be honest, it's why I'm so peacing good at what I do."

"Yes, ma'am." Once again, Eli elected to go with a minimalist response.

"Also, there will be no fraternization with anyone under your command," she stated with a level of seriousness that bordered on threatening. *Adrienne Tenney.* The name rose up inside his head of its own volition, but he knew who the colonel was referring to. Maybe. Perhaps the comment was part of the same, standard speech she gave to every captain under her command. He hoped so.

"Of course not, ma'am." The words spilled out and landed flatly on the desk between them. The colonel's eyes never left Eli's and she bobbed her head in a manner that let him know the seriousness of the issue. She let the air and the warning settle for the space of three heartbeats before continuing.

"And so we've arrived at the final topic we need to discuss today."

That sounded ominous and grew even more so as the colonel rose from her chair, circled the desk and put her hand on his shoulder. Her grip was iron and her blue eyes drilled into his brown.

"It's time you used your real name, Captain. You won't get any special treatment from me, and I already know who you are."

It took Eli a few moments to compute the words, but he finally realized their meaning. He struggled to form a response, offer a reply, provide an explanation, but came up with a big fat zero, just like his new rank. He realized she was right. He also realized he had to close his mouth. It had unconsciously gaped open at some point.

"Yes, ma'am," he finally acceded.

* * *

Lieutenant Colonel Becca Conway watched the young captain exit her office with mixed feelings.

He reminded her of his father, certainly, which brought back long-buried memories of their struggles together against the Minith in the Battle for Waa. She was a young sergeant (4) when that fight went down.

The younger Justice had his mother's dark eyes and hair, but his body and his military mind seemed on par with his father's. Well-honed muscles, obviously developed through years of exercise and training, sat atop a tall, angular frame that could only be passed down through good genes. The vid reports she had viewed revealed another trait that had been passed along from father to son: the refusal to give up, despite poor odds. The younger Justice's actions on the Telgoran plain in the tower assault exercise were nothing short of . . . amazing? Inspired? Becca was never very good with words, so she decided finally that "creative genius" was the description she'd go with. He also displayed flashes of true leadership at times and hoped he would develop that trait to mirror his father's ability. If he could manage that, he'd do well for himself. And for her, and the Shiale Rangers.

She hadn't been completely honest with Captain

Zero, though. She had studied most of the vids and reports that came out of his training unit. She knew the reasons why Sergeant Twigg had been named first sergeant, and she knew the issues that Private—lieutenant, now, she corrected—Crimsa had caused within the unit. She approved of the younger Justice's decisions on both counts and was pleased that he hadn't taken the easy way out with a problem subordinate. Shipping poor performers to another unit rarely solved the real problem. And most importantly, while she *had* given up her top-rated company to make room for the new, armored unit, the change hadn't been forced on her. No. She had lobbied long and hard with her Minith superior for the new unit to be assigned to her battalion. When word of the advanced armor had gotten out, she immediately saw the benefits of having a company of mechanized soldiers to complement the Shiale Ranger Battalion that she led. Putting the PEACE-armored company under her command only made sense, she had rationalized. Her battalion of ranger forces consisted of two companies of Minith and one company of humans. It was recognized as the most elite unit on Telgora, designated to be the first unit deployed when the shout hit the air. But the Minith colonel had balked, for whatever reason. It was often hard to understand *why* the Minith who ran the forces on Telgora did what they did. In Colonel Conway's opinion, the Minnies just liked to flock over their human counterparts whenever and wherever they could because . . . well . . . because they could.

In the end, she had finally reached out to her old commander, General Justice, the man in charge of *all* of the alliances forces, not just the ones on Telgora. She didn't like going over anyone's head, even when they were green and firmly planted in the anal cavities of their Minith owners, but she felt strongly about the situation. Fortunately, the general had seen the logic behind the suggestion and immediately put the wheels in motion to make it happen.

Although she hadn't known before making the request, Becca intuitively understood that the general might have been swayed in his thinking by the fact that his son would be in her unit. According to the father, his son wanted to earn his own way, so was using an assumed name. She respected that, but it no longer mattered. She had met him first as a seven-year-old child, then continued to observe him from a distance on regular occasions over the years at various events and training exercises. To the younger Justice, she was just another face in a sea of nameless military uniforms, but she had watched him grow up. There was no reason to keep his identity hidden in her unit. She already knew who he was, but more importantly, she didn't care about his lineage. She suspected the general's decision to put his son under her leadership had a lot to do with the fact that Lieutenant Colonel Becca Conway would never give preferential treatment to anyone. In fact, the general knew she was likely to expect even more from someone with Captain Zero's parentage. In that, he was correct.

Captain Zero had a lot to prove, and she was committed to making sure he proved it.

* * *

"No flocking way," Lieutenant Gale Benson, the new leader for Eli's former platoon argued. He was having a difficult time wrapping his mind around the news. "Your dad is *not* General Grant Justice."

As had become their routine during the Sift, the newly appointed officers for Alpha Company of the Shiale Rangers were seated together in the mess hall. As usual, they were at a table at the rear of the room, surrounded by the normal hubbub of activity and the buzz of conversation of fellow soldiers sharing their mealtime. It was their first meal together at their new unit and Eli had just informed the group the truth about his background. Tenney sat to his right. Lieutenants (0) Johnson, Benson, and Crimsa, the platoon leaders for first, second, and third platoons, respectively, sat on the other side of their table.

"He is, Benson," Tenney stated simply, speaking for the first time. She had remained quiet, her eyes on her tray as Eli laid out his background and upbringing for the other officers. "The captain and I spent time on-planet when we were just kids. His father *is* the general."

It was Eli's turn to be shocked. He had assumed that Tenney hadn't remembered their time together on Earth—it hadn't been long, no more than six months or so, and it was more than a dozen years ago—but apparently, he was wrong, and he had put off asking her about it. She had kept it to herself, though.

"I didn't think you remembered," he said, looking at his XO.

"It took me a while, honestly," she admitted. "I didn't recognize you. We were only seven or eight years old the last time we saw each other."

"I was six. You were nine," he corrected automatically. His XO furrowed her eyebrows and frowned. The look alerted him to the fact that the detail wasn't important—or perhaps it was the age difference that bothered her. He had no clue and dropped his eyes to his food tray. “Sorry.”

“As I was saying,” she continued. “I didn’t remember what you looked like then. It was so long ago. What clued me in was how you took charge and got us all moving in the same direction. After that forced march, remember? When you went back to help the stragglers.”

“You mean where I nearly washed out?”

“You can look back on it at as nearly washing out if you want,” Tenney chided. “The rest of us remember it as the turning point. Where we finally realized it was us against them.” She nodded her head in First Sergeant Twigg’s direction to reinforce who she meant by “them.” The Minith warrior sat on the far side of the room, eating his meal alone.

“I didn’t figure it out all at once,” she continued. “I just had this nagging feeling at first. But it came to me over the next couple of weeks as I worked it over in my mind. Your mannerisms. The way you think about a problem, put a plan in place, then act on it. It was the same when we were playing at paint ball and blades. Remember the last battle against Jonah and his team? We totally flocked their reps with the older teams.”

Eli smiled, remembering. He hadn’t thought about the simulated battle games in years, not since he had turned his focus to training for real battles. He wondered what Jonah was doing now.

“I remember.”

“Anyway, I figured you had your reasons for hiding who you were, so I kept it to myself.”

“Thanks,” he replied, grateful for her consideration. “I’ve been worried you’d out me ever since I first saw you. I recognized you right away. It was almost like we were kids again, to be honest. You were the older kid I always looked up to."

"Really?" she asked. She beamed with pleasure, then looked down at the table. Her eyes squinted, and she seemed to be searching for a way to say what she wanted to say. "You were younger than the rest of us, but we were the ones who always seemed to be looking to you for direction. Your dad was the general, of course, and that was part of it. But you had this . . . way . . . about you. You could see a problem and knew within seconds the best way to meet it. It was both strange and endearing. Honestly, most of us didn't know what to make of you, but we were glad to have you on our side."

She nodded her chin at the rest of the table. "Just like we're all glad to have you on our side now." The rest of them nodded in agreement, and Eli felt his cheeks redden.

"Thanks," he offered weakly, unsure of what else to say. He decided to return to the matter at hand. "Now we need to decide how to tell the rest of the company. Ideas?"

"Seriously, Jayson," Benson began. "I mean Justice—"

"*Captain* Justice," Tenney corrected. They were still getting used to the new ranks and needed the occasional reminder to use the correct title.

"Ahem, sorry," the other lieutenant started again. "*Captain* Justice . . . Hey, that sounds like one of those ancient superhero characters!"

"Yeah," Crimsa added. "Captain Justice. Defender of the Shiale Alliance!"

"Captain Justice! Peace Warrior of Earth, and a man among men!" Johnson made his contribution to the teasing, and the four lieutenants fell into a round of chuckles and grins.

Eli placed his elbows on the table, put his head in his hands, and rubbed his eyes. This was quickly turning into one of those situations that he had hoped to avoid, and that had caused him to hide his name in the first place. He silently thanked peace that his first name wasn't "Grant," like his father. He knew it was a lifelong irritant for the man, and now he fully understood why. *Captain* Justice sounded hokey enough. Captain *Grant* Justice would have been even worse.

He briefly considered keeping the "Jayson" moniker, but tossed the idea almost as quickly as it entered his head. Everyone would soon know his real name was Justice anyway. He couldn't hide it, and frankly, he didn't want to. He was proud of his father and proud of the name he had been given—despite how corny it sounded. It was something he would have to live with, and there were much worse burdens he could have been asked to bear.

CHAPTER 16

"That's politics, Captain Zero. Surely you're familiar with the concept of politics?"

The inference was clear. Because of who he was—correction, who his *father* was—he should know that politics often influenced military decisions. And she was correct. As much as the notion grated upon his sense of right and wrong, he had observed his father grapple with similar situations on too many occasions to claim ignorance or naiveté. Instead of continuing to argue further, he recognized the case was lost, and focused on negotiating the best compromise he could. It was a tact his father often used when presented with a no-win scenario.

"Colonel Conway, what if we find a place for him in one of the support teams? Mechanical, supply, or food service. His presence there could benefit the unit without causing distraction or being a hindrance."

"Captain," Colonel Conway pushed herself up from her desk and leaned toward Eli. Her tone was firm and measured but carried the unmistakable authority of command. She was speaking to a subordinate, and obviously wanted that subordinate to recognize the situation for what it was—unarguable. "You have three platoons in your company. I don't care which one you put him in. Any questions?"

So much for negotiating. Eli fell back to his standard approach when dealing with his new commander.

“No, ma’am.”

“Good. Will there be anything else, Captain Justice?”

“No, ma’am.”

The colonel gave a slight nod, pointed to the door, and sat down. Her eyes never left Eli.

Dismissed, Eli turned on his heel and walked through the door without another word. His mind was already worrying over the problem of integrating a young Telgoran civilian into his company of mechanized warriors.

* * *

“He doesn’t have armor! How’s he going to keep up with the rest of the unit?”

“Benson, it’s obvious you don’t know much about our planetary hosts.”

“Don’t tell me, EJ—I mean . . . Captain Justice,” Benson began. Like all of them, he was still adjusting to the recent changes in rank and authority. In his case, he had gone from being Eli’s friend and peer to being his friend and subordinate. “You’re an expert on Telgorans as well?”

“Not an expert,” Eli replied. “But I’ve just finished up some quick research.”

They were alone in his new office, so he let the lack of title slide without a second thought. Shedding their old roles and sliding into their new ranks was anything but seamless. It was a work in progress.

“Telgorans are a lot more complex than they appear at first glance. In addition to being taller than a human, they also possess quite a bit more strength."

"Those skinny guys? No flocking way!"

"Yes, flocking way. Their arms and legs might look like they'll break in a strong wind, but they're . . . wiry, I guess you could say. Their muscles have been compared by human scientists to steellike bands, which makes them both incredibly strong and extremely quick. You saw how fast Free led us through the tunnels. We were sprinting, but that pace is roughly half of what they can maintain, and for much longer periods of time."

"Whoa."

"Yeah. I haven't seen a Telgoran at a full sprint, so I can't say for sure how accurate the info in our systems is, but that should be easy enough to test. I do know how strong Free is, though. He pretty much had his way with me back in the cave. I felt like a rag doll being tossed about when I grabbed his staff."

"Looked like one too," the lieutenant offered with a smile.

"Yeah, let's see how well you do against him, shall we?"

"Hey, he's an ally," Benson argued, his hands raised in mock surrender. "Besides, if he's going to be one of my subordinates, I'd just as soon enter into the arrangement with my ego intact."

"Good call." Eli grinned. It was good to know he and Benson could still joke, despite being placed onto separate rungs in the chain of command. Eli never wanted to lose that.

"So, where do we go from here?"

"I'm going to ask First Sergeant Twigg to set up a schedule so we can bring him up to speed with team maneuvers and protocols," Eli answered. "I want you involved, so make some time. Ideally, we'll have him integrated fully in a few weeks."

"That's a bit optimistic, don't you think?"

"Yes, but I'm not sure how much time we have. The colonel hinted we might be up for a deployment soon. Plus, we don't have to train him on armor, so that will shorten our timeline. We also don't need him to know everything that we learned during training—just the basics. Everything else he can pick up along the way."

"I'd like to set up some tests to see just how quick and strong he is."

"Good idea. Let me know when those are scheduled. I'd like to observe, if I can."

"Will do, *Captain Justice*," Benson chimed with a halfhearted salute and a wide grin. His emphasis on "Captain Justice" was not meant to go unnoticed. Eli understood, with a clarity that he'd never experienced, why his dad was always rolling his eyes at his own name. Having Justice as a last name was tough, but having a full name like "Grant Justice" had to be doubly bothersome and hokey. Thankfully, his father had studiously avoided any first name that was similar to his own when christening his firstborn.

"You get a kick out of saying that, don't you?" Eli asked.

"I'm not sure what you mean, *Captain Justice*."

* * *

Colonel Drah paced around the path in his too-small office and considered the device in his hands and wondered how such a thing was possible. Even the Waa, with their technological advances couldn't match this marvel. He had been given the device, and the instructions for its use, three years earlier by the Zrthn Trade Minister, who was posted to Waa.

Drah, a major at the time, had been in charge of the Shiale Delegate's Guard. The Guard's purpose was to ensure the visitors' security and to serve as local guides. That was the story offered to the Zrthns anyway. The truth was something completely different and was recognized by all parties. The real purpose of the guard was to watch over their visitors, report on their activities, and prevent them from wandering into areas where they weren't welcome.

Drah had unfettered access to the minister, and had used it to his advantage. The long, three year wait since that final meeting seemed to be reaching a tipping point—a point Drah had worked for tirelessly since agreeing to the minister's plan. He had lobbied for, and received, a promotion and a posting to Telgora. That posting was leveraged at every possible turn to set the stage for a change in control. Humans were a weak scourge that had somehow managed to destroy his home planet and despoil his races' legacy. As a result, the Minith colonel was committed to their downfall with every muscle, tendon, and drop of purple blood in his body.

"Drah."

The device relayed the single word with a clarity that belied its complexity. The ability to transmit communications in real-time, over hundreds of light-years, was beyond the Minith colonel's technical comprehension. But the miracle of the ability was not. It took weeks for Shiale Alliance transmissions to travel between Telgora and Waa.

“Yes, Oinoo,” the Minith replied. “I am here.”

“It is nearly time.”

CHAPTER 17

Free squatted down in his assigned corner of the large "barracks" room and pulled the *ninal* skin across his shoulders. He had been issued a long, oversoft pallet the humans called a "bed" upon joining the unit three weeks earlier, but had requested it be removed after a single evening. He had encountered many strange customs and rituals since being placed among the human fighters, but the bed had been one of the most confounding. How any living being could sleep on such an uncomfortable platform of torture was well beyond his comprehension. He rolled his thin shoulders and enjoyed the welcome firmness of the brick wall on his back. *This* was how true comfort felt.

He observed as the other nine humans in his "squad" went about their evening rituals. Their habits were becoming familiar now, but the memory of how strange they had seemed on that first night was still fresh. Now, he understood what many of their movements and actions meant. He understood why they cleaned their weapons and armor at every opportunity. They were warriors. The weapons they carried were the sacred tools of their profession, and he emulated the practice with his own pulse rifle. He also understood—intellectually, anyway—the drive many of them had toward activities that injected levity into their group. They pointed out and laughed at one another's misfortunes and errors with animation, often fabricating mistakes where none existed for the purpose of amusement. The jokes they told—

although he rarely understood them—and the games they played were for recreation and diversion. These things he understood. The ability to sleep on the soft beds, their apparent need for meaningless, unceasing chatter, and the obsession for brushing their small, white teeth were still a mystery.

Despite the mysteries that surrounded him and the unusual customs of his hosts, Free still felt more comfortable in his current environment than he ever had among his own people. Among the Family, he was an outcast, a cripple—incapable of inclusion or understanding. He was "Alone." Here he was just one of many, a single entity among a mass of similar, individual entities. All were alone.

Free gasped as an unexpected realization swept over him. Humans talked incessantly because—like him—they were alone. Like him, their thoughts and feelings were individualized—blocked off and hidden from others. And the primary method for sharing those imprisoned thoughts and feelings was through verbalization. It was their way of seeking understanding and gaining *shiale.*

The clarity of the epiphany was quickly overtaken by a second, more insightful thought. For the Family, *shiale* was reached when the common mind was unanimous in a decision or a belief. From what he had observed so far, humans seemed incapable of reaching true *shiale.* Disagreements and debates were common among his squad-mates. They seemed to argue incessantly, and over the most inane topics. What was the best way to clean a rifle? Which food tasted better, the brown paste or the green? Who was the best marksman in the squad? Sometimes, they reached *shiale*, but most times, they did not. For humans, true *shiale* seemed possible only when the answer was obvious: What planet were they on? Or, what is the color of the wall? Even then, it seemed possible only with smaller groups. The larger the group, the less likely that unanimous agreement could be reached.

Free was certain of his thinking. The inability to reach unanimous agreement on important matters required hierarchical structures and leader-based governance models. Leaders were chosen to speak for a group because, left to their own, an ungoverned mass of humans will devolve into disparate units of like-minded individuals who have reached—and argue for—their own conclusions. It was in humanity's best interest to have leaders capable of, and willing to make, important decisions for a group, even when some of the group did not agree with those decisions. As certain as Free was in the need for leaders, he knew many humans would debate the issue, despite the compelling evidence.

Suddenly, he felt less comfortable in his new home. There was something to be said for the *shiale* that comes with a mass mind. But that world was closed to him—always had been. For him to succeed, he had to assimilate more fully with his new family. He had thoughts, ideas, and emotions. If he wanted to influence the *shiale* these humans achieved—despite how limited it might be—he would have to make his voice heard.

Until now, the work and the learning had been difficult—the most difficult experience he had ever endured. It was made worse by the extended proximity and his subordination to a Minith savage, who was unforgiving in his expectations. Free fought a constant battle with his emotions over the relationship. For him to join this unit, he had to learn what they already knew. This he understood. But to have to learn it from an alien being that he had been taught to revile from infancy was almost too much. He split his time between trying to impress the Minith and struggling not to kill him.

Yes, the struggles so far had been trying. But he now understood the real work was just beginning.

The Telgoran squared his back against the wall, closed his eyes, and shut out the voices surrounding him. The other members of his squad had become used to his solitary inclinations, so would not bother him. He ran through his life's memories, allowed his past to wash over and through him. He immersed himself fully into his final hours of being Telgoran.

Tomorrow he would work to become an individual among a race of individuals.

Tomorrow, he thought. *Tomorrow*.

* * *

"How's the new addition to the unit coming along?"

"Free is catching up quickly," Eli replied. He had been called into Colonel Conway's office and stood at ease in front of her desk. The holographic vid pic of the colonel with his father on the wall behind her still teased him, and his curiosity almost forced him to ask how the major knew his father. Almost. "He should be fully trained on all protocols and weapons in another couple of weeks."

"That's good, Captain Zero," the major said. "It will take your company about three weeks to reach your destination."

"Our destination, ma'am?"

"Rhino-3, Captain. It's a comm station on the border of the Alliance territory." The lieutenant colonel went on to describe the loss of communications with the outer Rhino stations, and the need for boots on the ground.

"Excuse me for asking, Colonel. But there's an Alliance mother ship in the region. Couldn't they investigate?"

"They could, Justice. In fact, they did," she answered. The slight smile of knowing condescension that seemed painted on her face morphed into a scowl as she relayed the events to Eli. It indicated just how serious his superior felt about the situation. "They dropped a carrier of soldiers onto Rhino-3, just like they did on Rhinos -1 and -2. All three of those went silent and haven't been heard from since. And the last two were armed and ready for contact."

The information hit Eli like a slap. The shout had apparently hit the air. And his company was being sent to investigate.

"You'll be joined by B Company," Conway continued. "Captain Zin and his company are experienced fighters, but your unit will be the initial landing force. We don't know what to expect when you land, so it makes sense to put those armored suits of yours to work."

That announcement was another surprise. Company B was an all-Minith unit. Led by Captain (13) Zin, it also happened to be the most respected company-size fighting unit in the Alliance Defense Force. The company was made up of highly experienced Minith warriors, most of whom had been together since before the start of the Peace Wars. He couldn't help but wonder if Drah's influence extended into their ranks, then realized with a mental shrug that he didn't really care. He had lived around the Minith for as far back as he could remember. If they wanted to cause problems, he would address them as they arose. With the PEACE armor in play, he'd put his unit up against any Minith force—even B Company.

As far as Eli was concerned, A Company was potentially the most deadly unit in the Alliance. All he had to do was turn that potential into reality, and their first test was less than three weeks away.

CHAPTER 18

The standard class daughter-ship dropped out of FLT drive and entered the solar system. Song, the solitary planet in the system, showed up at once on the ship's cameras and scanners. From this distance—still a full day's journey out—little seemed amiss, expect for the silence. Rhino-3 should have been broadcasting, but it remained quiet. Had been quiet for nearly two months now.

At a fourth the size of an Alliance mothership, the daughter-ship was filled to near capacity. The two ranger companies were accompanied by a squadron of jet carrier pilots, a company of artillery, and all of the standard support personnel required for any military mission. In total, five hundred fighters and support personnel, along with their assorted equipment, sped toward the silent planet.

The mothership assigned to the Rhino sector remained outside the solar system. Its five thousand troops remained in reserve, less than forty-eight hours away, should they be needed. Eli hoped they wouldn't be, because he and his soldiers would be in a world of hurt should that possibility become reality.

He pushed the thought of what *might* happen to the back of his mind and focused on the things he could control: his unit and their preparations. They were ready to go, he knew. But his lieutenants were showing signs of anxiety. If he was being honest, he had some of those feelings as well, but he stayed busy as much as he could to keep them at bay. Activity helped, so he made sure everyone stayed busy. Armor was checked and rechecked, as were the carriers the unit would use to reach planet-side. The jets that would accompany the carriers were also given repeated inspections that were jokingly referred to as "once-overs." All in all, it was busy work, but it was important on several levels.

The activity levels were maintained around the clock, with regular periods allowed for sleep and rest. Finally, when they reached a point that placed the ship within an hour's approach to an orbit around Song, A Company of the Shiale Rangers donned their armor and entered the thirteen personnel carriers that would deliver them to the surface. Twelve of the vehicles carried the company's three platoons and their leaders. The thirteenth carried Eli, Twigg, Tenney, and Free. The personnel carriers had no offensive capabilities—they existed for the sole purpose of moving soldiers from one place to another—so they were escorted by a half-dozen jet carriers. If they ran into trouble on the surface, the jets would provide air support. Numbering just under 120, it was a small but lethal force.

Although Free had been assigned to Second Platoon, Eli had made that placement only as an interim measure. It wasn't meant to be permanent, and the Telgoran's lack of armor caused a problem for the company. Eli's initial thought was to leave him on the ship, but Twigg and Benson had convinced him the tall, thin warrior was capable of holding his own, even without the armor, should they find themselves in a fight. As a compromise, Free was directed to join Eli and the rest of the command team in their vehicle. It wasn't a perfect solution, but it would have to do, at least until they settled on how he should be permanently integrated into the company structure. For now, Eli would keep an eye on the young Telgoran and see how he handled himself once they landed planet-side.

At the ten-minute mark, Eli activated his comms and spoke to the soldiers seated in the carriers.

"Alpha Company, this is Captain Justice," he began. He had observed his father do this exact thing on numerous occasions and tried to channel the calm, commanding presence that seemed to come so easy to the older Justice.

"I don't have to remind you, but over the past month we've drilled on this more times than any of us care to count. I'm confident that every one of you knows what to do when we land on the planet and these doors open. Follow your directives and know your role. If the shout hits the air, and things get crazy, remember this. Lean on your training. Rely on your equipment. Trust your fellow rangers. That combination will help you navigate the loudest shout storm more effectively than you can imagine."

Eli paused to gather his thoughts. Delivering a message to those he was about to lead into the unknown was difficult—much more difficult than it had ever seemed coming from his father. The weight of responsibility for their well-being was on his shoulders, and he was feeling it, in its entirety, for the first time. The sensation was crushing, and he wondered how his father managed. In what seemed like the longest second of his life—in all of eternity—he considered the burden his father carried. As the supreme military commander of the Alliance forces, he was responsible for the survival of several races and civilizations. In comparison, the weight he felt for a company of armor-clad troops seemed insignificant. It was a stark realization. How could the man he called "Dad" have carried such a heavy load, for such a long time? It seemed impossible. For the first time in his relatively short life, Eli could imagine how terrible and consuming his father's existence might be.

Control what you can control. Focus on the mission.

"Okay. We're under ten minutes, so do a final weapons and systems check before we depart the daughter-ship. I want all helmets on at the five-minute warning, so scratch your nose and rub your eyes while you still can. And one more thing . . ." He paused for just a moment. "Let's show the Minnies in B Company how it's done!"

He heard several gleeful shouts over the comm net and looked across to see Tenney give him a thumb's up. Twigg, seated next to the lieutenant, seemed less than pleased.

"No offense, Twigg," Eli offered to the Minith warrior with a shrug and a smile. "Are you ready for this?"

The scowl was quickly replaced with the Minith version of a grin.

"I've been ready for this for the past twelve years," Twigg growled. The sudden twitch-twitch of his overlarge ears confirmed his excitement. Even with the PEACE armor as an equalizer, Eli was glad the green giant was on their side.

* * *

The Rhino-3 communication station was perched

on the highest tip of an elongated ridge of empty, mountainous terrain, near the equator of the relatively small planet. A giant array of equipment was placed at the apex, and included an assortment of long-range radars, antenna, and deep space penetrators. A small, green building that housed a ten-person monitoring team sat just below the array. The barracks, mess hall, and other buildings that made up the remainder of the outpost spread out below the comm station, along the eastern slope of the rocky, snow- and ice-covered mountain. Small, roundish shrubs that the soldiers had christened 'ewe-bushes' dotted the mountainside like a well-scattered shepherd's flock as far as the eye could see. Small, isolated and barren by any race's standards, the facility was an important site for the Alliance.

As important as it was, though, it was just as hated by those who were stationed there. The small, yellow star that the planet circled every thirty hours provided just enough light to make each day a dreary, seemingly overcast existence. Though not as cold as the dark side of Telgora—few habitable planets were—the temps rarely got above freezing. It wasn't on the top destinations list for members of the Alliance Defense Forces. Instead, it was a place to be avoided, if possible. The only positive—other than the positive of serving the Shiale Alliance—was that postings to the outpost were relatively short, at just under twelve months, and were usually followed up by a posting of choice.

Using his suit's enhanced optics lens, Eli scanned the station from the company's placement six kilometers away. Located farther north on same mountain ridge, the summit they occupied was a near-twin of the one where Rhino-3 sat. The spot provided an ideal location for observation and planning. Their landing had gone smoothly, with all thirteen carriers settling onto the mountainside without issue. The company was now settled into a circular, defensive position around the carriers while deciding on their next move. A half-dozen carrier jet escorts circled far above, out of sight, but within striking range should their support be needed.

After thirty minutes of seeing no movement in or around the comm station, Eli had seen enough.

"I think it's safe to say no one's home," he announced to Tenney and Twigg, who lay prone on either side of him. Their eyes were also trained on the distant mountain top. "Would you agree?"

"Yes," both agreed.

"Okay then," he continued, this time on the command frequency so his platoon leaders and sergeants could hear. "Lieutenant Benson, get Second Platoon ready to move out. Lieutenant Johnson, get First Platoon loaded up onto your carriers in case the shout hits the air and second needs backup. Third Platoon will remain on the defensive perimeter here, around the carriers."

Choruses of "yes, sir" rang through the net. Moments later, the platoons began moving into their respective positions as the orders were relayed through the company. Eli monitored the various platoon and company nets for chatter and was glad to hear it was kept to a minimum. His troops were doing exactly what they were supposed to be doing: executing their duties with no complaints, no unnecessary questions, and no grab-ass.

"Yo, Eli," Lieutenant Tenney called out to him on a direct frequency.

"What's up, Tenney?" he asked, anxious to be off now that everyone was in place.

"I, um . . . just wanted to tell you to take care of yourself," she muttered. Her typical confident nature was absent from her words and he immediately noticed the change. "Some of us like having you around, and would be very upset if anything happened to you."

Eli double checked the frequency, noted with relief that it was indeed a person-to-person connection. No one could hear them. He closed the ten meters that separated them and looked into her helmet, found her eyes. They shared a look that made his insides flutter.

He had been avoiding her for weeks, afraid of the feelings that had been growing for her. His emotions often surprised him at the most awkward moments: during planning meetings, at the chow hall, once at a meeting with his executive team and Colonel Conway. All of that would have been okay, except that he often felt a strong element of reciprocation. The way she looked at him, the way she spoke with him when no one else was in the room; the time she reached for his hand under the dinner table and squeezed. The colonel's warning about fraternization was rarely far from his mind.

"I'll be careful, Adrienne," he told her softly. "Besides, you've got my back, right?"

"Always."

Eli tilted his head inside his helmet and returned her warm smile before turning back to the rest of their unit. Five minutes later, he was following Benson near the head of Second Platoon's line of armored soldiers, as they prepared to move toward the station.

Because he was without armor, Twigg was positioned near the rear of the column. As the company executive officer, Tenney remained behind with the two reserve platoons. Free had asked to join the unit moving toward the station, but Eli declined. He wasn't armored and his training was minimal. The Telgoran wasn't happy, but complied without complaint.

"Engage auto-spacing and move out at triple speed forward on my mark," Benson gave the preparatory command. Eli observed as his friend waited the requisite three seconds for any of his troops to activate a red light, which would signal they weren't yet ready to move out. When no reds appeared, the lieutenant gave the command to execute the order. "Go!"

As one, the line moved forward at a pace that quickly would have resembled their unarmored sprinting speed. In their PEACE suits, it was half what they could manage, if needed. Most importantly, it was a pace that Twigg could maintain over this distance and terrain without too much difficulty. Additionally, each suit was programmed to remain precisely ten meters behind the soldier he or she followed. The entire movement—one moment standing still, the next near-sprinting at perfect spacing—would have been impossible without the suits. Eli briefly checked Twigg's status on the suit's heads-up display and saw the Minith sergeant keeping pace, as expected.

At two kilometers out from the station, Benson slowed the column to "standard speed." At a kilometer, he slowed to a half-standard march, then stopped the unit fully when they were a hundred meters from the objective. When the unit halted, Eli scanned the buildings again. He still saw no sign of movement. He spotted two carriers on the near side of the comm center, and read their markings. They were the carriers the mothership had been sent out to investigate weeks earlier. The vehicles appeared undamaged, but there was no sign of their previous occupants. They had seemingly disappeared—like everyone else who had been stationed here. It was eerie.

"Lieutenant Tenney," he radioed to his XO. "Anything?"

"No, Captain. Still no sign of movement."

"Okay, keep your eyes open and let me know if you see anything," he stated, before realizing the absolute inanity of the comment. They both knew she'd be watching intently and would send word at the first sign of trouble. He winced and silently hoped she'd let it pass.

"No problem. I'll put the slop sandwich down and postpone my shower," came the matter-of-fact reply. *Nope, not gonna let it pass.*

"Sorry, Tenney," he apologized. "Nerves."

"No problem," she repeated, this time with a slight chuckle. "It was such a tasty sandwich too."

"Yeah, yeah," he acknowledged, grateful he wasn't broadcasting to the entire company. He quickly switched to the Second Platoon frequency. "Okay, Benson, move your teams out. Start with the comms building, and work your way down the slope."

"Yes, sir," the new lieutenant replied. He then turned his attention to the job at hand and began issuing orders to his platoon. "Sergeant Ellison, I'll take first squad and investigate the building. You and second squad deploy to the left down the slope in a covering line. Third squad, move up the slope to the right. Fourth squad, you stay here with the CO and watch our rear. Any questions? No? Okay, second and third, move out."

It took only moments for the two squads to position themselves as they had been instructed. When they were in place, Benson took first squad and moved slowly toward the station. Their weapons were up and ready for contact.

"Keep your heads up and your eyes open." Eli couldn't help offering a precautionary reminder. As with Tenney, just minutes earlier, the words weren't needed, but he felt better for saying them. "We don't know what happened here, so be alert for anything out of the ordinary."

He received a simple "affirmative" and a casual wave of an armor-gloved hand from Benson.

As the eleven warriors moved toward the comm building, a tight, hot knot of anxiety settled into Eli's stomach. This was his first venture at sending men into a potentially dangerous situation, and he struggled against a nearly irresistible urge to rush forward and join them—to be the first one across the threshold and into the building. He knew his place was *here*, managing the overall strategy of the mission, but he wanted nothing more than to be *there*, accomplishing the immediate task at hand. He took a deep breath, tried to settle his emotions, and forced himself to observe.

When the squad reached the small, green building, Benson halted the unit for a moment before sending two soldiers around to the right of the building and two more to the left. Within seconds, all four had returned, shaking their heads. Nothing out of the ordinary to report.

Next, Benson pointed to the four troopers and indicated they should take up positions on either side of the building's only doorway. He put the other six in defensive positions at the corners and to the front of the building. When everyone was in place, he moved to the doorway and, standing to the side, gripped the handle. He gave a nod to the four with him, turned the handle, and pushed the door inward.

As soon as the door cracked open, a beautiful, blinding white light burst outward.

The light was accompanied by a high-pitched, deafening whistle that sliced the air like a scalpel.

Eli clasped his hands to his ears, but found only helmet, and shafts of pain pierced his eardrums, unabated.

For the briefest of moments—before the agony became too intense, and he forgot himself completely—Eli felt an overwhelming desire to move toward the light, and his right foot lifted to take the first step.

CHAPTER 19

Eli awoke to a severe pounding noise, and only realized after several moments that the reverberations originated in his own head. Each dissonant thrum was accompanied by agonizing throbs that sent nails through his temple and slammed like a hammer into his upper back and neck. He groaned and tried to sit up, but immediately fell back in defeat. He raised a hand to his head and found that his helmet had been removed at some point. He cracked open an eye and found himself looking up at the familiar, gridded pattern that he had come to know so well: the bottom of a top bunk.

He flexed his neck and gently shook his head in an attempt to relieve the pounding but quickly decided the misery wouldn't be shed so easily.

With an effort, he turned his head to the left and came face-to-face with a gray, brick wall. He found himself staring at the surface and thinking the gray color—while somewhat dull—possessed a nice sheen, and the lines between the bricks were straight and uniform, just like they should be. His next thought was that his brain must be fried.

Who cares what the wall looks like?

He groaned and struggled to rotate the tired, pounding lump that was his noggin 180 degrees to the right. The movement—executed perfectly, after only a minute or so of painful concentration—revealed several rows of bunks. More than one was occupied. The closest was filled by Sergeant Ellison, who seemed to be sleeping. He managed to lift his head a few centimeters and scan the rest of the room. They were in a standard defense force barracks.

For a fleeting moment, he tried to consider how they had come to be here, but quickly gave up. His head wouldn't allow any degree of mental processing.

Satisfied there was no immediate danger posed to himself or to those around him, he surrendered his consciousness to that most effective pain reliever: sleep.

* * *

"Crimsa located what looked like an on/off switch, and well . . . it was," Tenney explained. The worry and the pain in her eyes were clear, and Eli knew exactly how she felt.

"So, someone put that device there knowing we'd investigate," Eli clarified. "It must have worked on the first two scout teams, and it almost worked on us."

"To be clear, it did work on us," Tenney reminded him. "Just not as well as they had planned."

Eli nodded and sighed. The pangs of grief threatened to push him to his knees, and he had to draw a deep breath to settle his thoughts. Losing two soldiers—and two key leaders, at that—hurt more than he could have imagined. He shook his head again and wondered what Benson and Twigg might have felt as they passed through the mysterious contraption. He struggled to reconcile the desire to grieve those who were gone with the need to lead those who remained. With no other choice, he made a conscious decision to push the grief away from his consideration. For now. Instead of thinking about those who had been lost, he struggled to focus his efforts and attention on getting the unit through this situation.

"So, there weren't any remains? Nothing . . . left?"

"Not a single drop of blood," Tenney answered. The waver in her voice let Eli know how shaken she was over the ordeal. "They just . . . disappeared."

"Disappeared through a door of white light."

He had inspected the device right after learning what had happened from his XO. It looked like a complex door frame attached by cables and wires to some type of generator-like equipment the size of a large ammo crate. The dazzling white light that he remembered was absent now that the weapon had been deactivated. "Any idea of how the thing works?"

"We don't have a clue, Captain. I'm not sure if our scientists—human or Waa—will be able to figure it out. It's so different from anything we've ever seen, a completely new technology. There are a couple of Waa engineers headed down from the Rhino mother ship now to investigate. They should be here this afternoon."

"Yes," he agreed. "Let's get the Waa on it. If anyone can tell us what that thing is, it will be those guys."

Though Tenney didn't seem to give them much credit, Eli knew better. He grew up on their home planet and knew what they were capable of. The small green aliens weren't strong, but they were intelligent and had a much better understanding of how "things" worked than any human or Minith ever would. They were responsible for the technology that provided the Shiale Alliance with their spaceships. A small crew of Waa was posted to every mothership for engineering work. With luck, they'd have the strange doorlike weapon figured out quickly.

Eli thought back to the vid Tenney had shown him when he finally woke up and was able to concentrate.

Taken from her vantage point, several kilometers away, the magnified view from which she had observed the events of the day showed the scene well enough. The first few moments mirrored Eli's recollection perfectly as he and Second Platoon approached the station. The scene unfolded as he remembered, right up until the moment when Benson opened the comm station door, and the white light poured forth. The vid had the sound turned well down, but he could still hear the unbearable, ringing whistle that had accompanied the light. Eli watched in fascinated horror as every member of the leading element raised their hands to protect their ears from the painful assault. He recalled his own initial response, including the strange, undeniable desire to move toward the doorway. Then nothing, until waking up in the barracks of the Rhino-3 station.

The vid filled in the blanks. Eli watched as the armored soldiers began moving toward the light that spilled from the station. Lieutenant Benson, being the closest, was the first to enter the building. He was immediately followed by the four soldiers that had been standing with him. Eli watched in wonder as the vid showed all of them—himself included—marching like thoughtless zombies toward the building, called forward like ancient sailors to the siren's song. Only Tenney's quick thinking, and her ability to remotely shut down the speakers in every trooper's helmet, had saved the day. It came too late to save Benson, though. He passed through the doorway without leaving a trace before Tenney could react. Once she did, though, the vid showed the remaining men and women drop like unfettered marionettes to the ground. It also showed Twigg, who did not have armor, keep moving toward the building and into the deadly device that beckoned from within.

Eli hung his head into his hands and struggled to fight back tears. Benson had been his friend, and though he understood he couldn't have done anything to prevent what had happened, his heart still ached. And Twigg. To think of the old Minith warrior dying in such a . . . dishonorable way . . . felt wrong. He deserved better. He deserved a death by combat, not by deceit. Once again, he made a conscious decision to push the grief away, ignore it completely until a more opportune time presented itself. Then he might allow it to consume him. He knew he would never be the same, but he also refused to dwell on the loss right now.

After reviewing the recorded events, Eli had visited the former comm station. It had been gutted; the electronics, comms, and sensing technologies that had filled the space had been removed—replaced by the mysterious empty door frame, with the beckoning light and whistle combination. The weapon was as devious as it was effective. It somehow enticed its targets to enter of their own volition and then . . . what? Vaporized them? Burned them? Separated their bodies molecule by molecule? Only those who designed and left the weapon for them knew for sure.

Fortunately for Eli and his company, the PEACE armor had saved them from a similar fate. Tenney's quick thinking allowed them to deactivate and capture the device. With luck, the Waa would be able to reverse engineer the thing to see how it worked and how their forces—the unarmored ones—could defend against it in the future.

His inspection didn't reveal anything more than Tenney and Crimsa's earlier attempts to understand the weapon had. Except for one thing. He recognized the alien characters printed on the control panel.

They were Zrthn.

He wasn't surprised.

* * *

He came to his senses slowly, lying facedown. He detected the sound of movement nearby. The next thing he computed was the soft, damp surface on which he lay. The squishy texture made his face itch, and he struggled not to scratch, lest he alert any enemies of his waking. On the heels of the itch, he detected a scent of brine, which quickly grew to a stench as the smell of stagnant water filled his nostrils.

Still, Twigg remained still.

He forced himself to be calm and take in his surroundings before opening his eyes or giving any observers a sign that he was conscious. A Minith's ears were quite sensitive, capable of picking up the smallest sounds. He had once heard a human describe his race as "large gorillalike creatures, with the ears of bats." He had no clue what "gorillas" or "bats" were, but he thought they must be very revered beings since the words were uttered in a whisper and revealed more than a small dose of fear. He used those ears to take in the noises that surrounded him and filter them into two categories: known and unknown.

In the known column: Deep breathing by multiple beings, of the type that often accompanies sleep. A rustle of clothing. Whispers in the distance.

In the unknown column: a humming that accompanied an undercurrent of vibration. Was he on a mothership? Possible.

The whispering ceased and was replaced by the sound of wet, plodding footsteps headed in his direction. He tensed his body as the steps approached, preparing himself for action should it be needed, and found that he ached from head to toe. A slight groan escaped his lips before he could retract it.

Giving up the act, he opened his eyes. He found himself looking at a dark, gray mat in a dimly lit space. The mat was damp and covered in mildew. Several meters away, he spied a set of large boots headed his way. Each step sank heavily into the mat as it landed and kicked up a slight splash of moisture. He tracked the boots until they stopped two meters away from his head. With an effort, he lifted his head from the watery mat and looked upward. The boots were attached to legs. The legs were attached to the body of a Minith soldier.

"Greetings, warrior," Twigg rasped.

"Greetings to you," the other replied. "Don't move too quickly. It takes a while for the effects to wear off."

The other warrior stooped down and helped Twigg roll over, then helped him into a seated position. The dampness that had soaked the front of his uniform now drenched the rear. He felt like an old, wet cleaning rag, and he made a face at the . . . sogginess of his situation.

"I'd like to tell you that you get used to the damp, but that would be a blatant falsehood," the other offered. "Unfortunately, this is how our captors like to live, so we're stuck with it."

"Captors?"

"Yes, First Sergeant—"

"Twigg. First Sergeant Twigg."

"We're inside a Zrthn prisoner ship."

Twigg growled.

"Yes, First Sergeant. That was the reaction of just about everyone here. Again, I'd like to tell you that you'll get used to it, but . . ."

* * *

Newly appointed Lieutenant (0) Gale Benson often asked himself "What would EJ do?"

Eli Jayson—*Justice*, he reminded himself—had become the directional beacon by which most of his actions and decisions were now made. It hadn't always been that way. When the two first became bunkmates in basic training, he had looked at the other man as just another orphan, someone to be used if and when needed. But EJ had quickly proved that he wasn't like the orphans Benson had grown up around. He now knew why. Eli wasn't a product of the orphanage system—a harsh, cold system that had only one purpose: grow Earth's youngsters into men and women capable of defending their planet and their race. The need for such a system was both real and vital. Benson understood that much. Earth could continue embracing the false concept of peace that the previous six hundred years had led humans into. But genuine acts of caring, consideration, and goodwill were rarely seen by the children who were raised by the soldiers, teachers, and administrators who oversaw the system. As a result, most learned to fight for what they wanted, take what they could take, and look out for their own best interests. Because of their upbringing, most were unable to blend in with the billions of humans raised outside of the system, so they had little opportunity save entering the Alliance Defense Forces. In that respect, Benson surmised, the orphan program did its job.

It wasn't until EJ came along that Benson saw another way of interacting with his fellow recruits and orphans. EJ cared what happened to those around him. He viewed them as a unit of individuals, who shared common goals, rather than as individual units out to protect their own interests. He guided, he tutored, he supported. In short, he showed them what it meant to be a leader, and provided an example for each of them to follow. For most who spent time with their fellow recruit from Waa, it was a life-changing experience that they soaked up and tried to emulate. It also led to Benson's ongoing internal query when presented with a daunting challenge or some new, undefined task. It was the question he was asking himself now.

What would EJ do?

What would Eli Justice do if he woke up and found himself strapped to a table? What would he do if he spied a tall, squidlike alien—*Zrthn,* he somehow knew—holding a circular cutting tool in one of his slimy, gray, tentaclelike hands? What would he do if the Zrthn brought the tool to whizzing, electrical life, and brought it into contact with his right, armor-covered arm?

Easy answer.

Benson flexed his armor-covered appendages.

The power generated by the PEACE suit easily snapped the straps that held him to the table. The alien, surprised by the sudden movement backpeddled. Once freed, Benson threw his body to the right and landed gracefully on the soft, sodden floor beside the Zrthn with the cutting tool. He didn't understand the alien's features well enough to be sure, but he assumed the open-mouthed look that appeared in the middle of the squid's head was surprise.

He scanned the room and noticed two other Zrthns on the far side of the table. One had been facing away, and as Benson watched, the soft-looking head spun 180 degrees on the body to face him.

Freaky.

The same open-mouth look that Cutter Holder had shown suddenly appeared on the distant alien's face.

Yeah, that's gotta be surprise.

There was no surprise showing on the third face, though. Instead, Benson noted a tentacle being raised and pointed in his direction. The large tentacle was as big around as his arm, and ended in several smaller tentacles. Those smaller tentacles—his mind registered them as fingers—held a shiny, metal object that was undoubtedly a weapon. The alien seemed to be struggling with it, which was just fine with Benson. He didn't wait for the ugly guy to work out the issue or to see what type of danger the weapon posed. Instead, he allowed his training, instincts, and armor to dictate his response.

He flicked his right hand out, plucked the tool from Cutter Holder and tossed it as hard as his armor would allow at Weapon Holder. The cutter had some weight, but the suit handled it easily. The aim was spot on, and Benson watched in repulsive wonder as the tool entered through the front, then exited the back, of the Zrthn's large, bulbous head. The gory spray of gray that accompanied the tool's exit splashed freely across Head Spinner, and the look of surprise turned to something else. Fear? Disgust? Anger?

Benson didn't really care what the follow-on emotion was. These three had somehow captured him, strapped him to a table, and were about to cut into his suit. That called for a response.

He pivoted right and put an armored fist through Cutter Holder's soft dome. The punch was gross, but effective.

He shook his hand to clear it of the clinging gore and turned to face Head Spinner. The third alien wiggle-walked backward on his leg-tentacles until he was flat against the far wall. His arm-tentacles were stretched out in front of his body, the sides of the thin mouth turned downward, and his head quivered like a bowl of jelly.

Yeah, that's fear right there, Benson thought as he moved toward the cowering creature.

CHAPTER 20

Both his pulser rifle and side arm had been removed at some point prior to his being taken into the "examination" room—or what he now thought of as "the Zrthn death room"—so Benson picked up the item that Weapon Holder had aimed in his direction. It was covered in the slimy gray gore of the alien's head, so he tore a swatch of cloth from the alien's gray, apronlike covering.

He cleaned the strange device as much as possible, then inspected it. Obviously, it was an alien design. That much he could have surmised even if he hadn't known its origin. Somewhat tubular in form, it looked like a length of bent pipe that had no flat edges. Though it wasn't designed for a human hand, the sizing was such that he could grip it easily. Fortunately, the business end of the weapon was quite obvious. He would have understood which end to point away from his body even if the device had never been turned in his direction. The firing mechanism wasn't so obvious, however. He searched for a button, trigger or switch that might activate the gun, but came up empty. There was nothing on the device that offered any indication as to how it operated.

He squatted down beside Weapon Holder's body and inspected the Zrthn's "hands," anxious for a clue. The two tentacles that the Zrthns used for arms each ended in a series of—he counted six—smaller tentacles that acted as fingers. Each finger-tentacle was roughly six inches in length and was covered with tiny suckerlike pads. All of Weapon Holder's finger-tentacles had been wrapped around the handle when he pointed it at Benson. Benson imitated the grip as best he could with his five armored fingers. He detected some give in the handle and wondered if a squeeze did the trick. He aimed at a spot on the far wall and applied pressure. All he received for his efforts was a tiny "click." There was no explosion, no laser, no arrow . . . just the click. He squeezed again.

Click.

"Crud," he spat, suddenly angry. He had a weapon, but couldn't make it work. He pointed it at the gray form lying at his feet and squeezed again, intent on taking his anger out on something.

The click of the gun was accompanied by an unexpected blast of angry red light that drilled a neat, inch-wide hole in what was left of Weapon Holder's head.

"Whoa!"

Benson pointed the weapon at the far wall and clamped his grip.

Click. Nothing but click.

He turned the weapon toward the Zrthn's body again and squeezed.

Click. Flash. Hole.

"Aha!" He pivoted and pointed the weapon at Cutter Holder's body across the room.

Click. Flash. Hole.

Again, at the wall. Click.

He turned the weapon toward the ceiling, and fired. Click.

"Now that's engineering," he muttered. The weapon was somehow designed to fire only when it was aimed at organic material. That explained why Weapon Holder appeared to be struggling with the weapon. Its internal sensors had apparently registered his armor as nonorganic, which had prevented it from firing.

That had to be distressing for the Zrthn, he mused.

Satisfied he had worked out the details of the weapon, he took time to run a systems test, then tried all of his comm channels to see if he could reach anyone. His suit's systems were fine and working as expected. The comm check . . . well, that didn't go as well as he had hoped. For now, he was on his own.

What would EJ do?

Benson looked around and with a nod, decided to find out what lay beyond the doorway to his left.

* * *

Benson opened the door slowly and peered into darkness. He activated the auto-lighting system built into his helmet and the darkness was replaced with a clear view of a passageway. Seeing nothing that would indicate a threat, he poked his head past the doorway and looked to the right. Nothing but a short hallway that ended in a "T" intersection. He looked to the left and saw a longer hallway that ended a hundred meters in the distance. Several doorways and two intersections lay between his position and the end. There was no sign of additional Zrthns.

He wondered where he was and how he had gotten here. The last thing he recalled before waking up on the table was standing outside the doorway of the comm station on Rhino-3. He remembered reaching for the door handle, pushing the door open—then nothing. If the low-level hum he detected through the floor and walls was any indication, he had somehow ended up on a spaceship. A Zrthn spaceship. How that was possible, he didn't know.

Right now, he didn't really care. His primary thought was to try and find another human—preferably one from his unit—and then decide on next steps. If he was indeed on a Zrthn ship, he had no idea how that could ever end well, but one thing at a time.

He stepped into the passageway and turned to the right. When he reached the intersection at the end of the hallway, he quickly scanned around the corners. He looked first to the left and spotted a glass doorway at the end of a short hallway. The room beyond the glass was dark, but there seemed to be movement on the far side. He then scanned to the right. Another darkened, glass doorway mirrored the one on the left.

Left or right?

Doesn't really matter.

He picked the left and quickly crossed the ten meters that stood between his current position and the doorway. He stood to the side of the door and peered in as best he could. The electronic lighting systems in his suit didn't help much, but he soon made out what was moving on the other side. The room was filled with Minith, in a variety of poses. Some stood; others were prone, most squatted. But it was obvious they weren't engaged in any real activity. They just seemed to be . . . waiting. None were armed, and if he had to guess, they were prisoners of the same Zrthns who had managed to capture him. He debated for a few seconds, then stepped fully in front of the door and waved.

Nothing.

He waved again, with both arms. They had to see him. They were in a darkened room while he was in a lit—albeit dimly—hallway.

Still no reaction from those inside.

He finally tapped on the glass and waved again. The action caused the nearest of the Minith to look in his direction, but they still didn't react to his appearance.

What the flock?

It was like they could hear him, but couldn't see him. He suddenly suspected he was tapping on one-way glass. It made sense if they were captives. The Zrthns would be able to observe without being observed.

Benson considered his options, then turned to the doorway at the opposite end. He paused briefly to scan the long corridor he had originally come from, and seeing it still empty, continued across to the second glass door. Confident that it was similar to the first, he stepped up to it and looked inside the darkened interior. It was similarly occupied, but for once difference. The figures lounging inside were all human soldiers.

Again, he tapped on the glass, and again, he received a lackluster response. A few heads turned in his direction, but most of the men and women inside ignored him.

He didn't have to consider his options any further and immediately looked for a way to open the door. There was no handle or any other mechanism on the doorway itself. A small glass panel was built into the wall beside the door, and he scanned it for a clue as to how it worked. There were six blue circles, each an inch or so in diameter, printed on the glass. A code of some sort? He had no way of knowing. He could probably break through the glass, using his armor, but that was a move he didn't want to make unless there was no other option. Who knew what kinds of sensors were built into the doorway? Seeing as how it was a cell door, there was a high probability that sensors or alarms were a given. The last thing he wanted to do was call out a large force of squid-soldiers when all he had to defend himself with was a single alien pistol.

This situation called for stealth and quiet. With that in mind, he turned his attention back to the glass panel. Something about the arrangement of the six circles nagged at him, and he reached out to touch them with his armored glove. The contact caused the panel to light up, and he knew he was on to something. The device was waiting for him to enter a code or—scan a fingerprint.

That's it!

The panel wanted him to place his six finger-tentacles into the circles. The only problem was, he didn't have finger-tentacles.

But he knew where he could find a full set.

* * *

Twigg squatted against the wall and flexed his muscles one at a time in a ritual that was as old as the Minith race. The exercise was meant to ease the pain of prolonged inactivity while also helping to keep the body toned and ready for battle. He started with his ears and worked downward through his body, flexing, releasing, and flexing each muscle individually, then each group of muscles in turn.

He was on his sixth repetition, and he was just as tense and anxious as if he hadn't even tried the exercise. Minith were active by nature. They needed room to roam, pace, and tromp for their well-being. Unfortunately, their captors hadn't afforded them any such luxury. They were three-hundred-plus warriors, crammed into a space that should hold half that number. And the overbearing dampness only made things worse.

Twigg added his growl—completely unbidden and irrepressible—to the chorus coming from the warriors around him. Despite the danger, he considered throwing his strength against the doorway across the room. The three crumpled bodies that lay at the foot of the door—victims of previous attempts—were the only deterrents.

His routine was interrupted by a high-pitch tone, and he opened his eyes to see those nearest the doorway moving slowly back. He had been told early on that the Zrthns wouldn't hesitate to kill anyone who stood near the entryway when they arrived. It was a lesson they had apparently learned the hard way—only after two dozen or more of their number had been culled. Still, this was Twigg's first encounter with the aliens he had heard so much about, so he observed closely, anxious to detect any weakness or opportunity.

After several seconds, the warning tone ceased and the doorway retracted quietly and quickly into the wall on the right.

Twigg stood up to get a better view, anxious to catch a glimpse of the aliens.

When Lieutenant (0) Gale Benson of the Shiale Rangers entered the room, decked out in full PEACE armor, Twigg couldn't have been more surprised. Or relieved. It appeared as though he wouldn't have to throw himself against death's door after all.

"What took you so long, Lieutenant Benson?" he growled.

The young human looked in his direction, and Twigg noticed the human lips turn upward. The movement usually indicated human mirth, happiness or sarcasm. He wondered briefly which of the three the man was feeling.

"Ah, First Sergeant Twigg," the lieutenant replied with a wide smile and a wave. "Did you miss me?"

Twigg growled.

Apparently, the smile could represent a combination of all three.

CHAPTER 21

"So, you're telling me this is a transportation device and *not* a weapon?"

"Yes, Captain," the small, green engineer replied. He and his partner had arrived on Rhino-3 and performed a complete inspection of the strange doorway. Now, the two Waa stood shoulder-to-shoulder, a seemingly identical pair, except for minor differences in the wrinkles on their faces. Their arms were folded in front of their bodies, with each of their hands tucked neatly into the opposite sleeve of the standard off-white robes the Waa wore. Eli watched as they eerily blinked their large, black eyes in perfect, synchronized unison. "It moves things from here to . . . somewhere else."

Eli had to strain to make out the words. It was an unfortunate trait of the Waa that they rarely spoke, and when they did, it was in a quiet whisper. He had grown up around the little green aliens, but hadn't had much need for direct interaction. Except for his father's assistant, Sha'n, he had rarely traded more than a hundred words with the fourth contingent of the Shiale Alliance.

Though most humans would find it strange, he had always felt more comfortable with the larger, more aggressive Minith than with the quiet, diminutive Waa. You knew where you stood with most Minith. They were open with their feelings, and they rarely tried to hide their intentions. The Waa were just the opposite. He could never shake the feeling they were hiding something. They rarely spoke, and when they did, it was never in their own language. He didn't even know if they had a shared language. He couldn't deny their intelligence and their ability to build and design the most amazing and complex systems—like the mother ships the Alliance used, or even the new armor that Eli now wore. Unfortunately, in Eli's opinion, they were just . . . too weird and secretive for his liking.

"And where does it move them to, uh—" Eli was suddenly embarrassed that he hadn't made the effort to learn their names.

"I am called Aank. This is Ta'an," the Waa on the left whispered. The announcement was accompanied by a casual wave of long, delicate fingers toward his partner on the right. The hand was immediately returned to the sleeve opening. "We do not know the exact destination of the device."

"The *exact* destination," Eli stressed. His knees might have buckled had it not been for his armor as a wave of lightheaded cool splashed across the heat of his suppressed grief. Benson and Twigg might still be alive. "So you have a general idea of where it's taken two of my soldiers?"

"And probably hundreds of others," Tenney chimed in. She was inspecting the strange Zrthn doorway, which still sat in the middle of the comm station where they had found it.

The two Waa shared a small look and blinked their large eyes once. Twice.

"May we speak with you in private, Captain," the one called Aank asked?

"You can speak freely in front of Lieutenant Tenney," Eli answered. "She's my XO, and can hear whatever you need to tell me."

"It's not a problem, Eli," she replied. "I can wait outside."

Eli was preparing to respond to the contrary when he felt a . . . touch. Only it wasn't a physical touch. It was entirely mental, and it carried a sense of caution and urgency that he felt compelled to obey.

"What the—" he began, but a second "touch" stopped him from completing the sentence.

We must communicate with you privately, Captain Justice.

The words entered his head, but not through his ears. He clamped his jaws closed in surprise and listened, suddenly anxious to understand what had just taken place. He watched silently as the two Waa looked directly at him and blinked again in unison.

Please, Captain. This cannot be shared with others.

He saw-felt-heard the urgency in the request as a breath of mental calmness settled his thoughts. The combination let him know with complete certainty the request was both rational and necessary. With a sense of wonder, he knew the two Waa had just communicated with him in a fashion that seemed beyond real. Until now, he had assumed only the Telgorans were capable of such communication, but this proved otherwise. He wondered if his father knew the Waa were capable of mind-speak.

Of course he does, Eli. The reply was immediate, and he felt it as much as heard it. *And it is on his orders that no one else should know how we communicate.*

"But you let me—" he began before another mental touch—this one pleading for secrecy and discretion—stopped his voice.

Lieutenant Tenney does not mind waiting outside.

You only need to ask her to do so. Then we can continue.

"Lieutenant, can you give us a few minutes?"

"No problem, Captain," she answered and headed for the door. "I need to check on the company anyway. I won't be far away. Just let me know if you need anything."

"Thank you. We shouldn't be long."

When the door to the comm station shut behind Tenney, Eli turned to the two Waa. He had a thousand questions to ask and didn't know where to begin.

He needn't have worried; the Waa took over and explained everything.

* * *

"Let everyone know the situation. We don't know where we are going to end up. For all we know, we'll get dumped into the middle of space and die, so our efforts might be wasted."

"But the Waa said we'd end up on a Zrthn ship," Tenney argued.

"No," Eli countered. "They said we'd *probably* end up on a Zrthn ship. It's not a certainty. According to their inspection of the transport device, the far-transfer location is constantly changing. It moves through space like a ship would move, and it's on a trajectory for Telgora."

"Which means it's a ship."

"No. It means it's *probably* a ship," Eli reiterated. "The Zrthn tendency to capture their opponents, and use them as slave labor instead of killing them, reinforces that probability. But it still isn't a certainty. Whoever agrees to go through that doorway needs to understand the difference. This could very well be a suicide mission."

"Everyone will agree to go," Tenney stated. "Captain Zin, the commander of B Company, has already volunteered his warriors."

"The fact that this isn't a certainty means we *can't* take everyone, Tenney. We can't risk two ranger companies on a mission like this. At most, I'm willing to lead a platoon from each company. One platoon of armored humans, combined with a second platoon of experienced Minith."

"Oh, so *you're* going to lead this suicide mission?" The exasperation on his XO's face and in her voice was clear, and he understood how she was feeling. He'd feel the same in her position.

"Hey, I can't ask anyone to go through that door unless I'm willing to do it also," he stated, then smiled. "Besides, it's *probably* not a suicide mission."

* * *

The Waa engineers had located and disabled what they believed to be the auditory device from the door, which they now knew to be some type of transportation portal.

Eli hadn't wanted any mistakes, so only Second Platoon of A Company was stationed outside the comm station doorway. Their external speaker systems had been disabled. The forty Minith warriors from B Company were in a holding position fifty meters back from the comm station. If the device's sirenlike call wasn't disabled, Sergeant Ellison, who had been tasked with switching the unit on, would receive notification from Tenney, who waited with the rest of the company at their original landing and observation point. He'd quickly turn the unit off again, and they'd regroup to try something else. Aank and Ta'an, the two Waa engineers, waited with the Minith. Their task was to shut down the transporter after the last soldier went through.

When everyone was in position, Eli, who stood at the head of the line of PEACE-armored rangers, gave Ellison a nod.

"Hit it, Ellison," he said simply.

Ellison took a second to locate the switch and activate the doorway. As soon as he did, the interior of the comm station was filled with a bright light. The light came from the door frame and, to Eli's surprise, appeared to outline a view of what lay on the other side. To his relief, he didn't see the cold emptiness of open space. Instead, he spied what looked like a darkened room or hallway. What little he could make out of their destination seemed damp and dark, but there was no indication that a Zrthn reception committee lay in wait. For the most part, as these things went, it looked like an ideal situation into which to throw oneself along with eighty fellow soldiers.

Eli lifted his Ginny shotgun, took a deep breath, and waited for the signal from Tenney, verifying the siren wasn't working its magic on the unarmored Minith outside the station.

"You're good to go, Captain," he heard seconds later.

He took another deep breath of canned air and took the first step toward what was—*probably*—the interior of a Zrthn spaceship.

* * *

"Senior Leader Ootoon, the sensors in the receiving room have just been activated. It appears as though we have more of the bi-peds incoming."

Ootoon opened his eyes slowly and twisted his head 360 degrees to remove the kinks from his neck. Being awakened from a deep slumber was never pleasant. To hear the reasoning was another incoming bevy of the pale two-legged creatures made the awakening even less cheerful. With luck, it would be another small catch like the last. Two of the ugly creatures were much easier to handle than the hundreds they had previously taken in and processed.

"Very well, Ohlo," the senior officer of the captivity ship sighed. "Send the catch to sorting bay two, and alert Senior Sorter Ah-loon of the incoming."

"Yes, Senior Leader." Ohlo lazily activated the conveyor belt that would deliver the bi-pends to the sorting facility, then sent an alert to the jailer responsible for the processing phase of their work.

As he went through his routine, Ohlo once again pondered his fate. As he had done a thousand times over the past weeks, he asked himself the now-hated question: why had he been posted to this monotonously boring captivity ship, instead of to a fighting unit aboard the main battle cruiser? He was the lone swimmer of all his pod-mates to be handed this existence, and he had come to grudgingly accept that he would never see a real fight. Prone forms on a conveyor, or a room stuffed with unwilling captives, were his life now.

Ugh.

He would trade a year's worth of undersea rations to trade places with his mates on the main ship. They were no doubt beginning their preparations for the upcoming battle.

All he could do was sit tight and wait for their eventual delivery of more pink and green bi-peds.

CHAPTER 22

Eli stepped through the doorway and noted his suit's display register an immediate change to the atmospheric temperature and humidity. He landed easily on the floor and felt it give slightly. As they had discussed, he passed through the doorway and spun his body immediately to the left. His Ginny, aided by the armor's weapons targeting system, sought out targets or threats. He quickly found himself facing a wall and spun back to the right.

The first trooper of the platoon had already stepped through the doorway behind him and had encountered a similar occurrence on the right. They were in a long corridor that was approximately three meters wide. The walls were moist with condensation and Eli watched as a trickle of condensation formed on the wall to his left. It ran down the wall to the floor where it was absorbed.

Zrthns certainly like to keep things a bit moist, he thought.

The doorway they had stepped through was positioned against the back wall of the area. As a result, the armored soldiers stepping through the door only had one direction to travel. Forward.

He was giving orders to the third and fourth soldiers through the doorway to keep moving forward when the floor beneath their feet suddenly jerked into motion and began a slow, but steady conveyor belt-like carry, which moved them toward the darkened doorway at the end of the corridor.

"Jenkins," he called out to the first trooper in the line. "Move forward with the floor, but hold up at that door and wait for the rest of the unit."

He got a nod from the soldier, then began to walk backward against the flowing floor. He easily maintained his position next to the portal and passed along similar instructions for the others entering the ship to move ahead. He paused long enough to look back through the portal to the far side. It appeared normal. He guessed he could easily pass back through to the other side if he wanted.

Interesting. It leads both ways, he thought.

His curiosity satisfied for the moment, he turned and trotted to the far end of the corridor where the first troopers had begun to assemble. He joined their reverse-walk maneuver to maintain their position just this side of the open doorway that lay ahead. The moving, spongelike floor took a sharp ninety-degree turn to the left just beyond the opening, and he wondered where it led. They'd find out soon enough. He looked back over his shoulder and saw the first of the Minith soldiers come through the portal. Not wanting to group his force in such a confined space he decided it was time to move forward.

"Lock, load, and lookout, rangers. It's time to see what lies ahead," he announced to the men and women surrounding him, then took a step forward.

* * *

Ah-loon moved quickly toward the sorting room. His blue-colored body paint had been reapplied just hours before and shimmered as he moved through the passageway. He wore the paint with pride, satisfied with his rank and place in the pod that was this ship. His three assistants followed closely behind. The natural gray of their skin—while beautiful in its own way—seemed dim and dull when compared to his paint. *As intended.*

Rank had its privileges, and he wore his with pride. Blue paint might be in their futures if they worked hard, and made satisfactory contracts with their superiors, but he saw little potential in this lot. Ah-loon could tell by the way their arms drooped by their sides and by the lack of bounce in their collective gait, that none were pleased with their lot in this particular navy. No doubt they felt they should be on board the main ship, preparing for the battle. He had once been of the same mind, but had long ago fallen into his assigned role with something resembling bored resignation. They too would eventually learn to accept their place, or they would be destined to a life as a mere gray-skin. Not that there was anything wrong with that.

They needed a good, long sort to take their minds off their current existence, and Ah-loon wondered what waited ahead. He hoped the room was filled with unconscious bi-peds awaiting their attention. The work was sometimes interesting, if not overly exciting. They were responsible for inspecting the catch closely, removing weapons and other potentially interesting equipment, sorting them into categories—specifically pink and green on the last few hauls—and sending each of the strange creatures off to their respective pens. Each haul was usually good for a surprise or two. They had found several new weapons in the last few catches, for instance, as well as a new category of bi-ped. They had called that one "metallic" and had sent it off for inspection. He reminded himself to check in with Antoo, the researcher who had been given that task. He had neither seen nor heard from the other since he had started his work. If he knew Antoo, he was tentacles-deep in the inspection and wouldn't come up for air until he had all of his questions answered.

Ah-loon and his small contingent of sorters reached the doorway. He placed his fingers into the appropriate circle-scanner position and pressed. The doorway retracted to the right, just as he expected.

The catch that waited inside, however, wasn't anything like he expected.

* * *

Eli and the leading contingent of the force had just ridden the moving floor into a large room filled with tables, bins, and strange equipment when the door on the far side of the room slid open. Just outside the door, stood several large aliens. For a long moment, neither group reacted. That changed when one of the aliens lifted a tube-shaped object and pointed it in their direction.

Eli jumped toward the aliens, allowing the powered suit to launch his body halfway across the wide area, in a single bound. At the same time, he lifted the shotgun, which was only effective at shorter distances, and tracked the group of Zrthns. Only one had raised a tube (weapon?) so he focused his aim there and pulled the trigger. The hundred or so tiny ball bearings crossed the distance in a fraction of a second. As they were designed, they spread outward in a brutal spray that sliced through the Zrthn and two of his (her?) unfortunate companions.

The fourth Zrthn fell backward awkwardly and

was spared from the blast of deadly metal. Eli watched the now-scrambling creature as its tentacles wriggled in fear. The slick gore that coated its body and the floor was making escape difficult. This one's body showed tints of light blue, he noted, which contrasted with the other three. Perhaps he was the leader. Unfortunately for the squid, his blue was now liberally painted with bits, pieces, and spray of grisly gray blood.

Eli moved closer to the struggling alien and took aim.

Do not kill him!

Aank's mental plea was both heard and felt. It was also something of a surprise as the short alien had been instructed to remain behind. Eli's initial reaction was to ignore the Waa, but a mental vision of the little green male's reasoning halted the squeeze of his right forefinger. Barely.

"Hold fire!" Eli ordered to those behind, as he sprinted forward.

He jumped over the pile of Zrthn dead and landed next to the still-struggling Zrthn. He put an armored boot on the alien's (chest?) body and pointed the Ginny at the gray dome of the alien's head.

"Don't you flocking move." He had no idea if the alien could understand the words, but something got through. The squidlike being stopped struggling and lifted both arm-tentacles in the air. The six finger-tentacles spread out in a wide pattern. To Eli, it looked like the human equivalent of "Don't shoot. I give up."

That is exactly what he means, Captain.

So you can read their minds too? Eli remembered to "speak" with his mind as he had been instructed earlier. It felt strange, but it would help maintain the Alliance's secret and would prevent getting weird looks from his soldiers. Talking to himself might have that effect, he guessed.

Of course. That is why I did not want you to kill him.

Good call, Aank.

Five minutes later, Eli had his troops deployed outside the entrances and down the nearest hallways. The Zrthn was no longer pinned under Eli's boot, but was closely guarded by two Minith rangers. Satisfied that their position was secure for the time being, he turned his attention to Aank.

Weren't you and Ta'an supposed to be on the far side of the portal?

Ta'an is there now, awaiting further instructions. We felt it best to keep the portal open, seeing as how it acts as a doorway between our present and prior locations.

Eli bit down on his tongue and stared into the Waa's large, black eyes. Aank and Ta'an's instructions had been clear. Wait for the last soldier to cross over, then shut down the doorway. Seeing as how it was their only way home, though, Eli admitted it made much more sense to leave it open, as long as both sides were guarded. Once again, the tiny Waa's thinking had been ahead of his own, and he had acted in their best interest. That bought a lot of leeway and forgiveness. Still, orders were made to be followed, not ignored.

Aank blinked once. Twice.

You're reading my mind right now, aren't you?

Again, two blinks. Eli thought the action probably stood for "yes" or "understood" or something similar that meant no real response was needed. So why even ask?

He received two more calm, even blinks and couldn't help but growl, much like a Minith.

So, what's our next step, Aank? We need to locate our people and find out as much as we can about this ship. Also, if we discover what the Zrthns have in mind that would be great.

"I will interrogate the prisoner now, yes?" Aank's words were gentle and issued in a near-whisper. It was obvious they had to speak out loud so as to not draw attention from those around them. The secret of their mental communication had to be kept, and Eli kicked himself for not thinking of that not-so-small detail before the Waa.

"Yes, Aank," he replied, his voice tight and controlled. "I assume you speak Zrthn?"

"I speak enough," Aank answered, then turned to the alien who still had his arms raised and fingers splayed. He began talking to the Zrthn in a chirping-squealing-chattering fashion that reminded Eli of the sound made by the dolphins or whales of Earth. The slimy, grayish alien responded in a similar fashion. Eli had an ear for language and followed the back and forth closely, trying to pick out patterns that would translate to understanding. The Zrthn appeared to be repeating the same patterns over and over, and Eli wondered what he was trying to communicate.

He is trying not *to communicate.* Aank answered without giving any outward indication that he was addressing Eli. *He repeats his name, which is Ah-loon, the ship's name—Captive Taker One—and his position on board. Apparently, he is a "senior catch sorter." Those items of information are all he is allowed to provide should he be captured. Unfortunately for Ah-loon, I don't need verbal answers. His thoughts are very clear.*

You know where our soldiers are being held?

Aank turned away from the still-chattering Zrthn and spoke to Eli.

"All captured human and Minith soldiers are being held in pens on the deck below this one. The doorways on the far side of the room lead the way."

The Waa sent Eli a mental picture so he would know exactly where to go and what to expect. Moving floors, similar to the one that brought them into this area, delivered inert prisoners to large round doorways set into the floor. The doorways were opened, and prisoners were unceremoniously dumped into holding pens below. To Eli, the process seemed inhumane and disrespectful. It was obvious the Zrthns considered their prisoners chattel—property to be collected, processed, and stored.

"The command center for the ship is one deck above. The ship is manned by relatively few Zrthn troops," Aank said.

"How many is relatively few?"

"The Zrthn was not specific, but less than two dozen. None are heavily armed and most are support personnel, like Ah-loon and his sort team." Aank waved toward the sputtering alien and his now-dead crew, tucked his hands into the sleeves of his robe.

"All right," Eli nodded. "That's enough to get us started."

CHAPTER 23

Benson paced back and forth along the long hallway of the ship, the solitary man in a long line of Minith walkers. The forgiving, spongelike matting beneath his feet squished as he walked, but he had learned to mostly ignore the strange surface. The fact that his armor protected his feet and legs from the damp flooring helped. He didn't know how the alien warriors who shambled along the hallway around him could bear the stuff. Most complained constantly, and he couldn't blame them. They had been trapped here for a lot longer than he had, and most were experiencing some form of ear mold, foot rot, or any number of other health concerns—all because of the constant, dank humidity that surrounded them. *Flocking squids and their crudding soggy enviro!*

He reached the end of the long hallway and did an about-face, robotically retracing the now-familiar path. He had silently watched the Minith captives for a full day before joining their line of movement. He didn't know what drove the Minith to move, but he was able to keep the pain of the suit at bay through action, so he fell in line.

He mulled over their situation as he paced, anxious to think of something he might have overlooked. They had tried everything they could imagine to find a way out of the hold where their captors had dumped them. After releasing the humans and the Minith from their rooms two days earlier, the group had searched for, but failed to find, a way to leave their current position. The Zrthn prisoner ship was well designed in that manner.

Although they had escaped the individual rooms where they had been locked away, leaving this portion of the ship had proved impossible. The long hallway, with all of its doors, led nowhere. With the exception of the initial exam room where he had awoken and killed the three aliens, the rest of this level was nothing more than a succession of more empty holding rooms. There had to be an entrance to the exam room, but he couldn't find it.

Apparently, the only way in or out appeared to be through circular, shutterlike panels set into the high ceiling of each room. Benson had never seen them function, but had been told new arrivals dropped into the pens through those entrances.

He was able to reach the ceiling by leaping upward, with the aid of his armor, but could find no way to open the shutters. Beating against the panels proved useless and, despite repeated jumps, his inspections revealed no way to open the doorways from this side. All he accomplished was to drain the already diminished power levels in his suit.

He was down to 10 percent charge and wondered how best to use the remaining battery life. Ramming the walls in order to break through to a far side seemed ill advised. They were obviously made from agsel, which meant any attempt was doomed to failure. Even if he was successful at penetrating the wall, how did he know he wouldn't be damaging an outer hull?

A clamor from the direction of the cell he had first opened drew his attention. Was that cheering he heard?

He and the Minith around him raced toward the sound and, upon reaching the intersection at the far end of the hallway, turned toward the human holding cell. At the end of the short hallway, stepping from the room at the end where his human peers waited, was another armored PEACE suit. Benson could only watch as the suit approached.

"Benson, what the flock are you doing?" the suit challenged. He recognized the voice but his mind almost refused to believe what he was hearing. "You wanted to become the first Shiale Ranger to get captured by the Zrthns, huh?"

"EJ?" Benson felt as though someone had doused him with a bucket full of cold water. "Are you here to rescue us, or have you been taken?"

"Rescue, Lieutenant Benson. Rescue!"

"Well, it certainly took you long enough," First Sergeant Twigg growled menacingly from behind Benson. "I can't take another minute being stuck on this damp excuse for a ship."

"First Sergeant, I hate to be the bearer of bad news," Eli replied. "But we have another stop or two to make before we're done here."

"Do I get to twist a Zrthn neck, at least?"

The captain smiled and nodded. "Perhaps, First Sergeant. Perhaps."

"Then, please. Lead the way."

* * *

Colonel Drah marched quickly through the hallway that led to his superior's office. As he moved, he considered the steps that had already been taken. He could not help but feel satisfied with the progress so far. He only had one remaining task to accomplish before his final plans could begin.

The warriors that were loyal to his cause—casting

off the shackles of the human-led alliance and fostering a new Minith resurgence—were already in place. At over a thousand strong, the relationships and affirmations that bound them together had been carefully cultivated over the past two years. It hadn't been easy to identify, recruit, and place so many of his fellow warriors into crucial positions, but he had pushed forward knowing the Zrthns would support his movement. In fact, their support was a critical step in its success. Taking and holding Telgora would be relatively easy once the wave grew and started its inevitable crest. That was no concern.

Drah was confident that an upswell of Minith pride and aggression would help sweep away the fraudulent "alliance" that he and his people had been forced to endure for the past twelve years. Even those Minith who knew nothing of what was about to take place would join his ranks—with both speed and ancestral enthusiasm—once they understood what was happening.

The forces and capabilities that remained on Waa were the only real concern. Would the Minith there support his movement and join it, or would they remain blindly obedient to the human leadership that they currently bowed before? He did not know, and that's where the Zrthns came in. He needed their support and recognition to ensure Waa remained a nonissue. Once he solidified his hold here on Telgora, not even the forces of Waa would be able to unseat them.

He grumbled for a moment over the favorable trade terms he had agreed to with Oinoo. The agsel sales would provide an influx of wealth and influence to his new dominion, but he was nearly giving the ore away. He considered the potential for renegotiating once his hold on the planet was secure. He decided it would be needed and smiled at the thought of alienating his new alliance. Oh well. Such were the circumstances of trade and profit. For now, though, the future trade arrangement was but a minor detail. His primary goal was to break the subservient hold that these weak, puny humans had placed upon his race.

He approached the doorway of General Tuun's office and paused briefly outside the large, wooden doors to clear his thoughts. He had been in this place hundreds of times over the past two years. Unlike previous visits, he ignored protocol and did not offer the perfunctory quiet *tap-tap-tap* that announced his intention to enter. Instead, he simply grabbed the handle with his left paw, gave a quick twist, and threw the door inward.

General Tuun, his superior in the Alliance Defense Force, raised his head, obviously startled by the sudden intrusion into his private work space.

"Drah! What's the—"

He got no further with the thought or the words behind it. The blast from the pulse pistol in Drah's right paw made sure of that.

Coup d état, Drah reminded himself. That was the human phrase for his act of deathly insubordination. Such funny, foreign words that made no sense at all. He much preferred the Minith equivalents of "mutiny," "overthrow," or—his personal favorite—"taking what is rightfully mine."

Regardless of what one called it, he was enormously pleased with how simple and fulfilling it had been to complete the final task on his list.

Now, the real fun could begin.

He pulled the communication device from the bag tied to his waist belt and activated the send mechanism.

"We will be ready in six hours."

* * *

Eli and the eighty rangers—forty human and forty Minith—were currently holding position at the base of a long, winding ramp that led upward to the first deck and the command center of the ship. Aank's mental interrogation of Ah-loon was thorough, and he had passed all the info he received, via mind speak, to Eli. Although he had never been aboard the ship before today, Eli knew what lay ahead and what to expect. He marveled at the ease with which it had been accomplished, but Ah-loon's knowledge had been transferred directly into his head.

It is not an exact transference, but should suffice, Captain.

Oh, yes. Aank was also with them. Now that Eli understood how important the tiny engineer could be, he wanted him close. But not too close. He stood near the rear of the assembled group where he could be protected.

We are secure here, Captain. The closest potential combatant is at the top of this ramp.

Thank you, Aank.

Eli shook his head and briefly wondered why the soldiers were even necessary when the Alliance had the ability to read the enemy's minds.

We are nonviolent, and only wish to serve.

Okay, Aank. Enough of the running commentary. I don't expect an answer to every unspoken question.

Eli couldn't see it, but he somehow felt the Waa's eyelids slide slowly and deliberately down over the large black eyes. Once. Twice. The blinks carried a hint of offended annoyance at the slight rebuke. Eli smiled. He couldn't help but wonder if all Waa were as sensitive. The absence of two more mental blinks probably indicated they weren't, and he felt a twinge of guilt.

I'm sorry, Aank. Just feeling a bit anxious about the current situation.

A rush of soothing calmness quickly settled his thoughts, and Eli understood at once the feeling had come from the Waa and that he was forgiven. He silently thanked the engineer and focused on the present situation.

"How's it coming, Benson?"

"Almost there, Captain. Just a minute or so to go."

As soon as they were retrieved from the holding pens, Eli sent the Alliance soldiers who had been held captive back through the portal to Rhino-3. The weeks aboard the Zrthn ship had taken their toll, and they needed medical attention. Many were suffering from moderate to severe skin conditions, while others displayed some type of respiratory infection. Both illnesses were likely caused by the damp conditions on board the ship.

All of the prisoners were malnourished, a result of the poor Zrthn diet. Eli had paused to inspect a bowl of the putrid, fishlike soup that the prisoners had been given day after day, and pushed it away at the first smell. Eating that particular gruel wasn't something he ever wanted to experience. He'd take the processed food pastes served in the chow hall over what these poor troops had been forced to endure, and silently swore to never complain about Alliance food—real or processed—ever again.

Of the former prisoners, only Lieutenant Benson and First Sergeant Twigg remained with the two platoons of Shiale Rangers Eli had brought aboard. Both were still fit for duty and refused to leave the ship. Eli understood and acceded. They had earned their place, and he couldn't deny their need to face what lay ahead. Each had been refitted with standard weapons, a cache of which had been found in a storage area near the sorting room on the second level. Benson retained the Zrthn weapon he had "liberated" from its previous owner, and it hung from a strap at his waist.

All of the human rangers were now taking turns connecting their armor to his. In this fashion, each passed a small percentage of their charge over to him.

"Okay, Captain," Benson gave a thumbs up and clapped the "donating" ranger on the back as he disconnected his suit. "I'm at eighty percent."

"Excellent," Eli acknowledged and turned his attention to the assembled force. "Okay, let's move out. Quietly. Armored rangers in the front, Minith rangers behind."

He heard the grumbling and the looks of anger cross the features of the large warriors. It wasn't unexpected.

"I understand you want to fight," he addressed the Minith. Although he could never say it out loud, he knew their aggressive tendencies and love of battle often overruled their common sense. "But the weapons we've encountered here on the ship don't seem to work against our armor. That's the only reason I'm asking you to stay back. We're protected. Also, if I'm not mistaken, we're going to need your battle skills soon enough."

The last comment got several nods, and Twigg stepped forward.

"We will follow your lead, Captain." He looked over the assembled Minith with a look that dared them to argue the point any further. "And we will be prepared to fight when the time is right."

Twigg was a well-known warrior among his people, and his words seemed to dispel any further discontent. Eli nodded to the first sergeant and turned toward the ramp. It was three meters wide, which accommodated two armored rangers side-by-side.

He and Benson took lead positions.

"We ready for this EJ?"

Eli couldn't tell him that he already knew what to expect. Or that this would likely be a cake walk. So he just hefted his Ginny into position, nodded and said, "Let's go."

The ramp wasn't steep, but it was long and circular. Because he now held some of Ah-loon's memories, he knew it followed a path that mirrored the ship's exterior. He also understood the gradual ramp was designed to best accommodate the Zrthn leg-tentacles. While Zrthns could navigate stairs, they weren't an ideal manner of getting from one deck to another. Eli noted and filed that piece of data away in his mental file, then made an official note in his suit's database. The official note, like the full vid of what they encountered on the ship, would be automatically transferred to the Alliance repository when they returned to Telgora.

Eli and Benson reached the top of the ramp and entered a hallway that led right and left. Eli turned left without pausing and picked up his pace. He tucked the Ginny into the sheath on his back and calmly drew his side-arm—a standard pulse weapon that could stun or kill—from its holster. Unlike the Ginny, it was near-silent when fired. Which is what he wanted just now. If his (Ah-loon's) memories were correct.

He turned right at the next intersection, spied the squid, and fired. The Zrthn appeared to be sleeping when the pulse entered his head, but Eli couldn't tell for sure. Not that it mattered. The now-dead alien crumpled to the floor with a soft, wet, plopping sound.

The intelligence they had gotten from Ah-loon was spot on, and Eli breathed a small sigh of relief. In the back of his mind, he had still held some doubt, still thought something might go wrong. But not now.

Sorry for doubting you, Aank.

Eli felt the mental blink-blink that he was coming to associate with the Waa, and smiled.

Eli and Benson held up just shy of the wide doorway where the dank, gray blood of the Zrthn guard had begun spreading across. It was being absorbed by the spongelike flooring.

"Good shot, EJ. Excellent reflexes."

They were on internal comms, but Eli still winced at the sudden voice in his helmet. "Not now. The command center is just inside. Remember the plan we discussed. This is a large room and will probably be occupied by a dozen or so enemy. Few, if any, will be armed. Take down any who look like a threat, but we need to capture as many as we can. You ready?"

"Sure."

Eli took a moment to switch out the sidearm for the Ginny. Firepower was needed now, not silence. He then turned his attention to the doorway and realized he had no way of opening it. He gaped at the panel next to the door and wondered how it worked. His (Ah-loon's) memory didn't provide an answer.

"What's the problem, Captain Justice?"

Eli shook his head and kicked himself for not thinking of this detail. He was on the verge of asking Aank for help when Benson reached down, grabbed an arm-tentacle, and dragged the squid toward the panel. With the armor's assistance, the movement seemed effortless.

"I got this."

Eli watched as Benson placed the six finger-tentacles on the circles drawn on the panel. Each made a small sucking noise and held in place when he pressed them down individually. When the sixth "finger" was in place, Benson looked to Eli, gave a nod, then pushed inward on the panel. The door whisked to the side, and the interior of the command center was revealed.

Benson beat Eli into the space and turned left toward his assigned zone. Eli moved directly forward, scanning for targets, confident the ranger behind him would move left, as he had been instructed.

Several of the aliens' heads popped up and spun in their direction. What appeared to be curiosity at their entrance was soon replaced with a buzz of activity and surprised urgency. The chirping-shuttering noises that made up their language shifted into overdrive as they no doubt recognized their guests as bi-peds. Armed bi-peds.

The alien on the far right of Eli's assigned zone lifted a weapon, but Eli was prepared and the Ginny quickly turned the threat into a gray spray of scattered flesh and blood. He scanned his zone for additional threats but saw only cowering figures. Several had their "arms" in the air and their finger-tentacles splayed in surrender. On a subconscious level, he heard the sounds of his fellow soldiers eliminating threats in their assigned zones. Those sounds abruptly ended and he heard announcements of "clear" before issuing his own "all clear."

The Shiale Rangers were now in possession of a

Zrthn space craft.

The question was, what would they do with it?

CHAPTER 24

Lieutenant Colonel Becca Conway sighed and turned to the next page of the training report. When she accepted the position as commander of the Shiale Ranger Battalion, she had envisioned so much more . . . excitement than what the job actually offered. Instead of leading her troops on dangerous missions that were crucial to the security of the Alliance, she spent her hours worrying over personnel issues and readiness reports. The latest mission to Rhino-3 was the most interesting thing to happen in years, and here she was—left behind while the least senior captain in the entire Alliance Defense Force got the call to action.

She was wondering how young Captain Zero was getting along on his first assignment when she heard the unmistakable sound of weapons fire erupt from the front of the building. She raced to the window in time to see a small group of Minith soldiers—her soldiers—step across two prone forms. The two forms—one human and one Minith—had previously been guarding the front entrance, but now lay dead or dying. And their attackers were entering the foyer just down the hall.

"What the flock!"

A thousand questions ran through her head, but she pushed them aside as she sprinted to the weapons cabinet at the back of her office. She was a firm believer in "hope for the best, prepare for the worst," and the worst demanded she arm herself. Her fears seemed to prove accurate as the firing continued down the hall and grew closer. She had just finished locking and loading a pulser rifle when the doors to her office slammed open.

She turned, aimed, and fired the weapon in a single, practiced motion. The well-aimed burst struck Captain Akko, the leader of Charlie Company, in the torso and slammed him backward into the two Minith rangers trailing behind. The trio fell and Becca advanced. She cast a quick look past them and saw the red and purple blood splatters that marked the deaths of her support staff. They hadn't been armed, so had no chance at defending themselves against whatever madness drove these three. That quick glance of confirmation took a fraction of a second and was all the proof she needed.

She returned her attention to the two remaining Minith attackers. Subconsciously, she noted they were bringing their weapons to bear on her, but the conscious part of her—that part that drove her warrior instinct and controlled her trigger finger—took precedence. Less than a second and a half separated the first trigger pull that killed Akko from the second and third pulls that dispatched the other two traitors.

She put a follow-up burst in each body to be sure, then rushed past their crumpled forms to check on her staff.

* * *

Drah was seated comfortably behind his previous senior officer's desk. He was receiving a steady influx of reports from the key leaders he had set into motion. Most were positive, with announcements that his forces were in control of the key installations around Telgora, including the mines, the Alliance human headquarters building, and the primary space landing facility. The latter was key to their success, and its capture had greatly relieved the stresses he had been feeling since putting his plan into motion.

There were only two apparent failures.

The first was his expectation that all of the Minith on the planet would rally to his battle cry and join the movement for emancipation and dominance. While his leaders had managed to sway a great number of their brothers to the cause, most—a full 80 percent—of the Minith on the planet had declined to commit themselves to the cause . . . yet. Instead, they expressed a desire to sit back and observe which way the tide flowed before taking a side.

He raged at the shortsighted weaklings, who refused to reach out and grasp their freedom from this sham of an alliance. With their backing, taking over this planet would have been a leisurely pace around the room. Without them—well, supremacy was still a foregone feat, but one that would require a bit more work. As long as they didn't take up arms against the movement, he would succeed. Notes would be taken, however, on where each warrior chose to stand. When the fighting ended, settlements would be made accordingly.

Yes, he would pit the thirty-thousand Minith warriors that now followed him against the human's fifteen-thousand without any worries over the eventual outcome. With Oinoo's ten thousand Zrthn troopers added into the fray, the odds became even more tilted in their favor. Thanks to the surprise element of the uprising, a quarter of the human force on Telgora—five thousand soldiers—had already been killed or captured. The remainder were scattered across the planet, running from the Minith, hiding from their fate.

The second apparent failure was their inability to seize the Shiale Ranger Battalion headquarters. The force assigned to assault and take that location had yet to check in, and several second-hand reports indicated that the human sheep, Colonel Conway, was still in control and had neutralized their advances. Oh well. He could hardly expect perfection, and in the larger scheme, the facility was minimal. Two of the battalion's ranger companies were off-world at the present time, which limited the danger. He would merely circle back around to her when he solidified his holdings elsewhere.

He put the failures out of mind and turned his attention toward more urgent matters. Now that the mines and the spaceport had been seized, the time had come to direct his forces against another major target of his movement to reclaim planetary dominance.

It was time to search out and destroy the Telgoran natives that lived beneath the planet's surface. Those ignorant bean stalks had been a thorn in the paw of the Minith for decades. Removing the thorn would be a pleasurable endeavor and would serve to sate the blood lust of his soldiers.

* * *

Once the Zrthn ship's command center was secure, Aank was brought forward. The engineer began speaking to the eight remaining Zrthns and immediately validated Eli's suspicions regarding who commanded the ship. The sky blue tint covering his body made the ship's captain—Senior Leader Ootoon, Aank discovered—the obvious choice.

At the Waa's urging, and after verifying the ship would stay safely on course without their direct interaction, the remaining seven squids were removed from and taken to a holding area on the bottom deck. It would be good to give the Zrthns a taste of the pens.

Once Ootoon was alone, Aank went to work.

The high-pitched back and forth between the Waa and the Zrthn sounded like a replay of the earlier interrogation. Aank asked his questions, and the Zrthn repeated the same information back in response to each.

Name: Ootoon.

Ship name: *Captive Taker One*.

His position: Senior Ship Leader.

To Eli, the repetitive nature of the Zrthns responses was clear. The same sets of squeak-squeals were uttered in the same fashion and cadence. He wondered if Benson, or the others in the room, picked up on the subtle nuance of the alien exchange. If anyone did, they gave no indication. The fact that none of them had ever heard a Zrthn speak, much less understood what they were saying, probably helped in that regard. The important thing, though, was that Aank was able to read the mental responses that Ootoon unknowingly provided.

Aank mentally passed his questions—and the Zrthns unspoken responses—to Eli, as they were intercepted.

What is the purpose of this ship? Aank asked. *The ship is a captivity ship. It facilitates the capture, retention, and disposal of enemy forces,* he relayed the Zrthn's response.

How many ships are in your group?

<Eight>

What is the purpose of the ships in your group?

<Six are captivity ships. One is a support and logistics vessel. One is a battle carrier.>

How many fighters are on your ships?

<Ten thousand. On the battle carrier.>

Who is your force leader and where is he now?

<Our force leader is Oinoo, of the Thmelia Pod. He commands the battle carrier.>

What are your leader's orders?

<Unsure. There is a rumor that he has no orders. He may be acting for the sake of his pod.>

What is the goal of your force?

<Support the overthrow of the Shiale Alliance on the planet Telgora.>

That response grabbed Eli's attention, and he projected a query to Aank.

He said they are supporting an overthrow, Aank, Eli interjected into the stream of mental questions. *That would mean someone else is leading the overthrow. Can we find out who?*

Eli, I cannot ask him a question based on information obtained through a mental response. To do so would reveal that I can read his thoughts.

Ugh. I hadn't thought of that. Sorry.

Eli struggled with a way to ask a question that might reveal the appropriate response, but realized it didn't really matter. There was only one answer that made any sense, and he didn't need to read the Zrthn's mind to know what it was. The Minith was the only force on Telgora that would attempt such a move.

Aank, ask him how he communicates with the other ships.

How do you communicate with the other ships?

<Standard communication protocol for most

interactions. Transportation maneuvers for face-to-face communications.>

"What the—" Eli muttered before he could stop himself. Benson gave him a questioning look and shrugged as if to ask *What?* "Sorry, I just had a thought."

Eli turned to the Waa engineer and asked, "Aank, what have you learned so far?"

In Earth Standard language, Aank quietly relayed the information he had obtained from the Zrthn for the benefit of the other rangers in the room. When Aank relayed the bit about "face-to-face communications," Eli stopped the engineer and keyed in on the piece of info that was of immediate interest. If the reply they got back from the Zrthn was what he hoped, they had a way to move forward.

"Aank," Eli asked out loud, again for the benefit of the other troops. "Ask how their face-to-face communications work."

"Yes, Captain," the little green alien replied in his quiet voice. He turned back to the Zrthn and resumed his squeak-squeal speech.

Five minutes later, Eli had his answer. He also had the vague beginnings of a plan. To implement it, he would need every available soldier he could gather.

"Benson, send word to our guard at the portal. We need Lieutenant Tenney over here as quickly as possible."

CHAPTER 25

Becca Conway was pissed. She had spent the last fifteen years of her life preparing herself and her troops for battle. The fact that it was *her troops* that had initiated the attack against her and her staff went against everything she believed in. In her view, the three Minith had no sense of honor and deserved a far worse death than the one she had given them. With the exception of Sergeant Boyle, who had been in the back room, all of her staff had been killed in the assault.

Now, she and Boyle were in route to the nearest human units—a series of basic training battalions three kilometers away. Fellow human soldiers would be there, and she planned to enlist their aid in repelling what appeared to be a limited Minith coup. She termed it a "limited" coup because of what she learned on her first stop, which had been to Charlie Company of her own Shiale Ranger Battalion. She wanted to find out why the leader of the company—her previous subordinate—had attacked his commander and her staff. What she learned only added substantial fuel to the raging fire that now drove her. Akko and his two followers were part of a larger group. And that larger group's plan was to take over Telgora.

Fortunately, not all Minith were fully on board with the plan. The three traitors had tried to co-opt the rest of the ranger company but had failed. That was good for Becca and Boyle, and was likely the reason they were still alive. The unfortunate news she had learned, however, was that while not all Minith were willing to join the coup, they also weren't willing to help stomp it out, either. For most, the preferred course of action was to sit back and wait for a winner to emerge, then pledge fealty to the victor. Not for the first time, she cursed the fact that a large part of the army she belonged to was made up of alien beings that couldn't be trusted to act in a predictable manner.

So, for now, she would ignore the Minith who sat on the sidelines. Instead, she would focus on those who were carrying the flag of Minith insurrection and aggression.

Peace help those poor flockers, she thought as she ran around the corner of the first basic training building. This was the unit where Eli and his fellow armored recruits had trained, she noted.

The absence of human recruits, and their Minith sergeants, was the first indication that something was not quite right. Normally, the area would be filled with activity as the soldiers went about their daily tasks and activities. As a result of the stillness, she assumed the coup had reached here and slowed her movement to match her sudden caution. She moved to the side of the building and peeked into the first window she came to. An empty barracks room.

She moved farther along the building, carefully scanning the area around her and Boyle. The young sergeant had never experienced battle, and she was pleased to see he was mirroring her movements. She inspected each window she passed but found the same thing in each. No sign of anyone. She reached the front entrance and debated whether to enter the building or move on to the next. This particular training facility was set up in a quad-type settlement: four long buildings, built corner-to-corner in a box fashion, with an open area—the quad—in the middle.

A sudden flurry of shouting came from the quad area. That pushed her into motion. She rushed into the building and passed through the entryway. Boyle kept his position behind as they entered, and she scanned the area, alert for the unexpected. No one. She then quick-walked past the central corridor and approached the doorway on the far side that led to the quad. She flattened to the side of the double door and looked out.

The first thing she noticed was the crowd of recruits seated in rows on the flat sand ground of the quad. Then, she noted the armed Minith soldiers. There were five in total, one at each corner of the quad with another in the middle of the group. The shouts were coming from where the Minith in the center stood. He had a pulser, and it was aimed at a knot of recruits, who were struggling to hold back one of their own, who seemed intent on attacking the alien.

She recognized the Minith from the vid of Captain Zero's assault on the tower. Sergeant Brek. It figured he was in on the conspiracy.

All eyes were focused on the skirmish, so none missed it when Brek pulled the trigger of his weapon and fired indiscriminately into the group.

The action caused an uproar from all of the seated soldiers, who were obviously being held against their will. As she watched, the two recruits nearest to the murdering alien jumped up and rushed the Minith. Each was cut down in turn, but it didn't stop other unarmed recruits from joining the one-sided battle. She felt a conflicting rush of emotion that was filled with pride, sadness, and shame. Those emotions were quickly replaced by the anger that she had been feeling since this whole thing started.

"Let's go, Boyle," she said over her shoulder as she pushed through the doors that led into the quad. Her finger was already applying pressure to the trigger of her weapon. "You move left, and I'll go right."

Her first shot was good, and she felt a surge of satisfaction as Brek was thrown backward in a spray of purple, alien blood. She remembered that splash with some degree of familiarity. She had killed more than a few of the large aliens nearly a dozen years before on Waa. She had been a sergeant during the Peace Wars and led a squad of untested, human soldiers against the Minith. They had beaten the aliens then, and she was convinced they would do so now.

Her second trigger pull produced another purple splatter as the guard on the far corner was dispatched. She had to admit, it was an excellent shot. The distance made it tough, but the fact that he was facing the doorway and had seen her take out the Minith in the center made him the necessary second target. She didn't wait to see the body crumple. Instead, she twisted her body to the right and drilled a shot into the large, green alien posted at the near corner. He was just turning toward her when her pulse round caught him in the chest and flung him away from the humans he had been tasked to watch over.

Once her side of the quad was cleared, Becca turned to the left and looked for how Boyle was getting along. She noted that the nearest Minith on his side was falling backward, a large hole in his torso. A slight twinge of pride slipped through her anger, and she turned just in time to see the last Minith at the farthest corner of the quad get swarmed by a dozen soldiers. Despite his larger size and stronger frame, he succumbed to the numbers and went down. His rifle was wrenched from his grip and was quickly turned on him, successfully ending the melee.

Although it still couldn't surpass the anger that coursed through her, the initial pride she had felt grew just a bit larger. She didn't know what week of training these recruits were in, but they definitely had the proper mindset for what she needed.

* * *

Oinoo received confirmation from his Minith lackey on the ground that all was ready, and he wriggled his tentacles in gleeful anticipation. After decades of having to work through intermediaries, and being forced to submit to irritating contractual necessities, the agsel deposits that filled the planet below would soon belong to him. No longer would he or his pod need to comply with the contracts negotiated with these backland heathens in order to obtain the valuable ore. Instead, he would be establishing contracts of his own. Contracts that others—pod and nonpod—would have to agree to and obey.

Not for the first time, he quivered at the notion of being known as the greatest tentacle to ever sprout from the Thmelia Pod.

He forced his body to still and focused on the final phases of his plan.

First, land.

Second, kill or capture.

Third, own and prosper.

He quivered once again. Then he issued the orders needed to prepare his fighters and begin the landing sequence.

* * *

"It's about time you let me join the fun, Captain."

"Sorry, Lieutenant," Eli turned to address his XO. "I needed you on Rhino-3. Until now."

He, Benson, and Twigg had been watching the ship's progress on the alien vid screen. The technology was similar to what the Alliance ships used, and he observed anxiously as Telgora grew with each passing minute. The Zrthn contingent of ships was close, and could land on the planet at any time. He wondered how the Alliance forces on the planet were faring. Not well, he suspected. It really depended on how accurate their assessment was of the situation. Aank stood quietly across the room. Two rangers stood with him, their weapons turned—probably needlessly—on the Zrthn who previously commanded the captivity ship.

"I know, Eli," she confessed. "I was just giving you a hard time. It's not easy to sit back and watch while others take the risks, you know?"

Eli did know. It's why he couldn't have sent anyone else in his place. He was responsible for their well-being and wouldn't ask others to take on a mission that he wasn't ready to take on himself. For now, anyway. If and when he rose in the ranks, he knew that would all change. He had grown up watching his dad struggle with the issue on a daily basis. As the leader of the Alliance Defense Forces, he was no longer allowed to venture out and face the enemy himself. Instead, he could only sit back and wait for others to take the risks, defeat the bad guys, and put *their* lives in danger. It wasn't something that Eli looked forward to ever experiencing.

"Yes, but now we need all hands on deck."

"We're ready, Captain. Give the word and I'll have every Shiale Ranger on that tiny rock called Rhino-3 here in less than an hour."

"That's exactly what we need, Tenney," Eli explained. His mind raced with possibilities, scenarios, and contingencies as the plan took form. "We're also going to need every non-ranger who's healthy enough to join us."

"The troops we just rescued?"

"The very ones. Most aren't ground forces, but they've been trained in standard tactics and know how to fire a weapon, so get them ready."

"That might take more than an hour, but we'll get it done," she replied with a furrowed brow.

Eli knew it seemed like an odd request, so he tried to explain what was happening in as few words as possible. When Tenney turned to leave, she understood the situation well enough. The Minith on Telgora were probably in revolt. The Zrthn battle carrier was preparing to land. Their presence on planet was needed.

"It has to be Drah, Captain," Twigg whispered to Eli when Tenney had gone.

"You're probably right, First Sergeant," Eli agreed.

He had been thinking the same thing. In a way, it was good to have a second opinion that mirrored his own. On another level, it caused Eli some grief. He trusted Twigg and felt strongly the first sergeant would remain loyal to the Alliance. He couldn't say the same for any other four-hundred-plus Minith he had under his present command. They needed to discuss this issue, and the timing wouldn’t get any better.

“We need to talk about your fellow warriors.”

CHAPTER 26

Colonel Conway assembled her five hundred young troops, many who were still in the process of getting kitted up.

After securing the first training battalion, she and that group had moved to the next battalion a kilometer farther west. They had encountered a similar situation as she and Boyle found earlier: the human recruits were huddled in the center of their quad, guarded by a small contingent of Minith. Before taking aim, Becca recognized the Minith guards as the training sergeants who had previously been tasked with looking after the young men and women. That fact apparently did not go unnoticed by the recruits. It certainly didn't go unpunished. The anger they displayed at the betrayal when the shooting began worked in their favor and the conspirators were quickly dispatched. Unfortunately, two recruits were also lost before the last Minith was taken down.

All Shiale Alliance defense units, including those going through initial basic training, are equipped to support full combat loads for the troops assigned to them, including comms gear, which Conway had quickly latched onto and put to work. Her efforts to reach out to other fighting units were more successful than not, but they hadn't resulted in overly positive news. All across the planet, Minith forces were either standing down, like her own Minith battalion of Rangers, or they were actively attacking human units and taking control of key facilities. The spacecraft landing base that stood twenty kilometers to the west was the first to be overrun. The agsel mines, defense force headquarters, and supply depots had quickly followed.

She had just made contact with a pilot with the Shiale Air Force, and the initial reports from that quarter weren't good. The air bases scattered around the planet, and the jets located at those bases, had been decimated. Minith didn't fly jets. *Because they're too stupid*, she angrily mused. As a result, they had no reason to capture the bases and every reason to destroy them.

"Alpha-21, how many pilots made it off the ground?" she keyed the comm set and asked. Alpha-21's pilot, Captain Gurney, was the only pilot she had managed to successfully contact, so far. She paced back and forth along her place on the quad and mentally pushed the troopers before her to hurry. They had work to do, and not much time to get it done. The longer they dallied, the more of their fellow humans would fall under a Minith boot.

"Colonel," Gurney replied in a calm-sounding voice that Conway knew was a front. She had been in enough battles to know what emotions the pilot was probably feeling right now. Calm wasn't one. "I've been able to reach twelve other pilots so far. Two from the local base, the remainder are scattered around the ring."

Twelve. Out of more than four hundred jets and pilots, only twelve remained?

"Roger, Captain," Conway acknowledged, struggling to match Gurneys calm demeanor. "What type of loads are you carrying?"

"It's a mix, Colonel. I'm carrying a full load of pulse and bombardment ammunition, but I was getting ready for my annual live-fire training mission. Three others have a lot less, but they can deliver some punch, if needed. The remaining eight have the jets they're flying and the fuel in their tanks. Sorry..."

Conway smacked her hand angrily against her thigh and bit her tongue.

"It's all right, Captain. Not your fault." She rubbed her eyes and thought through the problem. They were seriously outnumbered. She was leading a small force of half-trained soldiers. She had no idea how many humans were still combat capable elsewhere on the planet. Her most deadly unit was currently on a mission light years away. Her only real advantage—air superiority—wasn't much of an advantage. "How long can you stay airborne on the fuel you have?"

"With the new engines and fuel units we put into use a year ago, we can stay up for days, Colonel. We'll fall asleep in our seats before we need to land."

"Well, that's positive news." Conway had to smile at the captain's outlook. "Here's what I need. Save your ammo and avoid engagement with hostile forces. What I need is intel, so put the word out to your fellow pilots. Reconnaissance and reporting for now. We need to find out where we have units still capable of fighting, so I can direct their efforts. I also need to know what these green clowns have planned."

"I understand, Colonel. I'll— what the flock!"

"What is it, Gurney? Talk to me!"

"Do you have a line of sight to the west, Colonel? You'll want to see this." The calm voice and demeanor showed an initial, tiny crack.

Becca didn't have a view in that direction. It was obscured by one of the training buildings, so she sprinted for the corner of the building and looked to the west.

Holy Flock.

Approximately twenty kilometers distant, above the spaceport, a giant ship filled the sky. It was easily twice as large as a Shiale mothership and didn't have the standard features of one of their own. It was obviously alien. And it was landing.

She keyed the comms. "Recon, Gurney. Recon."

She received an affirmative from the pilot and looked up to see the small jet turn to the west. Two others followed close behind. In seconds, the trio of airborne fighters disappeared into the distant sky. The large, descending ship created an anomalous backdrop.

She raced back to the soldiers assembling in the quad behind her. The need for speed had suddenly been amped up even higher.

"Sergeant Boyle," she snapped into the comm set, her attention swiveling now to the Ranger NCO. "How are you coming on finding those carriers?"

"We're set, Colonel. Headed your way with the first group now."

"Excellent, Sergeant," she replied, glad that *something* was going right. He sounded much more at ease than she would have thought, and guessed why. "You haven't had a chance to look west, lately, have you?"

* * *

Oinoo rubbed his tentacles together in excited wonder as the ship settled into place. They encountered no resistance and he grudgingly afforded the Minith steward a silent, though pod-felt, moment of reflection. A reward might be in order. Though not the one the toady expected. Appearances would have to be maintained, however. He still needed assistance. For now.

He felt the ship tremble under his tentacles. The motion was an indication the dozen large ramps were descending into place. He felt somewhat lightheaded with excitement.

Moments later, ten thousand Zrthn soldiers and their equipment began a slow but steady exodus from the bowels of the battle carrier.

* * *

In seconds, the group of jets halved the distance to the Zrthn carrier.

"Alpha-22, cut speed to ten percent and proceed north around the alien ship," Gurney instructed his fellow pilot, a new lieutenant who had been in the squadron less than a month. "Maintain a five kilometer distance, and keep your eyes peeled. We don't know what these guys are armed with."

"Roger, Alpha-21."

"Alpha-23," Gurney addressed the third pilot in their tiny formation. The call signs had been assigned only moments before, and designated their new roles. "Maintain station here and observe. I'm going to proceed south and circle the ship from three kilometers."

"Roger, Alpha-21. Maintaining current station."

Gurney then tilted his command stick to the left, reduced his own speed to three hundred kilometers an hour, and peeled away, headed around the alien ship in a clockwise direction.

The ship was huge and, as the pilot looked on, it

settled firmly onto Terra Telgora. As soon as it landed, Gurney noticed several openings appear in the side of the ship. They were spaced evenly apart and ramps descended quickly from each. Once the ramps hit the ground, the first Zrthn appeared.

Gurney dialed up the magnification feature built into his face mask as high as it would go and focused on the creature, which was quickly joined by a score of others. They waddle-walked down the ramp on four strange leglike tentacles. In their two arm-tentacles, each alien carried a long, tubelike weapon, which he assumed to be their version of a battle rifle. A ring of mist—from his vantage point, Gurney couldn't tell if it was water or some other clear, wet liquid—surrounded each of their bodies. A closer look indicated the mist originated from a series of spouts that were attached to external harnesses that each of the Zrthns wore. As the crowd of aliens exiting the ship grew, the individual mist clouds joined together to form a giant, moving cloud of drizzle that surrounded the horde. *Interesting*.

He received a report from Alpha-22 that a similar crowd was making their exit on the far side of the ship, then radioed his observances back to Colonel Conway.

"That mist is likely water, Gurney. From what I know of these guys, they like it wet."

"Understood, Colonel. What would you like to do?"

"Hold on, Captain."

The pilot couldn't stop the light tapping motion his fingers insisted on making against the control panel. He barely resisted the urge to act on his own as the wait for her response dragged from seconds into a half-minute. He wondered what kind of leader this ground colonel was, and considered the thought process she was undoubtedly going through. Personally, he wanted to drop a load of high explosive plasma into the nearest cloud of squids, but this was her show. Despite his urgent desire to splash the forms below with plasma, he knew he'd follow whatever orders she provided.

"Captain, how many plasma drops do you have on board?" Gurney smiled. He was glad she was back with some direction, and he smiled at what the question seemed to imply.

"Three. Plus a full load of strafing rounds."

"Can you hit them with a drop and observe the results without getting your hind quarters shot down?"

Gurney had no idea what the Zrthn weapons were capable of, but he didn't say that. Instead he offered a simple, "Yes, Colonel. Not a problem."

"Do it, then retreat. We need you all in the sky if we're going to have any chance to repel these guys."

"You got it," Gurney replied and switched to the Alpha frequency. "Alpha-22, break contact and join Alpha-23. I'm going to see what a load of plasma does to our friends on the ground."

"What? I'd like to stick around and watch that!"

"Tune into my vid frequency then. You'll see what I see. But do it from ten kilometers away."

"Roger that, Alpha-22 moving back to ten kilometers."

Gurney waited impatiently for the seconds to tick by while Alpha-22 moved away from the ship. Finally, he got the word, then turned the nose of his own jet toward the growing crowd of aliens below. They were still pouring out of the ship, but the leading edge of the circle was almost half a kilometer in front, and they were now engaging with scattered, small groups of humans on the ground. As he watched, the small groups were quickly overrun, and he knew the timing wouldn't get any better. At a kilometer from the ship, he hit the targeting mechanism and released a single plasma bomb.

He watched as the bomb arced away from his aircraft and into the center of the alien crowd below.

The results were every bit as spectacular as he'd hoped. The blast turned every individual cloud of clear mist within a hundred meters of impact into a single, combined cloud of grisly gray blood and body parts.

If they only had a hundred more bombs, instead of just two, they could end this engagement in minutes. Unfortunately, that wasn't the case, Gurney rued. This battle would have to be won or lost on the ground.

He radioed the results of the drop to the ranger colonel, then turned his nose toward his two fellow pilots.

CHAPTER 27

"What you're saying is we can use these portals to reach the other Zrthn ships?" Tenney sounded incredulous, and Eli understood why. The room where they stood was round. Doorways, like the one they had stepped through to reach the ship, were spaced evenly around its perimeter. How could she expect them to know this room of portals led to the other ships in the alien armada? He couldn't tell her that Aank had read the mind of the ship's captain, so he told her the next best thing.

"Aank interrogated the ship's captain, Ah-loon," he said, and pointed to the squid seated across the control room. The Waa engineer stood close by the Zrthn captain, along with two Rangers who acted as guards. "He was very forthcoming. We learned a lot about the ship and how its systems work. We could land the thing, if we wanted. But that may not be necessary."

"And you trust this . . . Ah-loon? How do we know we won't end up back on Rhino-3 or—even worse—somewhere in the middle of open space?"

"I trust Aank," Eli replied. "You need to trust me. That's all I can say."

"Which means you have more you *could* say, but you won't."

Eli blinked twice, then mentally kicked himself. Flocking Aank. The engineer had him doing it now.

"I'm sorry. I can't," he said. He found that telling her 'no' was harder than it should have been, and that wasn't good. She she was his XO. The lines between them were becoming more and more blurred.

She nodded and heard her voice on the person-to-person frequency they had used earlier. "I need to tell you something, Eli."

"Of course, anything. You're my XO," he stated, then kicked himself for stating the obvious. They were on a direct frequency, which meant she wanted privacy.

"Maybe now, but not for much longer," she relayed. *What*? he thought, but didn't have time to say, before she continued. "When we get back to Telgora, I'm going to request a transfer to another unit."

Eli was stunned silent for several seconds at the announcement. "But . . . but why?" he finally managed to utter.

"Because I care deeply for you, Eli. More deeply than an XO should feel for her CO. If possible, I'd like to give us a chance to be more than just fellow officers."

Eli stared at her, struggling for the words to change her mind, talk her out of this nonsensical idea. He failed. It felt good to hear her admission—there was nothing he'd rather hear from her—but Colonel Conway's warning against getting too close with one of his subordinates stopped him from telling her how he felt. Then he understood. Tenney knew the regulations against fraternization and would have the same hesitancy to show any feelings for him…as long as they were in the same unit.

Eli looked to where Tenney stood. "I understand. On one hand, it saddens me to lose such an excellent XO. On the other hand… I couldn't be happier."

"Good, because my mind's made up," she said with a grin that he both saw and heard. "I can be a soldier in any unit. But I can't be your girl in this one."

His head reeling, he was still thinking through his response when Twigg approached and interrupted them.

"The troops are ready for your orders, Captain. Captain Zin and the platoon leaders for both A and B companies are in the staging room next door, awaiting your arrival."

The feeling of wonder and excitement that threatened to burst forth from his chest was new, something he'd never felt before. But it was good. He smiled as Adrienne—his girl?—passed by them on her way out of the room. She gave him a look that seemed to promise more than he ever could have hoped for.

"Um. Thank you, First Sergeant." Eli replied to the Minith sergeant as he struggled to dampen his emotions and put his and Adrienne's conversation behind him. He needed to focus his thoughts on the task at hand. He shook his head,took a long, breath of reprocessed ozygen, and went about the task of clearing his head. With an effort akin to lifting a carrier vehicle, he shifted his attention toward what Twigg had just told him.

Captain Zin.

Until now, he had been too busy to consider Captain Zin's thoughts about what was taking place. He could no longer put that off. It was time to face Zin, his more-experienced peer who commanded the Minith rangers in B Company, and convince him that the plan he had come up with was in their best interests. "How did Zin seem to you?"

The question was loaded, and both knew it. Eli wasn't only concerned with how the Minith captain felt about following a much less experienced company commander. He also had to consider Zin's personal affiliations. Did he stand with the Alliance, or did he stand with Drah?

"He seems . . . disgruntled that he and his warriors are not leading this mission. Otherwise, he seems his usual self."

"Hmm," Eli mused. It wasn't much to go on. Being angry was well within a Minith's standard response range for any situation. "Very well, we stick with the plan. Let's brief Zin and our platoon leaders so we can get this mission underway."

Ten minutes—and one angry, but resigned Minith captain—later, everyone was briefed and ready to lead their respective teams through the various portals down the hallway. Other than Tenney, no one questioned the decision to use the aliens' transportation technology against them, or if they did, they kept it to themselves. The technology that brought them to this ship from Rhino-3 had proved reliable enough so far. Perhaps that test was enough. Eli hoped so. Their lives, and the plan to help defend against the attack that had already begun on Telgora, depended on it.

The view on the ship's screens of the Zrthn battle carrier landing and expelling so many Zrthn fighters onto *their* planet had sealed the deal for Eli. It also helped convince the rest of the leaders in both companies, and in so doing, had alleviated Eli's concerns about Caption Zin, to some extent. Not enough for him to change the plan but enough for him to think the Minith would do his job.

There were eight ships in the Zrthn force: one battle carrier, one support ship, and six activity ships. B Company of the Shiale Rangers, led by Captain Zin and his platoon leaders, were tasked with porting to the support ship and the five remaining captivity ships. This allowed for a force of twenty rangers per ship. Based on the intel he had received from Ah-loon, those ships were manned by crews similar to what they had experienced on Captivity-1. In Eli's estimate, twenty Minith rangers would be more than enough to capture those vessels. He couldn't be certain, but it was likely that they would find the previous occupants of Rhinos -1 and -2 aboard one or more of those ships. If so, Zin was also tasked with rescuing them.

The battle carrier was in another category, however. Though intelligence from Ah-loon was lacking regarding the carrier, Eli assumed it would be heavily protected. Although most of the occupants had obviously already departed the ship, there was no reason to believe they hadn't left behind a substantial contingent of armed fighters. Because of this, he assigned the remainder of his forces to that direction.

The rangers from A Company would lead the assault on the Zrthn carrier. The size of the portal limited the number of soldiers that could make the journey at once. It wasn't ideal, but groups of three armored soldiers would go through the portal at a time, side-by-side. Eli planned to be one of the first three. If all went well, the entirety of A Company—all 120 armored soldiers—would make it through the portal in under three minutes and establish a secure perimeter on the ship that could be defended.

Eli's company would be followed by the 350 Minith warriors who had been stationed on Rhino-3. That group would be led by First Sergeant Twigg. Eli had some reservations about this contingent of fighters, but Twigg's assignment as their leader, combined with the fact that they were posted to a remote rock where Drah had no influence, convinced him that it was the right move to make. Once aboard the Zrthn carrier, they would need every available soldier, and the Minith filled that bill. Last, the Minith contingent would be followed by eight hundred of the human troops that had been posted to the Rhino comm station.

If they succeeded in breaching the carrier defenses, and joining the fight on the ground, Eli knew they would still be severely outnumbered by almost ten-to-one. There was nothing he could do about that, though. He had a job to do and soldiers to lead.

Sending Zin and his Minith through their respective portals took under a minute. Once they were clear, the line of armor-clad rangers that stretched out behind Eli moved forward to take their place. He looked back at them, took a deep breath, and tucked his Ginny into his shoulder.

He gave a nod of readiness to Aank, who stood next to the portal controls, then watched as the portal flickered to life.

"First group moving in three . . . two—"

He didn't get a chance to reach "one." A pair of squids appeared on the far side as the portal opened. Eli moved forward, firing the Ginny as he went. Beside him, Ellison and Benson matched him step-for-step and round-for-round.

* * *

Drah pounded the desk that had once belonged to his superior. He had taken the office for his own and installed his own staff of loyalists in the remainder of the building. For the most part, the plan was working well, despite the unwillingness of most of his people to readily take his side. No bother. He knew who had joined him and who had chosen to stand idly by while he did the work and took the risks.

His anger was now directed toward the video feed from the pacers he had deployed at the space pad. Everything had been going as expected for the landing force. The Zrthn troopers had begun to spread out across the tarmac where their ship landed. He had been informed that all resistance in that area was cleared, so the sudden appearance of human soldiers, though few in numbers, startled him. But the ease with which the Zrthns overran them quickly settled his nerves. He made a mental note, however, to punish his sources there for their ineptitude.

What really bothered him was the human jet vessel that had appeared and the plasma bomb it had released onto the Zrthn wave. He cursed his followers' inabilities to destroy the vehicle that created the ring of death and wondered what type of fallout he would hear from Oinoo for that particular failure. Fortunately, only one of the bombs had been released, which helped somewhat. The lack of follow-up drops told Drah that the humans had very few of the jets and—more importantly—very few bombs at their disposal.

Still, he put out orders to capture and man the antiaircraft weapons that stood vacant around the space pad facility. If the humans managed to rescue one jet, they might have rescued others. If so, they wouldn't get another free pass.

Having taken steps to counter the human threat, he turned his attention to another vid screen. That pacer showed his troops—nearly two thousand in total—as they neared, and prepared to enter, the Telgoran underground.

* * *

The spaceport was the largest facility on Telgora in terms of overall area. Measuring two and a half square kilometers, it was primarily a flat, open expanse of tarmac and concrete surrounded by a network of support buildings and a random scattering of abandoned equipment and vehicles. Designed to accommodate two motherships, the flat expanse was just barely large enough for the Zrthn carrier.

Becca studied the large ship, and the army that surrounded it, from a ridgeline on the east, that looked down onto the spaceport. Although she knew the ship was more than three kilometers away, the enormity of the alien craft made it seem almost close enough to touch. It was only when she focused on the thousands of alien troops circling the ship that she regained perspective. From her vantage point, she couldn't make out what type of weapons they carried, but assumed they were well armed.

The horde had spread out to encompass the support buildings that ringed the landing area. Here and there, she noted groups of human bodies—soldiers who had fallen trying to defend against the invaders. The hundred or so humans hadn't stood a chance against the numbers aligned against them.

Intermingled with the Zrthns, she spied large contingents of Minith soldiers. They seemed awful cozy together and Becca understood at once that these were more traitors to the Alliance. In total, she estimated the force below to be around twelve to fifteen thousand combined fighters. Fortunately, they were in a defensive perimeter that was enormous. As a result, their lines were thin. Thin meant they were vulnerable. Breaching the line would be possible, but to what end? She considered an attack that broke through the line, then focused on the ship in the distance, but quickly discarded the notion. The ship could retract the ramps that currently stood open, long before they reached the ship. That would leave her force trapped in the middle where they could be slowly eaten, bite by bite. They'd mete out a fair share of punishment but would end up decimated in the long run. That was less than ideal.

She noted the mistlike aura around the aliens that Captain Gurney had reported, and wondered if that presented a weakness that could be exploited. She didn't see how, but filed the notion away for future consideration, while her mind worked over the problem.

Lined up for a half kilometer behind Becca stood more than a thousand human soldiers, ready to do battle. It wasn't a significant force when compared to the numbers on the plain below, but she was glad to have it. After leaving the recruit training grounds an hour earlier, she had managed to collect five hundred more fighters on her passage here. More and more straggled into the ranks with each passing minute as the humans they passed saw, followed, and caught up with the advancing force. She had put Boyle in charge of sorting them out and getting them into units that could be maneuvered for effect. She was especially glad that many of those who joined them brought the tools of their trade with them. In addition to the standard small weapons that all Defense Forces carried, she noted the addition of three tanks and two artillery units to her growing force. Those, along with the jets above, could provide long-range support for an attacking force.

If only she had enough soldiers to mount an effective attack. Again, she struggled with the odds and how to best use her small army against those below.

"Alpha-21, this is Conway," she reached out to Gurney, an idea starting to form.

"Yes, Colonel," came the immediate reply.

"How are you guys doing up there?"

"We're getting a little anxious, to be honest, Colonel. We want to light up some bad guys."

"Patience, Captain. I'm working on it," Becca replied. She liked the pilot's attitude and shared it. She wanted nothing more than to pull the trigger with one or more of the aliens below placed firmly in her sights. "How many strafing rounds do you and your fellow pilots have?"

"Full load in all three, Colonel. We can do some damage."

"Excellent, Captain. Do you see how the Zrthn defensive perimeter circles the ship?"

"Um. Yes." Becca recognized it was a dumb question. From his perch up in the sky, the pilot would have an excellent view.

"Let's thin the herd a bit, Captain," she began.

"Coordinated strafing runs around the line?" Gurney asked. He was ahead of her, apparently.

"Yes, Captain," she confirmed. "Save your plasma drops, but these guys are lined up nice and pretty. Let's make 'em pay."

"Oh yeah! We've got this. Give us a minute to coordinate and then enjoy the show."

Becca couldn't help but smile, despite their dire circumstances. They were severely outnumbered, but the human spirit always seemed to rise to the occasion.

“Roger that, Alpha-21.”

CHAPTER 28

"Alpha-22, on my mark, proceed to the target, turn south and circle the ship on a clockwise route," Captain Gurney ordered. There was nowhere else he'd rather be at this moment than where he was: nestled comfortably in the cockpit of his fighter carrier. He felt a small twist of nervous anxiety in his chest, but the sensation was quickly overtaken by an angry need to strike out against the enemy below. All of his training and work at becoming one of the best pilots in the alliance had been to prepare him for what was to come, and he had to smile. He had never felt so alive. "I'll turn to the north and attack in a counter-clockwise maneuver. Focus your fire on the outer ring and, with luck, we'll meet on the far side and continue the run."

"Roger that, Alpha-22, ready on your mark."

"Alpha-23, when we begin our runs, you work on the slice of the pie that directly faces the colonel and her merry band of ground pounders. I don't know what she has in mind, but we might as well soften things up for her."

"Roger, Alpha 21. I'm not sure what these things eat, but I'll give them some plasma to chew on."

"That's the spirit, 23," the lead pilot replied.

Gurney had only been in the air for a couple of hours, but outside of the single plasma drop, their time had been a monotonous game of watch and wait. He wanted to hit back at the aliens who had invaded an Alliance world and killed his brothers and sisters. He was especially anxious to pull trigger on those traitorous, Minith flockers that had joined the ranks of the gray, off-world misters.

Misters. Yeah, that's as good a name as any for the waterlogged creatures.

"Let's take out these misters and the Minith who've joined them, shall we?"

He received dual affirmatives, and gave the command to execute their assigned maneuvers. Upon giving the mark, he turned the nose of his craft toward the enemy and tweaked the joystick to initiate an approach that would take him around the ship in a counter-clockwise fashion.

Gurney placed his jet's automated gun sights on the conveniently arranged ranks of enemy below, began the wide, looping approach that would carry him around the ship, and triggered the dual plasma cannons built into each wing.

The purple-colored tracers cut the air and closed the distance to his target in under two seconds. His speed was such that he barely had time to register the damage he was bestowing on the misters below, before he was past them and engaging more of the invaders. Occasionally, a large, green, two-legged target registered in his view. When that happened, he made a slight juke to the right or left to accommodate those special targets. He didn't know how effective those moves were, but he felt a pleasant tingle in his chest that made them worthwhile.

He was halfway through his pass when a sudden, powerful punch tossed him sideways.

The punch was followed by a loud clap and an immediate change in elevation.

A second punch slammed his helmeted head

against the jet's clear canopy. *Flock!* His instincts kicked in, and without thinking, he peeled away in a roll that changed his course, and initiated a steep climb. He had suddenly gone from the hunter to the hunted, and he switched his mindset accordingly. He didn't want to feel a third punch, so he raced upward and away, his goal now to outrace or outmaneuver whatever might be tracking him.

"This is Alpha-23," Gurney heard his fellow pilot yell. "I'm under fire from Alliance air defense!"

Gurney didn't have to tell the other man that those were no longer Alliance positions. The Minith aligned with the misters had obviously taken over the air defenses in place around the spaceport.

But he now understood who was tracking his own craft. That knowledge gave him both hope and despair as he made another, sudden change in his course and altitude. The hope came from knowing exactly what he was up against. He knew the systems that were targeting him, had trained against them hundreds of times and knew their strengths and weaknesses. The despair came from the same place. He knew he had a fifty-fifty chance at outmaneuvering a handful of the weapons. Unfortunately, the spaceport was surrounded by more than a handful. There were dozens of the air defense weapons deployed around the facility. The only question now was how many were in the hands of the Minith traitors?

"This is 22, I'm hit!" The previously calm demeanor was gone and Gurney listened helplessly, embroiled in his own struggle for survival. "I'm going down!"

Gurney cursed. He then juked right, dropped the nose, and pushed his craft as hard as he could. Distance between his ship and the weapons below was paramount, and he fought for control as his aircraft began a violent, teeth-rattling shimmy. At least one of the hits had done damage. He offered a silent prayer to the pilot in Alpha-22 and fought to stay airborne.

The view of the ground in front grew larger as he dropped altitude and gained speed. He was thinking he might just make it out of this jam when he spotted an unexpected sight ahead. He put his damaged vessel on a course to get a closer look, then keyed his mic and sent out a query. He understood the danger of multitasking at this moment, but had to get a message to Conway.

"Yes, Gurney, I'm here," came her immediate reply.

"Colonel, the shout's hit the air," he keyed. "We're under fire from the air defenses around the alien ship."

"I'm tracking that visually, Gurney," the colonel answered. "I saw one of your guys go down a kilometer south of my current position. He landed hard, but he looks to be okay. I've got a couple carriers of my troops headed out to retrieve him."

Gurney offered a silent "thank you" at the positive news, but it did little to relieve the tension in his body.

"Great, Colonel, but we've got other problems," he relayed, unable to delay his report. The constant, all-out shaking threatened to drop him from the sky at any moment. "There's a large force of Minith ten kilometers west of the spaceport. They appear to be entering the Telgoran underground, and they're heavily armed. I think our green, former friends intend to pay our gray, current friends a visit. And it doesn't look like a friendly one."

"Flock me! As if we—"

Gurney didn't hear the rest of the colonel's response. An explosion rocked his craft and cut off radio contact.

"Ahh!" He shouted, banged his fist against the canopy that surrounded his body, and struggled against the controls. The propulsion unit on his right side was gone. He could stay in the air using only the left for a short while, and he argued with himself over what to do. If he initiated a landing now, he *might* walk away from the impact.

Or he could do something about the large force of greenies that were marching toward the Telgoran entrance below.

It wasn't really much of a choice.

He fought the carrier through a rough banking curve that put him on a course with the traitors below. He was lined up on his target when the left-side engine gave out. He suddenly found himself surrounded by the relative, rattling silence as his dying carrier jet went into a glide.

His fate now sealed, he did the only thing that could make him smile.

He sent the last two plasma drops on their way, then calmly pointed his jet into the Minith soldiers below.

* * *

Oinoo cursed the incompetence of the Minith. His people had traded with the large, green bi-peds for decades before the humans had defeated them. He should have known that they were incapable of keeping their side of any bargain.

Before this "Alliance" had been put in place, the

Minith incompetence had been a joke among his pod—a fact to be taken advantage of and exploited at every turn. His agents had routinely shorted their trading "partners" of their full payments. Along the same vein, they regularly made off with greater loads of agsel than what they paid for, and they had never been found out. That should have been an indication to Oinoo that they would be incompetent in all areas, including the one they claimed was their greatest strength: war.

The Minith certainly seemed menacing enough. Giant, angry monsters, always eager to fight and quick to show their aggression and violence. Their reputation as fierce warriors had been the primary reason why his own race had never tried to wrest control of the agsel-laden planet before . . . well, that and the ease with which they could be stolen from. But now, when he needed them—no, when he *counted* on them—to be strong and wield a heavy tentacle against the much weaker, but smarter, humans, they failed miserably.

Oinoo watched the vid screens before him with rising anger. A fourth of his fighters—fighters that should not have even been needed, if that imbecile Drah had delivered on his contract—were dead or dying on the ground outside the ship. He had some small measure of satisfaction that the three human aircraft had been blown from the sky, but that wouldn't bring back more than two thousand Zrthn mercenaries. Now he owed a death-rate payment to each of their pods in compensation. Even if successful—Drah claimed it was still a certainty, despite the "minor" setbacks—his costs for this mercantile venture had just tripled. His initial return on the investment would drop, and his influence within the pod would diminish. His head rotated with concern, and his tentacles tangled with anxiety. Hostile takeovers were always a questionable endeavor. Unsanctioned takeovers were even more so.

Unsanctioned takeovers, that were unsuccessful, were often a death's sentence.

He pondered what to do with Drah when this was over. They had a verbal agreement—not quite a contract, but most would consider it a valid negotiation. He could break it, of course, but that might color his credibility when making future agreements. If anyone found out, that is. Accidents happened all the time that negated agreements.

Oinoo was mulling over the type of accident that he could manufacture when the sound of weapons-fire grabbed his attention. He looked to the vid screens but knew instinctively that the sounds hadn't come from that direction. They had come from the ante-room on the far side of his personal command center space.

But . . . how? And more importantly, who?

* * *

Eli was pleased. The movement from the portal room to the battle carrier's command center went quickly and without major incident—for the humans. The Zrthns aboard the ship hadn't fared too well. Benson was correct. The strange, tubelike weapons the invaders carried did not work against their PEACE armor. They could move virtually without worry. There had been one situation just inside the portal doorway when Ellison slipped while stepping over a dead squid and landed face-first on the floor . . . but that hardly counted.

For the most part, they had found the corridors of

the ship vacant, which made sense. Most of the alien force had been off-loaded onto Telgora already. Presumably, only support and command personnel still remained on the battle carrier.

Eli marched into the command center of the carrier, scanned the area, and held his fire. None of the dozen or so squids seemed to be armed, or if they were, they kept their weapons lowered and out of sight. *Smart.*

Seeing the situation was under control, Eli asked to have Aank brought forward.

As he waited, a door on the far side of the large area opened. Eli and the rangers with him pointed their weapons in that direction, but a diminutive Zrthn stepped through the doorway, unarmed. He was the smallest squid they had encountered yet. Where the rest of the Zrthns stood roughly two meters tall, this one fell a good half-meter short of that mark. *Interesting.*

Even more interesting, at least to Eli's mind, was the coloration that decorated the Zrthn's body and tentacles. Brilliant swirls of various blue and purple hues covered every inch of the alien's features.

"If the coloration is any indicator," Eli announced to his fellow rangers, "this guy must be the leader of this armada."

You are correct, Aank informed Eli. The Waa engineer had arrived.

"You are correct," the multi-colored Zrthn answered, speaking Earth Standard language. "I am Oinoo, a senior member of the Thmelia Pod. What are you doing on my ship?"

Eli was surprised the alien spoke their language. The words carried a heavy dose of the squeak-squeal that Eli had come to expect, but they were easily understandable. The current of arrogant superiority that accompanied the words was also easily understood. The urge to squeeze the Ginny's trigger and silence that arrogance was intense, but he refrained.

"I'm Captain Eli Justice of the Shiale Rangers" Eli replied, through gritted teeth. "What the flock is your ship doing on *our* planet?"

The senior member of the Thmelia Pod—Oinoo—moved forward, closing the distance that separated them. Unlike the other Zrthns Eli had encountered, the small leader of this Zrthn venture seemed graceful in his movements. Instead of the wriggle-walk movement he had come to expect, Oinoo's leg-tentacles moved in a short, fluid motion that seemed to float his body across the floor. His subordinates, which were a mix of the higher-ranking, blue-tinted squids and the standard, pale gray, moved quickly aside to accommodate his passing. He stopped three meters from Eli, certainly aware that every Alliance weapon in the room was pointed in his direction.

"I'm here to complete agsel negotiations with the supreme Minith commander, who now controls this planet," Oinoo stated. His enunciation was improving, Eli noted. "If you and your . . . people . . . exit the ship immediately, without causing further damage or harm, I will speak to him on your behalf. You may receive a lesser degree of punishment for your deference. Do we have a contract?"

What the flock? There were more than a dozen weapons aimed at his overly large head, and he thought he held the upper hand. Eli considered pointing out the obvious.

"How about you recall your soldiers to the ship,

and I won't pull this trigger," Eli countered.

"I understand your position, human," Oinoo said, his voice like honey—sugary sweet and full of promise. "Here you stand, on my ship. You have me at a momentary disadvantage because of your weapons. But you should think long-term. What is going to become of you and your . . . men . . . when you leave this ship? You are surrounded by ten-thousand Zrthn mercenaries, who are backed by one hundred and fifty thousand Minith. Surely, your force cannot stand up to those odds. Accept my advocacy and I will ensure your wellbeing. Do we have a contract?"

They had swapped less than two hundred words in their short time together and Eli was already tired of that question: do we have a contract?

His Zrthn forces have been cut to just over seven thousand after encountering Alliance carrier jets, Aank inserted his thoughts into Eli's consciousness. Eli welcomed the Waa's mental presence, happy for his ability to see into the Zrthn's thoughts. *The number of Minith backing Drah is also greatly exaggerated. He is uncertain of the true number, but it is a fraction of the total population.*

Not all Minith are on Drah's side?

No, Eli. Most are sitting by, waiting for a victor to emerge. Again, Oinoo is unsure of the exact numbers, but it is a majority. He is not pleased with Drah. Apparently, the colonel promised a full rebellion.

So, he's trying to bluff me?

Eli, we both know you would not accept his offer. But the Zrthns, by nature, are masters of trade and business. They are skilled negotiators who value contracts and agreements. This one places much value on his negotiation abilities. Bluffing is merely a tactic he uses to sway issues in his favor. Also, he is highly intelligent and has already surmised how we arrived on his ship. Because of that, he believes you aren't aware of the events happening outside.

Interesting. And he has no clue we know what he's thinking? Eli considered the value in knowing what your enemies and your trading partners thought. No wonder the Waa ability to read minds was such a closely guarded secret within the Alliance.

Blink. Blink.

Okay, Aank. Keep me on track here. If there's anything I miss, let me know.

Blink. Blink.

"Come now, Oinoo," Eli addressed the Zrthn. He tried to mirror the alien's honeylike tone. "We both know that thirty percent of your forces have already been killed or injured by our aircraft. And Drah has less than a thousand followers. The remainder are sitting on their paws waiting for this to end."

Although he wasn't familiar with Zrthn facial tics, Eli saw a change in Oinoo's features at that news. The low ball estimate of a thousand Drah followers was a complete fabrication. Fortunately, two could play the bluffing game.

"If you recall your forces now, we will allow you all to leave Telgora unharmed. If you don't . . . well, we'll have to take the appropriate steps to eliminate you. All of you." Eli allowed the threat to hang in the air. The weapon he pointed at Oinoo left no question about who would be the first to die.

"The fighters outside are contracted mercenaries, Captain," Oinoo replied. "If you kill me, they will fight to the death. Then where will we be?"

That is a truth, Eli.

"I believe you, Oinoo. But if you're dead, their continued struggle doesn't help you or the Thmelia Pod. And they will end up dead anyway."

It would cost his pod a great deal in compensation to their families, Eli. He does not want that.

"Perhaps there is truth to your words. But their sacrifice might weaken your defenses enough so that a future foray by my pod would be successful."

Not true. He is here without authorization of his pod or the Zrthn executives to whom all pods pay tribute. A future assault is possible, Eli, but not from this one's pod. Compensation payments and the negative reputation over this failed attempt will prohibit that.

He's a rogue?

Somewhat. It is not unusual for their kind to take unilateral actions against worlds like this one. Senior pod members who lead successful subjugations are hailed and applauded.

And those who lead failed attempts?

Ridicule. Loss of Position. Sometimes death.

So, why would he agree to leave? He has nothing to lose if his forces fight to the end.

Do not underestimate loyalty to the pod. He may agree to a deal that spares his pod from ruin.

"Oinoo, are you loyal to your pod?"

"Yes!" The word was delivered with a sense of what Eli assumed was righteous indignation. The alien's finger-tentacles quivered and waved as well. Good.

"Here is my proposal," Eli responded. "Recall the mercenaries you have deployed outside the ship. Leave Telgora, and do not attempt future forays against us. In exchange, we will guarantee safe departure for you and all of your forces. In addition, the Shiale Alliance will agree to negotiate only with the Thmelia Pod on future shipments of agsel. No other pods will have a seat at the negotiating table."

"You would do this? You would deal only with my pod?"

That has his interest, Eli. For him, being the only recipient of the Telgoran agsel is nearly as good as his agreement with Drah, who he feels may be unable to uphold his end of their bargain. Such an agreement will also rescue his reputation within his pod. He now envisions a prosperous arrangement, where before he saw little chance of success.

Good, Eli thought. *Let's increase the pressure then.*

"Yes, Oinoo," Eli replied. "We can make this deal. However, to compensate the Alliance for our loss of life and for the damages caused by your actions, we will retain five of the six captivity ships in your fleet. You will be allowed to keep your battle carrier, your support vessel, and the last captivity ship."

Eli didn't disclose why he wanted the ships, though it was likely obvious. The transportation portal and real-time communication device alone would move Alliance technologies forward a hundred years. Who knew what else the Waa could find on board?

Oinoo's arm-tentacles started a slow, rhythmic side-to-side wave as he considered the offer.

He is wavering, Eli.

"If you do not agree to these terms," Eli continued, pressing the advantage. "We will seize *all* of your ships and eliminate all of your crew and mercenaries. The Thmelia Pod will be left with nothing but heavy debt, failure, and ridicule."

Oinoo's tentacles stopped their strange waving rhythm. Eli knew the other had no choice but to agree.

"Do we have a contract?" he asked the Zrthn.

CHAPTER 29

Becca looked down across the plain where the ship waited. She had no idea what was happening. The Zrthn forces there had begun a slow but steady retreat back inside the large spacecraft, and she wondered what they were up to. The attacks by Gurney and his crew had taken a heavy toll on the ground forces around the ship before they were brought down, but that didn't explain the movements taking place.

Her forces were still ready to move out—had been since the pilots started their assault. But she held them back, unwilling to commit until she had a good idea of the situation. Now, she had no one left outside the ship to attack, except for several hundred Minith, who wandered about, seemingly just as confused as she was.

She had no desire to throw her forces—now two thousand strong—against the ship itself. Though the ramps were still down, she doubted their ability to storm the craft with any degree of success. She considered Gurney's final transmission and debated bypassing the ship altogether so she could help the Telgorans against the Minith forces headed below ground. Still, she held back. Indecision was a fatal error in any battle, but so was committing your forces without knowing what you were committing them against.

She decided to wait another ten minutes. If nothing changed by then, she'd move to support the Telgorans.

With five minutes to go, Lieutenant Colonel Becca

Conway received the greatest shock of her life. She watched in stunned wonder as a line of armored Shiale Rangers exited the alien ship and headed up the hill in her direction.

"This is Captain Eli Justice of the Shiale Rangers," she heard over the comm unit attached to her ear. "Who's in charge of the force on the hill?"

Becca slowly fingered the transmit button. How in the flock did her troops get on board a Zrthn ship?

"Captain Zero," she announced, shaking her head. "You have some serious explaining to do."

* * *

"Captain Zero," Eli heard Colonel Conway's voice come across the headset. "You have some serious explaining to do."

He couldn't hold back the smile, and he put the suit into triple speed, anxious to reach his commanding officer. He should have known the colonel would be at the center of the human response to this rebellion. She hadn't been put in charge of the ranger battalion because she lacked skills or initiative.

"Colonel Conway, it's good to hear your voice, ma'am."

"How the flock did you get aboard that ship? Aren't you supposed to be on Rhino-3?"

"It's a long story, Colonel, and I'd like an opportunity to share it with you. But we've got a few things to accomplish first."

"Agreed, Captain," Conway said. "What's going on with our Zrthn visitors? Since you're coming from their ship unharmed, and their soldiers have suddenly left

Terra Telgora, can I assume they are no longer a threat?"

"That would be an accurate assumption, Colonel. We . . . um . . . we've reached an agreement."

Eli felt a sudden stab of doubt. Until this moment, he hadn't really considered how his deal with Oinoo might be received by the rest of the Shiale Alliance. He was just a lowly captain (zero). What authority did he have to speak for the entire Alliance? Oh well, it was what it was. All he could do now was live with the fallout.

He reached the ridgeline where the human force waited and saw Conway waving from a hundred meters to the north. He looked over his shoulder to make sure the rest of his company was behind him and, satisfied that they were keeping up, moved in her direction.

When he reached her location, Eli offered a silent nod of recognition, propped the Ginny against his right leg, and reached up, suddenly anxious to release the clasps of his helmet. He turned the locking mechanism, flipped the clasps, and twisted the helmet a quarter turn clockwise. With a sigh of relief, he lifted the helmet from the suit and breathed nonprocessed air for the first time in two days. It was the hot, sand-blown air of Telgora, but it felt wonderful. Even the tiny pricks of sand hitting his face were almost welcome in a painfully familiar way.

With the helmet removed, he offered his commander a perfectly executed salute and a thin smile.

In return, the colonel surprised him by closing the distance between them and throwing her arms around his body. It was an unexpected greeting, and while he couldn't feel the embrace through the PEACE armor, he definitely felt it in the core of his being.

EPILOGUE

A crowd of more than one hundred thousand filled the stands that had been set up on the tarmac of the recently renamed *Captain Jamison E. Gurney Spaceport.* The large crowd arranged around the Gurney Spaceport was a healthy mix of Minith, human, Telgoran, and Waa; all of whom had reason to observe the medal ceremony and cheer on their own races' medal recipients. The damage caused by Gurney and his fellow pilots had been mostly repaired, and the Zrthn ship that had occupied the space was now gone. Still, all of those in attendance understood the significance of holding the ceremony here, where the majority of the battle had been fought.

Eli had never met the pilot whose name the spaceport had been given, but he had heard of the man's actions from Colonel Conway. He had also viewed the vids from the pilot's final flight. While many no doubt credited Eli and his company of rangers with playing the largest role in quelling the rebellion and defeating the Zrthn invasion, Eli thought the pilot did more than he ever could have done. He and his fellow pilots had reduced the Zrthn forces around the ship by 25 percent before being taken down by the Minith rebels. Gurney had then single-handedly destroyed nearly half the Minith who were marching on the native Telgorans and sacrificed his life to accomplish the feat. His actions were the turning point and provided Eli with the leverage he needed to convince Oinoo to cut his losses and retreat.

Eli stood at attention, a position that he had

somehow managed to hold for the past hour without wilting in the face of the ever-present sand-pricks that bit at his uncovered face.

The ceremony was being projected on a giant vid screen that resided somewhere behind Eli and the other recipients. The audio projected out over the large crowd and gave the waiting soldiers a running update of the proceedings. By following along, they were able to estimate just how much longer they had to wait—either to receive their award or to wait for the others to have their turn.

The end was nearing. The hundreds of former prisoners from the Rhino stations had been the first to get their medals. They were issued Meritorious Agsel Awards en masse, a company at a time, to expedite the ceremony. The next level of awards—Bronze Agsels—were given out to those who had been instrumental in freeing the captives being held by the Zrthns and securing the alien battle carrier. Tenney—who had just received approval for a transfer, and was in her final days of being his XO—Crimsa, Ellison, Captain Zin, and the rest of rangers were included in this tier.

Eli and the rest of the assembly listened as the last of those awards were made. From his periphery, he saw the award presenters appear on his far right. Finally, they had made it to the rank where he and the final recipients waited.

The first person in his rank to be pinned was Colonel Conway, and Eli listened closely to the announcement. His commander was awarded the Silver Agsel—her third, he was surprised to hear—for her actions during the rebellion. The announcer noted her resistance against the initial assault on the ranger headquarters and her ability to assemble a large force that was capable of defending the Alliance. Her bravery and leadership while leading that force against the eleven hundred Minith who survived Captain Gurney's final attack were cited as the primary reason for the award.

The award was appropriate. After they met on the ridge above the spaceport, he and the colonel had discussed next steps and settled on a plan. She had taken her force and moved to help the Telgorans, while Eli and his company of rangers had moved toward the building where Drah was still holed up with his most loyal supporters.

Next in line was Free. The young Telgoran who had worked so hard at becoming a ranger had been assigned to help Colonel Conway's attack against the Minith. He had been instrumental as a guide into the underground tunnels and at communicating with his people to help locate, outmaneuver, and ultimately defeat the Minith force that was successfully rampaging through the Telgoran homelands. For his efforts, he was also awarded a Silver Agsel. He had also, from what Eli had been told by Titan, been universally accepted back into the Family that had once shunned him as being "Alone." He was still alone, but he was now a hero among his people.

After Free received his medal, the three individuals who were presenting the awards stepped up to Aank. Eli couldn't see the trio very well. Twigg stood between them, and the first sergeant's bulk blocked much of the scene. But he listened as they presented the Waa engineer a Silver Agsel for his efforts at figuring out how the portals worked and for his translation services aboard the Zrthn ships. Besides Eli, only two others knew just how important the diminutive engineer's services had been to repelling the invasion and defeating the rebellion. If his abilities hadn't been a secret, he would be receiving a Golden Agsel, not Silver.

The Silver is more appropriate to my contributions, Eli.

Really, Aank? Even here?

Blink. Blink.

Eli smiled and sent a feeling of thanks and appreciation toward the Waa.

You are welcome, Eli. And congratulations.

Eli didn't have a chance to question why he was being congratulated. Aank sent a mental vision of a smiling Adrienne Tenney, accompanied by a sense of excited well-being and eager anticipation, into Eli's thought stream. Eli knew the feelings well. Those same emotions filled his body every time she entered a room, or smiled in his direction. The feelings were followed up with a sense of mirth and knowing that let Eli know he had no secrets from the little green alien.

Flock you, Aank, Eli replied, and tried to suppress a grin.

When the presenters moved on to Twigg, Eli got his first good look at the three. Titan, the human emissary to the Telgoran people, held a large tray where the medals lay, waiting to be handed out. Beside him, General Treel, the newly appointed Minith general in charge of the defense forces on Telgora, read out the verbiage that went along with each award. The third individual, General Grant Justice, the supreme commander of the Alliance Defense Forces—and his father—was doing the actual pinning of the awards.

This was the first time in more than six months Eli

had seen his father, but he turned his attention forward, and focused on the ceremony taking place beside him. General Treel's low, gravelly voice recited the first sergeant's accomplishments.

Twigg was awarded the Golden Agsel, the Alliance's highest military award.

Twigg was credited with turning the vast majority of the Minith who refused to choose sides back toward the Alliance. He was also recognized as the Alliance soldier who captured Colonel Drah. Eli noted there was no mention of the fact that Twigg had badly beaten his former superior when he found Drah trying to make his escape to the Zrthn battle carrier. Apparently, Drah did not realize how low his standing had fallen with Oinoo, or he might not have run in that direction. Not that it mattered. His return to a Zrthn ship was a foregone conclusion.

As a point in their negotiations, Eli had permitted Oinoo to retain one of the captivity ships. His reasons for doing so were clear and well considered. He expected the Zrthns to remove every rebellious Minith that could be identified from Telgora. That especially included Colonel Drah. No one in the Alliance gave much thought to where the Zrthns planned on taking the traitors, or what they intended to do with them, but it was assumed they would not be well treated. Eli hadn't known until recently, but apparently the Zrthns were known for capturing their enemies and negotiating their eventual release through completion of lengthy labor contracts.

Suddenly, as if by magic, the trio appeared in front of Eli. His father turned to retrieve the medal from the platter that Titan held, then stepped forward. The two men, meeting as soldiers in the same army for the very first time, looked into each other's eyes. Eli couldn't help but note how much his father seemed to have aged in the six months they had been apart. Eli understood how that was possible. Leading men, sending them into situations where they might be killed was one of the most difficult things he had ever done—and his father had been doing exactly that for most of his life. A twinge of doubt crossed his thoughts.

Can I be a good soldier, a good leader? Can I send soldiers into battle, and if I do, can I live with the consequences?

His internal struggle was interrupted by his dad reaching out to grip his right hand. The handshake was strong, and the look in the older Justice's eyes seemed as controlled and resolute as ever. That was good, Eli thought. Those things should never change.

The younger Justice shook off his reservations as he released the handshake.

He was vaguely aware of Treel's voice as the details of his award were recited, but he didn't hear the words.

He didn't need to hear them.

The pride he saw in his father's eyes as the Golden Agsel was affixed to his chest was more than enough.

The End

Acknowledgements

If you've made it this far, the book probably held at least a tiny bit of appeal. If it didn't, I'm not sure what you're doing all the way back here, but allow me to offer my apologies. I did my best. Ideally, I hope you enjoyed the hell out of it. If you did, I urge you to take a few moments and tell others how you feel about the book by leaving a review on Amazon. In addition to helping a struggling writer (that would be me), your review will also help other readers like yourself.

It is important to name some of the key contributors to *Son of Justice*. This book took more than two years to write and it's not an endeavor I could have completed on my own. Just as it takes a village to raise a child, it takes a team to build a book. Some of the key team members for this book include my Kindle Scout editor, **Ty Johnson**, my pre-Kindle Scout editor, **Laura Kingsley**; my cover artist, **Yoly Cortez**; and my wife and best friend, **Juanita**. Thanks to all of you for your support, encouragement, and hard work.

I also had the help and support of some very important folks . . . my beta readers. This group worked with me in advance of submitting the final draft to the editor. The book is a better product than it would have been without their wise counsel and support. In no particular order, they include: **Dave Jenks**, **Dennis Riggs**, **Michael Porkchop**, **Chris Cefalu**, **Robert Allison**, **Roy Hawksley**, and of course, my wife, **Juanita**, and my brother, **M.L. Hawk**. Thank you all for your help, support and guidance!

Finally, I want to thank you, the reader. You've been very good to me over the past four books. Your continued support and encouragement are what keep me going. I love you all!

Take care, and happy reading!

Steve Hawk

January 17, 2016

About the Author

Steven L. Hawk spent six years as a Military Intelligence Specialist with the U.S. Army's 82nd Airborne Division before joining the ranks of corporate America. He has a B.S. in Business Management from Western Governor's University and is a certified Project Management Professional (PMP). He has traveled extensively across the United States and, at various times, has lived in Georgia, North Carolina, West Virginia, Massachusetts, California and Idaho.

He currently resides in Boise, Idaho with his wife, Juanita. Together, they have a blended family of five sons and two Chihuahuas.

This is his fifth published novel. For more information, you can follow him via the following channels:

Website: www.SteveHawk.com

Linkedin: http://www.linkedin.com/in/stevenhawk

Twitter: @stevenhawk

Facebook: www.facebook.com/Steven-L-Hawk-296463223817121

Also by Steven L. Hawk:

Peace Warrior
Peace Army
Peace World
Creeper Town

Made in the USA
Coppell, TX
09 October 2023

22629447R00203